Praise for J.C. Hager's *Hunter's Escape: Quest for Freedom*

Hager's best to date. 'Old friends,' familiar characters, return for more edge-of-the-chair adventures. Matt is a long way from Michigan's Upper Peninsula as he and his new bride face rapid-fire perils in what should be a tropical paradise, except for a surplus of killers, narco-traffickers, Cuban gunboats and clanking cell doors! You will definitely enjoy the read, but watch out for ricochets!
Joseph Greenleaf
Author, *Sudden Light, Donegal's Novel*

Praise for J.C. Hager's *Hunter's Secret: Wreck of the Carol K*

When I finished J. C. Hager's first book, Hunters Choice, *I asked the author, "Where's the next one?" I finally got my eyes on* Hunter's Secret *and got by on little sleep until I'd read it. The locales depicted are bang-on, the human characters are well-crafted and many return as the reader's old friends. Now, John, where's the next one?*
Joseph Greenleaf
Publisher, Swordpoint Intercontinental Ltd

Hunter's Secret *has action, intrigue, spot-on descriptions, unique Michigan settings....an entertaining and logical sequel to* Hunter's Choice.
Aubrey Golden
President, Michigan Karst Conservancy

Praise for J.C. Hager's *Hunter's Choice*

Superbly crafted, Hunter's Choice *documents Hager as a master storyteller whose attention to detail insures the reader's rapt attention from beginning to end.*
Midwest Book Review

John Hager knows the outdoors, he knows the human heart, and best of all he knows how to tell a hell of a story!
Steve Hamilton
Author, the Alex McKnight novels

In his debut novel, J. C. Hager has employed his expertise as a hunter to offer us quite a yarn that could probably easily make a great movie...What also shines in the novel is Hager's familiarity with the finer points of all things pertaining to hunting and boating that he cleverly interweaves into his plot.
Norman Goldman
Editor, BookPleasures.com

Hunter's Escape

9/16/17

To Diane,

Bon voyage with
Matt & Tanya,

John Hagen

Also by J. C. Hager
Hunter's Choice
Hunter's Secret: Wreck of the Carol K

Hunter's Escape
Quest for Freedom

J. C. Hager

A Matt Hunter Adventure

Greenstone Publishing
Rapid River, Michigan

Hunter's Escape
by J. C. Hager

First Edition

Manufactured in the United States

Book and cover design by Five Rainbows Services
www.FiveRainbows.com

Print ISBN: 978-0-9797546-3-0 $14.95
e-Book ISBN (ePub): 978-0-9797546-4-7 $4.95

Information: www.GreenstonePublishing.com
              1-906-280-8585

Publisher's Cataloging-in-Publication Data

Hager, John C.
   Hunter's escape : quest for freedom / J.C. Hager.
      p. cm.
   ISBN: 978-0-9797546-3-0 (pbk.)
   ISBN: 978-0-9797546-4-7 (e-book)
   1. Caribbean Area—Fiction. 2. Cuba—Fiction. 3. Drug traffic—Fiction. 4. Adventure stories.   I. Title. II. Series: A Matt Hunter adventure.
PS3608.A44 .H865 2012
813`.6—dc23
                                        2012939351

To Luis Ruiz
(Heriberto Luis Ruiz Ojeda)

His quest for freedom inspired this novel. He swam at night through shark-infested waters toward Guantanamo Bay, was blown back by a monster storm, sailed past patrol boats from the north coast (intercepted by the USCG fifteen miles from the keys) and finally took a plane to Mexico and walked, penniless (his money taken by corrupt Mexican Officials), across the border into Texas. Let us always applaud his indomitable spirit and realize it is the essence and core of our national greatness. Luis is now a proud U.S. citizen, living with his wonderful family in Escanaba, Michigan.

1

Adios Fidel

Dark beach, low clouds, no moon, May 10, 3:00 a.m.: the only sounds—the ebb tide sloshing and sucking at the old coral rimming the shore on Cuba's north coast. From a forest of shrubs, scattered trees and sea grapes, four figures appeared struggling to carry a battered catamaran. Behind them a woman followed with several bundles. They scanned the beach in both directions looking for horse patrols that were rewarded for turning in escapees. Whispers and grunts of accomplishment came as they set the catamaran down near the water, where its mast was stepped and secured with several previously unattached wires. Bundles were placed and tied to the trampoline surface that was the vessel's deck, a hand-covered flashlight checked the connections and ties. The sky glowed with the lights from the oil refinery to the west, and from the city of Matanzas further to the south at the end of a large bay. Four men finally carried the vessel across the coral, their shoes protecting their feet, but the three inches of water hid many treacherous holes. One man fell, his ankle hurt and scraped. Another twenty feet and the coral became sand, and the catamaran floated in knee deep water. They stood for a time, breathing the smells of the sea and the tidal flats, then one man hugged each of the others and carefully worked his way back to shore where his wife waited. The three boarded, took paddles, crudely made from tree branches with pieces of scrap wood nailed to them, and began their journey to freedom that waited ninety miles to the north.

Dead calm water, ebbing tide and strong quiet strokes of their paddles brought the craft over the fringing reef and into the sea. They bent to their tasks, two on the paddles, one man as helmsman. As silently as possible they moved the craft through the unusually calm windless night. Their progress soon gave them a view of the lights along the coast. A key point of reference came from the light on the thermoelectric power plant tower located on the west side of the bay entrance. The French-designed power plant had docks that were also a border patrol station for various patrol boats. As they moved farther north into the sea, the tower light soon blended with the lights of the refinery complex and the city down the bay. After hundreds of strokes, tiring arms and straining lungs were gratified as the Cuban coast over their shoulders became lower and dimmer on the horizon. Then they heard a motor approaching. Soon after, they defined the easterly direction of the engine noise, a bow wake appeared as a white specter. They stopped paddling, lying low on the plastic-fiber deck, praying the boat would pass them unnoticed. A bright beam from the approaching boat dashed that hope.

"Where are you going?" came as a yell from the pleasure craft.

"To freedom," the helmsman yelled back.

"You're crazy. Stop, we will tow you back to shore and say nothing. You are stupid to try this thing. You will probably die," came the reply as the patrol boat cruised to within fifty feet. The men on the boat wore uniforms. They were a coastal patrol, part of the *Guarda Fronteras* that used commandeered or impounded private craft. The men were not armed. They had a radio but it was either broken or didn't have the range to call the gunboat whose presence would mean the end of their escape from Fidel's oppression.

Looking away from the spotlight, the men continued their paddling. A second voice from the patrol boat shouted another warning, "Turn back now, they will bring out a Zhuk." A minute passed as the men on the catamaran strained with their homemade paddles. No more was said as the sleek powerboat's engine roared and it quickly came to plane, heading west toward the patrol-boat base.

The despair of being so quickly discovered vanished with some initial puffs, then a steady wind from the northeast. The men, giving no thought to returning, worked to fit the Hobie Cat sails they had jury-rigged into the Prindle mast. The mainsail and jib caught the wind; the catamaran came around, running close-hauled with as much reach as they could achieve and still speed toward their northern goal. The noise of the departing patrol craft quickly was overcome by the shudder of the lines and sails as the craft's asymmetrical pontoons sliced through the warm black water.

The speed thrilled the men. With paddles stowed and a tight grip on the steering arm, the men leaned low in the craft and smiled with the prospect of a successful escape from the tyranny and tortures they had each experienced. From the storage bag came a boat's compass they had liberated from a Canadian sport fisherman's yacht. One man held the compass; another used a now very weak flashlight to read the dial then used his hand and arm to give a course for the helmsman. They were going a little west of north, but freedom was a big target, and they needed speed more than accurate navigation. Passing around one of their four plastic bottles, they all took a refreshing drink. Two of the converted Coke liter bottles held water, two had water with lime juice. They had food also, a waxed paper-wrapped roll of crushed and compacted peanuts. They each broke off some of the rich, oily substance, ate and washed it down with more water. They did all their dining with one hand; the other was needed to hold on to the fast-moving vessel. The wind had also brought waves, the fast craft jumping through the building foot-high chop.

As they moved around the flat bouncing trampoline of the catamaran's deck, the man who had hurt his ankle moaned when it was touched. His two compatriots removed his shoe, rolled down his sock and looked at the now swollen and discolored ankle.

"The coral, *dientes del perro*, bit you."

"Put it overboard, cool it with sea water"

"No, it might slow us. I can still swim, I'll crawl ashore if I have to."

"Let me wrap it, it will help," offered one man. Skilled in athletic medicine and training, he took a towel from the bag, ripped it into four inch wide strips, wet them in the spray going by the pontoons and wrapped the ankle with a professional figure eight. He made a respectable ankle bandage by tightening the cloth and tying it with ends split from its own length.

"That's good, it feels better already," said the injured man above the sound of the rushing water and the vibrations of the sails and stays.

They exchanged smiles as the lights of the coast disappeared. There was a faint glow along the eastern horizon. Dawn was coming. One man had a watch, an hour had passed while under sail. They knew the horizon at sea level was about ten miles distant, the immediate goal was to sail twelve miles from Cuba, to reach international waters. That goal couldn't come soon enough.

Ten minutes later the water ahead of them danced; erupting in fountains of spray as shells impacted off their bow. Seconds later they heard the staccato bangs of machine gun fire, the sound rolling across the water from the south.

Against the dark southern horizon, they saw tongues of yellow-orange flash from the twin 12.7 mm machine guns they knew were mounted on the 78-foot gunboats provided by the Soviet Union. They could barely make out the bow wake in the low light. Splashes again churned the water ahead of them, closer now.

The message was clear—turn back or we will fire into you. The Zhuk was too far astern for hailing. They must be close to the territorial limits. The gunboat might not cross the line, but its crew had no qualms about stopping their escape with machine gun fire.

The catamaran helmsman maneuvered his fast-moving craft into a zigzag. The white sails luffed, and the mast strained against its wires. The maneuvering lost them speed but may have momentarily saved them as a hundred-shell salvo hit the waters they would have occupied had they held a steady course.

"What should we do?" cried the helmsman, bringing them back to maximum speed.

Before he got an answer, shells pelted the sixteen-foot craft.

The sound of the bullets varied depending on their point of impact: hitting the water made a slapping-sucking sound, the plastic and foam pontoons made a dull cracking sound, the shells hitting the aluminum crossbars or mast made a ringing-breaking sound, the shells hitting flesh- made an unspectacular sound- just a dull thud, no louder than a playful shoulder punch. Two men jerked and spasmed as the large bullets tore through them. One took a head shot: bone, blood and brains spewed across the craft. With a loose helm, the craft turned with the wind, the sail jibed and jammed in the lee braces as part of the mast came down—shot through above the braces and bow stays. As the second man reached for the helm, two more bullets joined the several that had already pierced him, and he rolled off the now slowing craft and slid into the dark water.

The heavy bullet that had brought down the upper part of the mast also creased the chest of the third sailor and passed through a portion of his lower calf muscle, knocking him into the water. He surfaced twelve feet from the vessel, took a breath and pulled the water over himself to get away from the rain of lead coming from a ship he couldn't see and from guns he could hardly hear. He swam under water, away from the catamaran and the sounds of gun fire. Surfacing twice for breath—fear and shock an anesthetic for his bullet wounds—he finally came up as several more short bursts from the closing gunboat skipped and slashed into the boat that was once his hope for freedom.

The partially filled sail gave the Zhuk's skillful gunner his target, the yellow pontoons absorbed holes, but foam filled, they would not sink. Chunks chopped out, a tip blown away, and the twin rudder mechanism gone with the cross bar that held it, the craft looked like a capital "A" with half a mast. The small, thin jib, its halyard pulley shot through, trailed in the water behind the barely moving wreck.

A third and forth short burst of machine-gun fire turned the sail into a strainer, took more pieces off the pontoons and shredded more of the black deck material. With a loud rumble of its twin engines, the gunboat came within a hundred yards, running parallel to its drifting target. A powerful searchlight swept the area. For several minutes they held it on the wreckage looking for movement, or maybe to see if the craft would sink. Then it went off, the poorly tuned diesels popped then roared as the ship swung around toward the south. With boat noise still in the air and water, the wounded man moved toward his only slim chance of survival—the wrecked catamaran.

His strength ebbed with each stroke, pain building in his chest and leg as tortured skin and muscles opposed his attempt to reach the moving wreckage. His breathing came in gasps, each a painful tear across his wounded chest. He tried to kick, his wounded leg felt detached, numb, he couldn't sense its movement. The catamaran moved away. He tried to swim toward it, the only floating object in his sight. It twisted, the shredded sail caught more of the breeze, and it moved away as did his chance for life. He took two pitiful and painful strokes. Something moved across his hip and right leg. He reached forward and down. His arm and hand touched the jib halyard line. With desperation he grabbed the line, then the sail, painfully pulling himself toward the floating debris. At the wreckage he climbed onto the slanting deck area. He saw a dark stain on his chest and the wound in his leg. Using the jib sail as a crude bandage he first wrapped his wounded leg and then used the rest to wrap up and secure himself to the bottom of the mast. Feeling nauseous and thirsty from swallowing salt water and the onset of throbbing pain, he threw up. Loosening the sail that covered him, he found the food and water bag still remained tied to the mast: one bottle still full, another half-full with a hole through its neck. The peanut wrap had exploded over the inside of the bag. He scraped two handfuls into his mouth, drank all the water left in the holed plastic bottle. He tore off his ripped shirt, making a bandage for his chest wound, hoping to stop the bleeding. His leg was numb. He could feel tissue coming out the exit hole- he pushed it back in, rewrapping it tightly with part of the jib sail, tying it off with a loop of jib halyard line.

The light from the east was good enough for him to see the deck area. With the last of his strength he maneuvered the mainsail around the side stays to better catch the wind, he didn't want the easterly current, and later a flooding tide, to eventually take him back to a Cuban beach. He looked at the wreckage, too weak and tired to try to fix the pontoon braces, and gave a final look at the gunboat disappearing over the horizon. He figured that must be south, the sun a glow in the east, the wind was taking him west. He also saw movement in the water—a small shark finned the water in the barely perceptible wake. Then another joined it.

He thought of his friends, how quickly they went from celebration to death. He recalled their flashing smiles and confident happiness, then he remembered them being broken apart, shells shredding and exploding their flesh and bones with little sound; he saw muscles, bones and skulls bursting. He would wait to join them.

"At least I'll die free and not in a cage," he said aloud as he curled around the mast and fell unconscious.

2

Cannons in D

Florida Keys, May 10, 11:00am

Matt Hunter gazed for the second time in twenty seconds at the mirror on the back of the Pastor's office door. His first look reflected a tanned, handsome bridegroom in a perfectly tailored white linen, three-piece suit, happily contemplating marriage to his fantastic bride, Tanya. The second look came after reading a hastily printed note on the back of a ceremony bulletin shoved into his hands by a man in a dark suit. The note read:

DO NOT START THE CEREMONY. KILLERS AMONG
GUESTS. NEED TIME TO FIND THEM. I TALKED TO
ORGANIST. I'LL BE THERE IN A FEW MINUTES. AL

Matt now found his reflection resembled an albino deer staring into the headlights of a speeding logging truck.

Numbly holding the note, Matt moved down the short hallway to an archway behind the lectern. The minister, in a high-backed chair, out of sight of the wedding guests, looked up. He waited for *Canon in D* to announce the gathering of Matt and his son, acting as best man. Then the men would begin their procession to the altar area.

Matt whispered, "There's been a delay, we're waiting to seat a few special guests. It'll be a few minutes." The minister nodded and patiently returned to a position of comfort and contemplation. Matt fought back a panic attack, a part of his brain wanted him to dash to the center of the apse and scream, "Run for your lives!"

Matt returned to the office to find Al with an attractive, petite woman inspecting the outside entrance door lock.

She said, "This is what I found when I made an inspection of the building this morning. The door lock is jammed with some kind of putty—it won't lock. This is all fresh." After opening the door just enough to inspect the handle and lock, she and Al closed the door and turned to Matt.

Al, an ex-Detroit police detective, and now chief bodyguard and security expert for the Russian gangster generally known only by his last name—Webb—introduced the woman as Kate Wilson, the bodyguard for Webb's daughter Carla, Tanya's maid of honor. Kate's background was in military security, and Webb had hired her from Blackwater, a contract security service.

Al said, "We have two more security people in the back of the church, and two on the grounds, Webb was going to be here ten minutes ago, but we called him, he will drive around until we give him the all clear. I had the organist agree to keep playing until we tell her we are ready to begin the ceremony."

Matt said, "How'd you know there's a problem?"

Kate answered, "We found snipers on the school building next door. They eventually told us there is another three-person team, two inside the church. They are to kill Webb and escape through this office. The snipers knew of, but never met, the other team."

Al broke in, "The door fixed like it is means someone wants in during the ceremony, probably to cover the shooters' escape. We want that person to identify the other two."

Matt checked his watch, 11:02. *Canon in D* was scheduled to start at exactly 11:00. Matt's son entered the office hand-in-hand with his daughter Suzy, three years and three months of energy. The little blonde girl, all white ruffles with a butter-yellow band in her hair and a matching cummerbund, tiptoeing in white patent leather shoes, announced, "My new grandma is so beautiful. I will have a whole basket of rose flowers to scatter. When do I start?"

Matt asked his son and granddaughter to go back with the ladies, saying there would be a short delay while they seated a few more guests. He didn't want to tell them they had killers to find so a powerful gangster would be safe to watch his daughter stand up in a marriage ceremony. He expected Tanya understood the problem to some degree—Webb at a known location at a specific time placed him in danger—and somehow, she would keep her mother, Anita Vega, from coming unglued and ranting about all the times Webb had brought ruin and unhappiness to their family.

Al was on the cell phone to Webb's limo, they would pull up to the front and one person would rush into the church. Anyone watching from the side parking lots would only see the vehicle enter the short circular drive before the entrance, but not be able to see who entered the church.

The limo driver confirmed the plan and said it would be done within two minutes.

Al and Kate took two weapons from under their suit coats. They looked made out of dull, gray plastic, but big, the size of a regular army .45. They each took dark green tubes about six inches long, an inch in diameter and screwed them onto the barrels, then moved to the corners of the room to watch the outside door.

Al whispered, "Stay out in the hall, close the door behind you."

Matt went to the hall, his mind spinning. He could peek into the sanctuary, half filled with expectant wedding guests. The bride's side was nearly filled, the other side had just a few pews occupied in front by several of his friends and relatives who had come down from Upper Michigan or were snowbirds staying in Florida or on Alabama's Gulf Coast.

What had initially been discussed as a simple civil ceremony on some palm tree-lined beach, had taken on a life of its own, directed by Tanya's mother. Anita had rallied her considerable resources among the Cuban community in Miami, invitations sent with only a three-month RSVP had been quickly returned with acceptance. Skilled Cuban tailors had cut and sewn in Miami. A Lutheran church had been chosen because it was available and the minister agreeable. A Catholic Church would have greatly pleased Tanya's mother, but Matt's divorce over two decades ago brought complex and intrusive procedures, too much for Matt in both time and long-buried emotions. The rejection never got to monetary considerations. Anita Vega begrudgingly had bowed to the positions and wills of Tanya and Matt.

The Lutheran minister appeared in the hallway, and pointed at his wristwatch. Matt went to him and whispered, "Only a few more minutes, we're expecting an important guest who's been delayed."

The minister returned to his chair.

Several minutes dragged by, the organ music paused a few times while pages of new music were unfolded before the skilled master of the pipe organ's multiple keyboards.

Matt heard voices in the office, sounds of scuffling and a popping sound. He opened the office door to find Kate and Al standing above a man writhing in pain on the office floor.

Al held the man by his throat, his pistol's silencer touching the man's right knee. He hissed, "Identify the people after Webb or I'll blow out your right knee, then your left, then your feet, hands, shoulders and on and on—I've got nineteen more shots in this cannon. You'll never have a day without pain again. You will tell us sooner or later—why not do it while you can still walk and still hold things? You're just a hired gun, how much is this job worth to you?

Probing with the silenced, formidable, semiautomatic weapon, Al spent several seconds concentrating on its position at the man's knee.

When a look of frightened surrender crossed the man's face, Al loosened his grip on the throat.

"Stop—I'll tell you everything. Two people, a man and woman. He's tall, got a beard, dark suit. She's mean lookin', blue dress, dark hair."

Moving like an athlete, Kate left the room, hiding her semiautomatic in her waist band and pulling her blazer over it.

Al rolled the man over, pulled tight two, white-plastic tie strips to bind his wrists, duct taped his mouth, then rolled him onto his back. There was no fight left in the man. Al picked up a mini-Uzi that he had kicked under the minister's desk. The man's left shoe showed where a bullet must have nicked his foot, a little blood seeping out of the hole in the leather.

Popping the magazine out of the Uzi, Al ejected the chambered 9 mm shell and put both parts into a wastebasket, covering it with some papers off the desk. He spoke quietly into the cell phone—telling Webb they would have the situation controlled in two more minutes. He speed dialed another number and a man came to the door to take the wounded would-be assassin.

Minutes passed, and Al moved Matt to the hallway. Matt watched his son come up the side aisle, stopping to assure his wife that their daughter was perfectly prepared for her role, and stood with Matt. Matt could only see part of the first few rows. By moving out into the archway he could see the main aisle, where a man and woman were being quietly escorted into the narthex at the back of the church by three large men. Kate stood in the doorway directing the ushers, seemingly in charge of the situation.

Before Matt could contemplate the fate or future of the ejected couple, the first few notes of *Canon in D* began, the minister stood, and Matt and his son followed him onto the platform to stand at the right front before the altar.

Matt saw Webb and his wife Karen being seated on Matt's side, four pews from the front; several bodyguards took up positions behind them, helping to balance the seating. Webb caught Matt's eye and winked.

Matt took a deep breath and looked down the nave.

3

Previously, with the Women

Looking at the clock on the wall of the church's nursery, Tanya waited with her mother, her bridesmaid Carla and her basket-carrying, soon-to-be granddaughter, all expecting the signal to assemble in the open area before the main aisle where George Vega waited patiently to offer his arm to his beautiful daughter.

Carla's bodyguard Kate rushed in, pulling Tanya aside. "I need you to peek out into the sanctuary, tell us if you know a couple of people." She moved Tanya to the heavy vertical blinds that covered the glass wall between the sanctuary and the narthex. Pulling them aside at their end, looking across the wedding guests, Kate directed her to a tall, bearded man sitting with a dark-haired woman in the sixth row on the bride's side, at the outside of the pew.

Tanya whispered, "With or without the beard, I know I never saw him. The woman isn't familiar either. I'm fairly sure I would remember that face."

Kate nodded while trying to move Tanya back into the nursery room. George Vega came over with a questioning look. Tanya, growing more anxious by the minute, shook off Kate's hand, while she and George Vega kept watching through the edge of the blinds.

Wasting no more time, Kate spoke into a miniature radio, and three men with their hands inside or close to their open suit coats surrounded the unknown couple. The lead man leaned down and whispered instructions to the seated couple. The man and woman carefully grasped the pew in front of them, slowly standing. The group of five made their way along the side aisle to the back of the sanctuary. Kate, moving to block the main aisle and ordering the ushers to stay in the sanctuary, herded the departing group to a corner of the lobby, out of sight to all but Tanya and her father, who watched—Tanya's brow furrowed; her father frowned. The two guests were thoroughly searched while Kate stood six feet behind them with her silenced pistol firmly leveled. Tanya's eyes widened when the security agents took a small pistol from each would-be assassin. One of the agents pried a sheath, holding a short-handled knife, from the man's wrist and—equally as sinister—removed a hypodermic kit from the woman's handbag. All tools of a deadly trade.

Now unarmed, the security trio, with Kate following, roughly pushed the pair out of the church through a back door of the narthex. Kate, her pistol now holstered, returned quickly with two of the guards. She beckoned to Tanya while opening the nursery door; the men quietly reentered the back of the sanctuary.

Tanya and her father stood together. They worked at calming each other. George held Tanya's hands, she in turn took several deep breaths, smiled and kissed her father's cheek. Then she moved toward the door held open by Kate, George Vega showed his watch to Tanya: fourteen minutes behind schedule. He reverted to his Air Force background and made a "wind it up" motion with his hand and arm. The wedding guests seemed not to mind the delay. They were quietly chatting between the pews with friends and family.

Tanya escorted her father to his previous station near the main aisle just as Webb and his wife Karen entered the church from the main entrance led by Al. The waiting ushers quickly escorted them to an empty pew on the groom's side.

Now back with the ladies, Tanya allowed them to make final, final adjustments on the dress-matching mantilla and a small, pearl-encrusted comb that had been adjusted several times before. She in turn rearranged the small, baby-orchid corsage surrounding a silver, jeweled pin that gathered the material in front of her mother's left shoulder. Tanya fought to control her nerves and fingers and to not betray more than the expected excitement of her wedding day. She focused on her mother, who smiled back with love and happiness.

The steel-gray, watered silk dress perfectly complemented Anita's salt and pepper hair. Tanya had never seen her mother looking lovelier.

Her mother, nodding at the clock, said, "We're late, what's going on, I peeked out for a second, who were those people that were moved out?"

Kate smoothly took the questions, "They were crashers—like the people at the White House—except we caught them. You will be starting any second now."

Kate stood behind them as the three women and the little girl looked into the low mirror that made up half the children's room wall. They saw a beautiful tanned bride in a white, halter-top gown with an empire waist, pearls covering the bodice, her dark hair up with one thick curl cascading over and down her right shoulder. The comb, used by the family's brides for many generations, came from 17th century Spain; it secured the floor-length mantilla that covered her bare back. Carla's gown had a similar construction, but shorter, butter yellow with a finger-length mantilla, her dark hair pinned up with tiny flowers that matched her dress.

White and yellow flowers came out of tissue filled florist boxes. Suzy's basket quickly overflowing with yellow rose petals poured from a plastic bag. The women were ready when they heard the entrance music begin.

4

With This Ring...

Matt stood contemplating the guests as the processional music began its first simple notes. Scanning the bride's side he recognized many of the people he had been introduced to at the groom's dinner the previous night. Together, they made an impressive group of handsome, successful people: doctors, realtors, insurance executives, stock brokers, bankers, retired Air Force and a few who had only mentioned they were in trade or importation. The group of Cuban expatriates had known Anita and George Vega since their first arrival in Miami during the '60s. On Matt's side, four of his closest friends fidgeted: Dick and Billy Lamoreaux and the Ferr brothers, Sam and Will. They had all driven straight through from the Upper Peninsula in a Sierra extended-cab pickup truck—bringing best wishes and gifts from relatives, including a cooler of frozen pasties, smoked fish and quart jars of canned venison—all destined for the afternoon's party. Matt's side also included two rows of friends who had vacationed in the south and lengthened their stay for a week or so to celebrate Matt's wedding. Some had given short notice of their coming, it got complicated, but all had received invitations and rooms booked in the area.

The music's cadence with increased volume caught everyone's attention as both ushers led Anita Vega up the aisle. Rather than risk a fight or hurt feelings, she had asked both to escort her. Both men were her lifelong friends, growing up in Cuba and rising to success in their new country. The three made an entrance worthy of stars at an Oscar presentation. The dark suits made a fitting frame for Anita's silver dress and shoes. Glowing with happiness, she made eye contact with several friends. Matt had never seen her dressed to this level of perfection. He remembered picture albums Tanya had shared with him when Anita was in her teens. She was still a head-turner fifty years later.

With Anita seated, Carla came up the aisle, slowly stepping to the beat of Pachelbel's baroque 1680s music. She was a picture of loveliness, worthy of a fashion shoot or a master's brush, a classic beauty in her late teens. Webb's daughter Carla was a stranger to many on the bride's side; whispers murmured through the attendees. Tanya had chosen her over many girlfriends from her youth and school days. The bond she and Carla had formed on their life-and-death yacht journey through the Bahamas and subsequent meetings on Carla's visits to the UP had made them friends for life. Like soldiers who had survived deadly combat, their kinship had become as strong as that of any blood relatives. Carla smiled at Matt. Looking over at Webb and Karen, Matt saw pride and tears in their eyes. As Carla turned, taking her place at the left front of the altar, the organist changed stops.

The music rose and so did the audience as Tanya appeared in the doorway of the sanctuary with her father at her side and Suzy in front of her, her basket overflowing with yellow rose petals. Suzy looked back at Tanya who nodded. Suzy took her task with seriousness and pleasure. Stepping to the tune, she scattered the velvety rose petals. They fell like fragrant pieces of sunshine on the white runner. Matt noted her age, perfect for the role: old enough to do the job and still young enough to feel all this was just for her enjoyment. Not nervous, glad to see all the people watching her, she smiled as several cameras flashed at her passing. Her timing, distribution and supply of petals came out perfectly.

The bride and her father started up the aisle just as Suzy cast the last petal and slipped into her special seat in the front row beside her mother.

Tanya's beauty sucked the air out of the room. No one could break the spell enough to crassly snap a picture. Matt's heartbeat pounded in his ears as his blood pressure altered the volume of the processional. Tanya didn't look right or left, just at Matt. They had practiced this entrance the day before dressed in casual clothes, but nothing had prepared Matt for the vision that approached him. He broke eye contact, looking down, widening his stance, and took two deep breaths.

His son whispered, "Beautiful." Stepping a little closer, perhaps thinking he might have to break the old man's fall.

As father and daughter came closer, Matt watched George Vega proudly walking beside his daughter and occasionally glancing and smiling at friends. George took his appointed position behind Tanya as she stood beside Matt.

The service began: Matt faced Tanya, her eyes showing love, trust, hope. George Vega replied, "Her mother and I," when asked who was giving the bride away, and sat down. The minister read the service from a leather-bound, red volume. He had big, worker hands. No one stood up and gave a reason they shouldn't be joined together. *You never know*, thought Matt, glad they got past that part.

The exchange of rings went smoothly. The day before, Matt had noted a worrisome air-conditioning duct in the front—he had had it covered with the white runner, worrying about a dropped ring clinking its way into the church's nether regions.

The message was from Colossians 3:12-17—"Clothe yourselves with compassion, kindness, humility, gentleness and patience." As verse after verse of Paul's words was explained Matt appreciated their wisdom and contemplated their meaning in a marriage. Near the end of the service, his concentration was broken by a smile from Tanya. Some words had stirred a thought in her; he would ask her about it later.

"You may kiss the bride."

At last.

Matt expected a ceremonial, "don't mess-up my make up," kiss. Instead, Tanya's lips met his with warmth, softness and purpose. His mind went blank; he was back at the little cabin, in a blizzard, their first kiss. Every sensation of that moment rushed into his thoughts and body. Time lost all importance. Matt closed his eyes, held her warm body close and enjoyed every feeling that accompanies a perfect kiss. He heard the minister announce them as a couple and the clapping of the attendees, but he was enjoying the kiss too much to really care. Finally their lips parted, Tanya's eyes glistened, and Matt came back to the reality of being in front of sixty people, and standing at an altar.

The recessional started.

5

Receiving Line

Applause faded as Matt and his bride exited the church's nave and formed their reception line, soon joined by the best man and bridesmaid. Family and special guests come out next.

The Webbs appeared, smiling and chatting, accepting compliments for their beautiful daughter. The recessional music was Clarke's *Trumpet Voluntary*, highlighting the skill of the organist, the range and power of a pipe organ, and matching the happiness of the people moving from the sanctuary.

Webb and Karen greeted, hugged and kissed their way through the line. Anita actually hugged Webb and allowed a cheek kiss. They all agreed to stay until the guests were greeted before returning to the altar for pictures and the official signing of the marriage certificate.

After Webb kissed Tanya and held her at arm's length to inspect her beauty, he whispered to Matt, "We have business; let's meet on your boat this afternoon."

Webb formed his own receiving line on the other side of the narthex. He knew many of the guests, from the early days in Miami or perhaps other business dealings.

Matt wondered what the minister would think if the mini-Uzi was still in his wastebasket. He hoped to relieve his fears when Al came into the lobby with Kate, and they took up positions near their charges: Kate near Carla and Al behind Webb.

Matt turned to Kate, "Is the office suitable for the minister?"

Kate whispered back, "Yes, you hardly notice the hole in the carpet and I even emptied his wastebasket."

Matt's face hurt from smiling, his nose was filled with a variety of perfumes and he was jealous of several very handsome, younger Latinos who spoke smooth, low Spanish and kissed Tanya. Tanya was astonishingly beautiful even in the mixed sunlight and over-head lighting of the narthex. Carla had at least a dozen invitations to be shown around the Keys—mostly by love-struck men in a wide range of ages who didn't know or care about her father or that she had an armed bodyguard standing behind her. Matt's friends and relatives filed past, several had been his students—only five or six years separated him from his earliest charges, Matt felt older when he saw several were balding, out of shape and had grandchildren with them. Cousins Dick and Billy Lamoreaux nearly broke his shoulder with punches of good will and congratulations. Friend Sam Ferr whispered to Matt, "You're going to need oxygen…" after he moved from hugging Tanya.

The line went quickly because everyone knew the party would soon begin at the Tiki bar at the Holiday Isle, where they would have time to talk in a more relaxed atmosphere. There would be no crowd throwing rice outside.

Talking groups had to be broken up to satisfy the lurking photographer, barred from working during the ceremony, and the patient minister wanting to get the signings completed and go home.

Matt and Tanya met in the office and signed the marriage certificate, completed by the minister. As they walked back to the altar Matt asked Tanya, "What made you smile near the end of the message?"

Tanya held Matt's arm, moving close to his ear so her words could not only be heard but felt, and whispered, "When he said, 'On top of all these things, put on love'…I had a thought that now and then my red teddy would be a good idea."

The photos took over a half hour, the photographer enthusiastically playing with exposures and filters to capture the impressive beauty of the ladies and the cute little girl. Webb and Karen were included in one group picture as well as a threesome with Carla. Matt went with the flow, following instructions, laughing every time he was asked to stand and look at Tanya. *Red teddy, indeed.* He hoped the makeup on his white suit from lots of female hugs wouldn't show.

At last they all left the church, their vehicles assembled in the front circular driveway. Loading people and wedding materials; they departed for motels, Vega's home and in Matt's case, a yacht, all back down US 1 about ten miles. The plan was to reassemble at the party, with Matt and Tanya fashionably late enough to make a good entrance.

As Webb came out, Matt, Al, and Kate each scanned the grounds and then looked across the side street into a bright sun reflecting off the big high school gymnasium roof—no snipers. Webb and Karen dashed to their limo: no rice, no lead.

It was a beautiful day.

6

Party

Matt drove with Tanya beside him, his son, daughter-in-law and granddaughter in the back seat. No one mentioned the uninvited guests. Suzy worried about who would pick up the flowers she had scattered. With the Vegas following close behind, they went to the Vegas' home to freshen up. The wedding party would remain in their formal clothes, but they wanted to give their guests time to change into more comfortable, casual attire. A half hour passed while they chatted and enjoyed the impression of the wedding from Suzy's perspective. Tanya had Matt take her cosmetics bag and a hanging wardrobe of clothes she had not already loaded aboard the Hatteras yacht that would be their honeymoon home and transportation for a month or so at sea.

Then back into vehicles headed for the Tiki Bar.

The partying in progress, Matt observed that fifty people made up of Cubans, Yoopers- lucky people living in the Upper Peninsula of Michigan, and Air Force personnel had no problems enjoying themselves. The buffet was organized on either side of the wedding cake, to be cut later. In lieu of gifts, they observed the Cuban custom of giving money to the bride during a dance. In turn, Matt and Tanya provided a gift to each guest: a small woven basket containing a tiny bottle of rum, a green lime and a small potted Mojito mint plant that seemed to please everyone. A box of Cuban *Cohiba Esplendidos* lay open on the gift table—no one admitting how they got there... A four-piece band, hooked into the Tiki's considerable sound system, treated the whole marina to lively music.

Matt and Tanya started the dancing. Without her mantilla, Matt's right hand found only smooth, toned skin. He reluctantly relinquished his beautiful partner to the ravages of sweaty-handed, male guests. A line had formed of eager men, many had changed into Guayabera shirts, the light linen, vertical pleated traditional shirt of Cuban weddings. Matt appreciated the faster tempo of the music , so there would be less Tanya touching going on. Shedding his suit jacket, he danced with Carla and then her unescorted mother, Karen. Scanning the bar and deck area, he noticed that Webb had chosen to stay away from the festivities. Karen, a performer with several Russian ballet companies, had moves that made Matt look very accomplished just by moving his shoulders to the beat and taking her hands as she extended them to him.

Mojitos and pasties, grilled shrimp and smoked fish, and even venison from the UP was sampled—probably a violation of some food ordinance—to everyone's enjoyment.

Matt and Tanya finally cut the wedding cake accompanied by many champagne toasts in glasses that magically had appeared.

Later, as Tanya chatted with old friends, Matt took some coffee to the railing that overlooked the harbor filled with moored boats. Rum drinks and champagne in the sun can be a deadly mix.

Karen came up to him, flush from many dances. "My husband would have liked to have been here, I hope you understand and forgive his absence." She handed Matt a small envelope with Webb's unmistakable bold printing, addressed to Matt and Tanya on their wedding day."This is for you and your lovely Tanya."

The envelope contained two plastic Visa debit cards from Lloyd's out of Gibraltar, in each of their names.

Karen continued, "He will explain more when later he sees you. Also, Tanya owes him a bridal dance. He apologizes for the disturbances. We hope you visit us in the future, we love you both very much." She kissed Matt, turning to find another young dancing partner waiting expectantly.

Moving to Tanya's side, he happily noted she had put his suit jacket over her bare shoulders and back to counter the cooling afternoon breeze. Clinking her champagne flute against Matt's coffee cup, she whispered, "I have a heavy purse of money, I think some men put in gold coins."

Matt showed her the credit cards. Her questioning look brought Matt's comment, "Karen gave me these from Webb. Who knows what he's up to. We will probably learn soon enough—after all, why leave a couple alone on their wedding night?"

Tanya led Matt to a table where her parents had held court, although they were now dancing. There, among purses, the mantilla and various articles of clothing shed by dancers, was a wooden box, probably mahogany, with brass corners and latch. Tanya opened the box, inside was a very expensive-looking telescope—red leather, shiny brass, nestled within green felt. A card, taken from its envelope said, "Congratulations, this may be useful." It was signed "Edward."

Matt took out the instrument, "A spy glass... Har. Leave it to the DEA to give us something useful—particularly to them. I can't see the string that I know is attached to this gift."

Tanya said, "Edward has helped us more than hurt us. He helped you get rid of a crashed plane and two bodies; he helped Webb with the problems at the Canadian Border and our battles with the Livingston brothers. Before that he warned us about the Cortada plots to kill Webb, his family and us."

Matt countered, "He also used you to incriminate Webb, making you walk a fine line between two deadly forces. Both the government and Webb got you to do covert or illegal work by holding prosecution or threats over you and your father. A lot of blood and lives have been lost in the adventures associated with Edward of the DEA and Webb of the crime underworld."

"I'll be interested in hearing Webb's thoughts about who sent these latest killers into our lives."

Matt thought, while holding the heavy instrument, *We will be seeing Edward again, he will want something and make it seem our duty to help him.*

As Matt put the spyglass back into its secure box, they were joined by many Yooper friends—they all posed for cell-phone pictures to be sent in many emails. Billy Lameroux asked Tanya to take off the jacket, saying, 'We don't want people back home to think it's cold down here."

With that statement, everyone had extra big grins for the pictures.

The sun was getting lower, still warm, with clouds of orange and pink on the horizon. The party was considered a success. Everyone had enough to eat and drink, all the proprieties of a wedding feast had been observed, all the pictures taken and quality time shared with new and old friends. Matt's son and his wife had taken Suzy to play in the pool. The Vegas were still having drinks and coffee with friends at a far table while the efficient caterers cleaned and organized the Tiki for the public that would be coming for the evening. Many of the Miami guests had left for their homes; others, staying over, had agreed to come to the Vegas' house for breakfast. Most of the Yooper group had rooms at the Holiday Isle, all planning to see Tanya and Matt motor the yacht out of the harbor around 10:00 the next morning.

7

Webb Aboard

Matt backed his SUV to the dock area. It was their last trip to stock the gleaming white Hatteras for their voyage. Fresh vegetables, salad material, cakes, cookies, steaks, eggs, fruit and many plastic bags of last-minute necessities foisted upon them by Tanya's parents. The sun had set, they were tired. Their vehicle would be taken back to the Vegas the next day.

"Let me help you," said Al, Webb's bodyguard, stepping out of the shadows of a pier post. Matt jumped; even though he had known Webb would likely come to the yacht sometime that evening.

The *Reefer* waited, stern to the dock, moored in the outer area of the marina. She was 54 feet of the best fiberglass, chrome, and diesels that Hatteras Yachts could make in 1993. The *Reefer* displaced 70,000 pounds, with seventeen feet of beam, drawing nearly five feet at the tips of her two costly, five-bladed propellers, partially hidden in prop pockets that allowed less draft and drag plus a reduced shaft angle, each prop connecting to a 1,200 horsepower MAN diesel. Built for high speed cruising, she had a checkered past. Her first owner ran drugs, got caught, and a government auction had allowed Webb to buy her for thirty percent of the appraised value. Webb had sold her to George Vega as a sweetheart deal even after he had put major money in navigation gear, interior renovations and engine work. Webb then had highjacked the boat to make a run to the Dominican Republic with his family, carrying a fortune in money, jewels and blackmail material. Webb's plan had snared Tanya and Matt and involved them in a hazardous journey through the Bahamas.

Matt and Tanya stepped down to the boat's aft deck, memories of the Bahama run flooding back. As Matt struggled with his bundles trying to find the handle of the salon door, it slid opened. Webb let Matt in and took Tanya's sacks. Al followed carrying a large box of groceries, with plastic bags balanced on top. Al made one more trip to the vehicle and returned with the last box of supplies.

Webb took a gold-green labeled, dark bottle of Dom Perignon from the Subzero refrigerator. Deftly removing the foil and wire, then twisting the bottle while holding the cork, he opened the champagne, pouring a splash into each of four glasses that waited on the counter. Then he poured in more, bringing each to half full. The counter had a platter set with toast points and caviar in a container nestled in a bowl of ice. He gave glasses to Tanya and Matt, took two more, one given to Al and proposed at toast.

"To the most beautiful bride and the most fortunate of men, may your lives be long and filled with joy and adventure." Webb lifted his glass and drank, Tanya and Matt did the same. Webb then touched buttons on the stereo, and a waltz tune filled the salon. He moved to Tanya, now in shorts, safari shirt and sandals, her hair in a pony tail: her makeup, shiny finger and toe nails testimony to a bride's careful grooming. He took her in his formidable arms and smoothly danced for several bars, moving easily even on the boat's carpet. He gave her a kiss on her forehead, then a hug. His eyes glistened as he turned away, moving the caviar setup to the salon coffee table, motioning Tanya and Matt to the couch behind the table. He refilled the glasses all around, emptying the bottle. He brought another, unopened bottle in an ice bucket to the table, then stood looking at the newlyweds.

Matt wanted to ask several questions but saw in Webb's eyes, as they looked from Tanya to Matt and back, that something important was going to be said.

Matt had not seen Webb up close since visiting him at Al's home outside Detroit the previous November. Webb looked older, even tired, and thinner. He had been a weightlifter in his youth, a scholar in economics, he had worked for the old Soviet Department of Administration, killed a man in a bar fight, gone to prison, made friends with gangsters, came out with a network of very tough, new friends, discovered he had the perfectly educated position and temperament to control a vast black market that grew even faster than the USSR broke up. He had made an official passport and obtained a visa to the USA, his prison records magically disappearing. Matt guessed he had to be in his mid-70s, but his short hair, big shoulders, barrel chest and forceful presence took ten years off the clock. Having Karen on his arm and a teenage daughter to worry about also kept him younger spirited.

Webb drank from the nearly filled champagne glass. Setting it down, he scooped some caviar onto a piece of toast using a special spoon that came with the setup. Taking the glass back, he made himself comfortable on the salon's other leather couch.

After a theatrical pause, he began, "I've known you, Tanya, since you were still a gleam in your mother's eye. I've been a part of your life because I wanted to be. We've been through some bad and good together, I've always been proud of you. Now I am very happy for you. I know Matt is a good man, I've seen him in battles. He is tough, even mean when he has to be, he is also smart and he loves you. You will do well together.

"I've been in negotiations with the Livingston sons. They are certain I had their fathers killed on their ship, they have no proof, but no denials came from me."

Mat broke in. "You're putting yourself between them and us. That's brave and kind. We are in your debt."

Matt thought, *You have to be making something out of this situation.*

Webb shook his head, "Not really, you just did what I would have done, given some time and planning, and by sending others. You know, with the exception of a drunken fight in a Moscow bar in my youth, I never personally killed anyone. That's a fact I wouldn't want getting around, it would hurt my reputation."

Matt thought, *There was the Venezuelan gunman—self-defense doesn't count, I guess.*

"Anyway," Webb continued, "the sons thought their fathers were cantankerous and a little weird, but not homicidal. They hadn't known of all the deadly attacks instigated by their aged fathers. I convinced them of their fathers' treachery, they were shocked and ashamed. Their present concerns are not on revenge but on keeping secret their grandfather's and now fathers' criminal acts. I underestimated their fathers, Jud and Jared. They shot deals then still came after us—almost succeeding.

"The sons are not made of the same stuff as their fathers—who grew up under the thumb of a murderous sea captain, learning life on ships, working railroads, drinking and fighting in mining towns. Not the same as the present Livingstons—who went to private schools, got MBAs, and now sit on Sierra Club boards while retaining public-ity firms to cover their logging, mining and manufacturing interests."

Tanya broke in, "Who sent the killers to our wedding? Who's after you now?"

Webb replied, "We're still working on that. I'm sure it isn't the Livingstons. That's what I'm going to report to you now.

"I could have them all killed and they know it. I met with them two months ago face to face. I showed them time-stamped, digital pictures of all of them: fathers, wives, sons and daughters. I played recordings of all their home phones and cell phones, showing videos taken in their bedrooms and offices. They clearly understand how vulnerable they are.

"With death as a consequence for any more broken agreements, we got down to business. Their only interest is to protect their name and their multibillion-dollar business. There is no statute of limitations in Canada, their grandfather's murders and the sinking of the *Carol K* may be seventy years in the past, but would still bring prosecution and financial ruin. Their fathers' crimes died with them unless evidence of their treacherous acts becomes known."

Matt broke in, "We've been here before, we trusted the Livingstons through several deals, they lied and later came at us. History shows appeasement doesn't work. I say let the law and our evidence destroy this family."

Webb took more caviar, drank from his glass, waving his hand as though to dismiss Matt's words, "Listen to the plan…

"The Livingstons, with large contributions that bring support from the proper officials and academics, will salvage the anchor and bow of the sunken *Carol K* and bring it back to Canada to make a memorial at their company docks in the name of their grandfather; this will destroy any evidence or concerns as to how the ship got close to Granite Island when it was reported sunk fifty miles away. The incriminating scratches on the rock that the two survivors made will be ground out, the surface reworked by rock experts. This brings us to the other evidence. I'll keep the slug, pistol, log and all the pictures and material you have on the wreck. It will join an impressive and well-secured group of blackmail material I control.

"Now to the nut of the deal, the painting you found hidden in the log book. It is an early and rare Camille Pissarro, it has providence by the painter's grandson's printing on the back, making it very valuable but damning to the Livingstons. If allowed to be exposed to the art world it would be poured over by scores of experts, intellectual pit bulls when it comes to a newly discovered 1851 painting by the father of Impressionism."

Webb took a notebook from his breast pocket, "The printing said, 'If you find this, I did not make shore. Here is my treasure, my grandfather's work. I hold Charlotte Amalie in my heart.' The note ended with the signature, *Saul P.*

"Every good art dealer is an historian and a detective. They will eventually track the note to a Saul Pissarro, a ship's wheelman, and the Lake Michigan shore, and the *Carol K,* sunk in 1930, will be a subject of worldwide focus. One way to eliminate this discovery is if no one sees the back of the remarkable painting. For these reasons the Livingstons have offered to buy it from you for ten million US dollars."

Tanya choked on the sip of wine she was taking, the too-full glass spilling champagne on her shorts and bare legs. She looked at Matt who just stared at Webb.

Webb continued, "This is my wedding present. I can take the painting with me, the money will go from Canada to your new account in

Gibraltar within twenty-four hours. You will never have to worry about money again. Even if you are scrupulously honest, a good accountant will allow you to net nearly seven million after taxes. Believe me, the laws regarding found treasures, treasure troves, are many and complex, this arrangement will avoid or satisfy them all."

Webb smiled, a real smile, and scooped more caviar.

Matt, turning to Tanya, found his tongue, "Do you think we can get the painting away from your mother?"

8

Money Matters

Tanya phoned her parents, they agreed the painting belonged to Matt and Tanya. But they would only part with it by bringing it to them. Tanya warned them Webb was holding court, but the news didn't dissuade them. They had guests at their home, but would come for a short while, curiosity and perhaps a little more alcohol than they were accustomed to spurring them on.

While they were waiting for the Vegas, Webb began talking about using capital to make more capital. He had switched from the champagne to cold crystal glasses of vodka. He rotated chilled glasses, filling them from a bottle in the freezer. He seemed to be happy he had gotten past the issue of the painting.

Waving caviar-mounded toast, several pea-sized spheres rolled their way to the gold carpeting, little light-gray eyes that stared up as Webb pontificated, "Take this caviar—Iranian, Beluga, six times more valuable than silver per ounce…I watch governments making rules, save the poor sturgeons, stop taking caviar from the Caspian: quotas, inspections, insulting the only real natural law of commerce—supply and demand. I make some Iranian friends; the fishermen do as they have always done—but now only one part legal and nine parts illegal… in the warehouses, caviar is caviar. Pre-ban, post-ban—the records blur and I enjoy a modest percentage of a quarter-billion dollar industry. As the unsuccessful laws change and relax, more, non-wild, caviar comes from farms, where they milk the fish like cows, or do C-sections in sterile operating rooms, the costs will come down as the supply and suppliers increase. Point being—if you have some money and you watch the stupidity of law-making do-gooders, you move your money around, making serious returns on your investments. I'll be glad to offer my advice to you from time to time."

Tanya got up and made some coffee, Matt busied himself with emptying the boxes and storing their contents for a sea voyage. Webb stopped drinking and talking, pitching in, reminding them, after all, that it was his boat at one time and he knew its spaces.

The Vegas were escorted in by Al, who carried the painting protected in a cardboard container that the framer must have provided.

Webb had never seen the original, so Anita and George Vega agreed to open the box and enjoy one more look at the exquisite work.

The frame was some dark hardwood, narrow and non-distracting, the matting also narrow and neutral, the painting seemed to bring its own light. It depicted a beach, rays of a rising sun touching the tops of a few palm trees, the calm sea reflecting the pinks and yellows of the sky of a new day. The work, truly a masterpiece, transcended its components of fiber, ink and oil.

George Vega spoke, "When we read the words scribbled in the log pages we vowed to avenge the two men who died on that cold, barren island. We also talked about bringing the painting back to St. Thomas—for no deep reason except the thought felt right."

Not responding to Vega's points, Webb told the Vegas about the money involved. They gasped, taking several moments to appreciate the changes the money would bring to the newlyweds and in turn to their own lives, not to mention the relief knowing their daughter would be well off.

George Vega spoke. "If I knew you would have so much money I wouldn't have shot such a hard deal for a rental contract. This boat hadn't paid its keep for the new owner, he didn't take the best care of it, and his charter captains were as messy as their customers. When we owned the dive shop and charter boats we made money on everything. But I guess the economy was better then.

Matt thought, *Yah, Webb and his smuggling friends kept you in charters, booked ahead, half the time they were no-shows with no refunds.*

No mention has made of the wedding gunmen, so George hadn't said anything to Anita. Good, sleeping dogs...

George Vega continued, speaking for Webb's benefit, "We spent several weeks getting her shipshape. We had a boat service here for ten days—working on spotted chrome, chalky fiberglass, bilges and heads that stunk, lots of dirt in the corners. I went over the engines and brought in a MAN mechanic to help me. I worry a little about gunk in the fuel tank, we gave it treatment chemicals and sucked what we could from the tank bottom. Setting around in the heat doesn't do diesel fuel any good. They didn't run it enough. She's ready for sea now."

Webb offered the Vegas a nightcap, they said no, then hugged and kissed Matt and Tanya, thanked Webb and secured promises that the honeymooners would check-in every few days. Anita was crying as George led her off the boat and down the dock.

Matt and Tanya took one more look at the painting as Webb carefully re-boxed it and commented, "You know this is such a wonderful work, I hope we aren't selling it too cheap. I didn't remember how impressive it is."

Webb held out a legal document. "Here's a bill of sale—it's made out to the Livingston Corporation—you both need to sign and date it where the little, yellow stickers indicate. I've got a friendly notary that will walk over hot coals swearing to your signatures."

Matt felt a little lightheaded when he tried to count all seven zeros after the one. Tanya just smiled and whispered something about it being some wedding gift. Finally finding her voice, she said, "A week ago we were juggling finances and questioning if it was wise to spend so much on a cruise."

Webb said, "You're now among the 1% of the U.S. taxpayers that pay about 40% of all the income tax."

They all had a cup of coffee. Webb became his serious self again.

Matt asked, "What is happening with our well armed wedding guests?

Al answered, "We have them all at a house at the end of a long deserted road on some no-name key. They are telling all they know, which isn't very much. A shooting, in daylight with witnesses, in the Keys—which has only one long highway and a dozen organizations that can track every boat, is not how to stay in business long."

Webb added, "Their instructions and money came from Canada—too obvious. They think we are checker players—but we play chess, four or five moves ahead—this is probably U.S. Government—they have to know about the Livingstons, my connection with the Vegas, the wedding, my daughter. But we will hold our conclusions until we check more leads."

Tanya spoke, "What about the Venezuelans—Cortada tried twice—maybe he felt three's the charm?"

Al looked at Webb, who paused for thought, then nodded. Al poured more coffee into their cups and spoke. "Cortada is no more, he thought he cleverly bribed his way out of a Dominican prison, even paying for a special helicopter ride back to his beautiful villa that overlooks Maracaibo. He was very impressed with the uniformed escorts in the helicopter, they even allowed him to call ahead to have his minions and family waiting to celebrate his homecoming. The party had a real surprise when, with the help of a stun gun, he came hurtling out of the machine about five hundred feet above his patio.

"There will be no more issues—Cortada had his chances and failed, twice coming at Webb's family. Payback is understood and failure has a high price in the drug business."

Matt remembered Webb's vow to show Cortada's family some blood when his hired killer, Carlos, had taken over the boat, and shot Ray, Webb's long time body guard, in front of Karen and Carla, with instructions to kill them all, by either bullets or by a trip to the bottom of the Gulf Stream in chains.

Webb put his emptied cup down. "Time to go, it's been a long day and I've got a wife and daughter to find.

"Just a little more business. There's a hundred thousand in the debit card, should buy you enough diesel to go around Cuba a few times. It's your money, I sold all the Livingston stock we were given as part of the nuclear-waste deal. I wanted to cash out while their stock was high. If the sons' plans to destroy evidence screws up—and all it would take is one good reporter or some smart university kid—the stock would tank.

"Also, you should know the rest of your stock money is bouncing around the world commodity markets—stewarded by a little guy named Otto Rugur—I call him Pal—after Palindrome. You two go have fun while Pal works at a big desk with six telephones and three computer screens in New York's Mercantile Exchange. Just like caviar laws bring profit, US ethanol subsidies and mandates that use up a third of the corn crop have far reaching effects on domestic and world supplies and demands. Pal assures me there are riches to be made."

Webb opened a leather pocket folder and took out three cards. The first was plain with just one number on it, the other two had color and printing. "Here is my number, the card of the banker at Lloyd's Gibraltar bank, I wrote down your PIN number—call him, set up security codes, e-mail passwords, get comfortable with him—and finally, here is a great tax accountant—actually wrote a book on international banking while serving federal time.

"That's a joke…Let's leave these people to their honeymoon night."

Webb got up, looking around for his jacket.

Al stood up. "I've got a gift for you, too." He took out his pistol, putting it on the galley table. "This is an FN Five-seven, made in Belgium. I think it's the best handgun in the world, light, great capacity, very accurate, little recoil, normally restricted to military and law enforcement. The US Secret Service uses it. It can shoot through body armor; over a pound lighter than a military .45. Here are two more magazines—each with twenty shells. You can buy more 5.7 by 28 mm from most ammunition suppliers. Shoot some plastic jugs. Don't waste the ammo in the mags on targets—it's very special, blended metal. You'll both like it. I hope you don't need it except for target shooting."

Matt picked up the pistol—working the action, ejecting a shell, locking the breech open—the weapon was light, plastic, nice balance and feel; grip a little large, adjustable sights, internal hammer, safety on both sides, controlled by the trigger finger.

Al continued, "Only 1.7 pounds loaded, and here's the suppressor too. It could get you in trouble, and maybe several years if you're caught with it."

Webb asked, "Do you know about the hiding space in the helm chair?"

Matt, still holding the pistol, now with the magazine ejected, said, "No, I just know about the space under the bed." He looked at Tanya, who shrugged.

Webb spoke as he gathered his suit coat, "The middle chrome flathead at the base of the seat back will slide, then the chair back opens from the bottom. There is a space that will hide a pistol or several pounds of illegal material. Work on it. I never showed it to you because I had a pistol in it and I wanted to keep an edge—just in case I needed it. I'd show it to you now, but its dark and a light on the helm could have us seen from most of the marina. Just play around with the bottom chrome bolt head on the back of the chair and you'll get the front to pop open. You'll figure it out."

Al shook hands. Webb kissed and hugged Tanya. Matt reluctantly stopped bonding with the new pistol to help them off the boat, the boxed picture firmly in Al's arms. A limo pulled up at the end of the dock.

Tanya and Matt watched the men get in and the black vehicle move away, with more sound from the crunch of gravel than the engine.

9

Love Nest

Matt carried blankets and pillows to the lounge area of the *Reefer*'s bridge. The boat faced away from the marina, the helm hid the inglenook from view, even from elevated platforms of other yachts moored in the calm security of the harbor enclosure.

After looking at the beautiful half moon from the dock, they decided to build a love nest.

He and Tanya had not been together, alone for what seemed like months—but was really just a week. They had stood on the dock for a while after Webb and Al had left, looked at the moon, made their plan, then went into the salon and cleaned up glasses and bottles. As they put things away, they tried some of the expensive caviar and decided it was an acquired taste.

Taking a second small scoop of the Caspian Sea's fish eggs, directly from the ceramic spoon, and then washing it down with some warm champagne Matt said, "I've fished salmon with spawn bags. It was orange, looked and smelled better than this."

Tanya went toward the master stateroom, "I'm brushing my teeth, taking off my make up…and putting on something special for you on our wedding night…"

Matt finished up the salon policing chores with superhero speed. Also washing up and brushing the fish egg taste away, he made the one trip with the blankets and pillows and came down again for the ice bucket and another bottle from the refrigerator—not Dom but Pommery, a champagne they had enjoyed before at Webb's cabin. He had worked hard to find it in the Keys. He just hoped it was still good. With bottle, bucket, two glasses he worked his way up the ladder to the bridge area: a slide show of Tanya in various wedding night attire jumping through his eager brain.

The setting was perfect. The large, low half moon hung over a vast, calm sea. A few stars were bright enough to be visible to the west and low to the south. Light from the setting moon came peeking under the bridge top. Music came from the marina bar. Matt arranged the blankets, pillows and himself.

The night sounds of the marina were muted in the confines of the boat's bridge lounge area, a bed-size padded plastic expanse—marina bar music, waves lapping at the boats and piers, the occasional squeaks of fenders or nylon spring lines and occasionally a car engine or a distant truck's Jake brake as it slowed to a few feet behind some octogenarian driver blocking its path on US 1.

Matt heard the salon door slide open and shut. The slight click of a new wedding ring on the chrome ladder rail and the whisper of diaphanous material as it brushed against the helm partition announced Tanya's approach.

She stood before Matt, wearing a dark peignoir.

"I wanted this night to be special so you remember it, like the first time we made love in your cabin, during the blizzard. I knew we were special together and I dreamed we would have the day we did, so this is just for you."

She pulled the belting, the covering opened, then fell from her shoulders, Matt leaned forward to see better in the dim light. Tanya, her right side bathed in moon light, stood in a dark, hip-covering garment. Matt moved to the edge of the lounge. Tanya wore the dark green

Packer Super Bowl XXXI t-shirt Matt had given her on their first night together; he chuckled as she moved into his arms.

The shirt didn't stay on long. They made love as the moon watched, remembering the wedding kiss and happy to fulfill its promise. Matt and Tanya were soon lost in the sharing of each other. They set a new bar for mutual pleasure. Their joining was the natural result of their desires, an enjoyment of their physical selves and an affirmation of their love for each other. They were lost in pleasure as the moon slowly moved across the evening sky.

With the moon closer to the horizon, they kissed, touched and cuddled under covers as their wedding day ended and the rest of their lives began. They talked about their love, the beautiful ceremony, Webb, money, her parents, and as the night got cooler and more humid, they decided it was time to make the run to their cabin. Just as they were trying to find clothes, Matt whispered for silence.

They heard steps shuffling on the dock: muted voices, shushes, a few giggles. They couldn't see the dock from the bridge lounge area without getting up and going aft.

Then Matt heard a name—Billy. It was the Yooper boys coming to call. Matt slipped into shorts, crawled around the helm area, seeing dark shapes tying items to the *Reefer*'s aft railings. More whispers, more giggles, a hiccup, a chorus of loud shushes, dark shapes bobbed in and out of fading moonlight beating an unruly retreat off the dock.

Matt came back to Tanya, who looked worried, "No killers, just friends tying cans and jugs to our boat, a proper marriage trip send off. It's one of those things that guys think up after midnight."

Matt watched in admiration as Tanya shook the blankets until her t-shirt fell to the helm's deck. Together they got the love nest materials and themselves back inside. The champagne ice was water, the bottle unopened.

10

Leaving Harbor Sunday Morning

Tanya was up before Matt. She hummed as she made coffee and split some whole wheat English muffins for later toasting. Their refrigerator produced a quart of large, fresh strawberries that came from the huge vegetable farms surrounding Homestead. She cleaned and sliced them for adding to bowls of cereal she would have waiting when Matt finally got his newlywed butt out of the bed. She had happily proven that there wasn't really a powerful chemical in wedding cake that destroyed a women's sex drive.

She had never felt more content and happy. All the struggles and pains of her life faded into ancient history. She never had faced a day with such near giggly glee.

She heard the toilet flush, Matt had lived.

Matt found his shorts and a fresh t-shirt. He looked into the mirror as he shaved. He had a lot of things to think about, taking a boat on a five or six hundred mile voyage is a serious responsibility. He had gone over preparations days before with his father-in-law and his Yooper friends. They had a long check list: extra storage areas in the bow, charts, updated GPS and harbor information, reviewing all the tricks the relatively new Raymarine, multifunction navigation system could do. He had stored a whole box of extra fuel filters, cinched ties and securing straps on all stored materials and completed a score more checks on equipment: tightening screws, checking gauges and emergency gear, filing plans with the harbor master. He had topped off the diesel fuel the day before when they had returned from a sea trial that they had combined with a little yellowtail fishing.

Motoring to Croker Reef he had tied up at the number 16 red-nun buoy. After an hour of active baiting and beer drinking, the yellow-tails and sea birds had formed behind their transom: cold beer, buzzing reels and a frenzy of fishing followed. On the way back, Matt had inspected the boat from underwater one last time. Everything had been perfect and the fishing provided a little bonus for his friends for their support and their long driving trip.

Matt finished his reverie and shave, while looking at his clouding image in the steam-shrouded mirror. Cleaning up the sink, folding his towels, Matt padded past the bed, enjoying a moment to reflect and be thankful for all the blessings of his new life.

In the salon, Matt's planning thoughts stopped when he saw Tanya. She wore short shorts and a t-shirt. In that moment, Matt had a vivid flash of what she looked like in just her sun tan.

"Good morning, Mrs. Hunter."

"Good morning, my handsome captain, we're two hours past high tide and the sun just got up too. When do you think we should leave port?"

Matt thought, "I expect visitors in about an hour. We said we would leave around ten, but we aren't really in any rush. Key West is only about fifty miles by sea, a few hours. We'll check for a good forecast before we make the run for Mexico."

They kissed, breaking to pour coffee and move out onto the aft deck to watch, and feel the warmth of the rising sun.

They saw the group approaching down the row of moored charter boats. Six of the Yooper group bearing more bags and two coolers.

Tanya put her coffee down, "I've got to put on better clothes, I don't want them thinking that I'm a slob."

Tanya went into the boat as Matt stepped onto the dock to greet the wedding guests.

The guests had brought their own breakfasts. Soon everyone had beer, champagne, or coffee in a variety of cups and glasses. Toasts and jokes accompanied hugs and best wishes for a fine journey—through the sea and through their life together. Tanya got a lot of attention from the Yooper crew along with a few stories exposing many of Matt's faults. They all agreed this fall would be her deer hunting baptism, they promised her a perfect blind and that they would do everything for her except pull the trigger.

The Vegas also drove up. George reviewed all the possible problems they might expect; Anita gave Tanya a silver St. Christopher statue with a peel-and-stick base for the helm.

After a little more than an hour of chatter and good humor, the mood changed and became quiet, and the group moved to the aft deck, then the dock. The engines warmed up, lines cast off or pulled in, then the space between dock and stern slowly widened as Matt at the helm engaged the propellers. Tanya gave a final touch to her mother's hand. Then the sadness turned to laughter and cheers as empty beer cans, with their openings taped, and multiple rubber ducks were pulled from the cross pilings of the dock by hidden fishing lines. Matt had seen them but had no intention of ruining the surprise.

The *Reefer* moved slowly out of the marina into the channel that ran southeast into the deep water. They carefully followed the channel markers through the extensive sand bar that lay off the Holiday Isle. The day was warm and sunny, the usual rafts of boats had already formed in the shallows along the channel, their crews enjoying their Sunday on the water and sand. Matt could smell the food cooking on grills on several pontoon boats. He watched the colorful swimsuits of office girls from Miami, muscular Latinos making impressive leaps and dives after Frisbees and footballs, and nearly a hundred people who watched him as the *Reefer* negotiated the rather narrow channel. Standing in thigh-deep water, only twenty feet from the channel, the spectators noticed the ducks and beer cans then gave waves and clapped, with several wishing them good luck.

Tanya joined Matt at the helm. Hugging Matt she said, "We can take the little honeymoon accessories off when we get into deeper water."

Fifteen more minutes at no-wake speed brought them to the deep water. Matt slipped the transmissions into neutral as they both worked to pull in and plastic-bag the trailing flotsam.

Matt had the charts and GPS settings prepared. Pushing chrome shift levers forward engaged the twin propellers, one hand brought the twin throttles two thirds forward then eased them back. The *Reefer* leaped to its natural element—smoothly planing at speed across a blue-green sea. They cruised at 24 knots. Experience and instrumentation had proven the speed to be economical and comfortable for a light downwind sea.

Tanya left, then returned to the helm area in a light blue cover-up, carrying a beach towel. She spread the towel, removed her shirt and let Matt inspect her new bikini: iridescent beads in blues and greens. After a slow pirouette, she said, "This is a gift from Steve, a longtime friend that runs the *Bikinis in Paradise* shop at the Holiday Isle. I bought two others, and he gave me this one. You can't get it wet! The beads get water in them or something. But it is beautiful and fits perfectly."

Matt agreed about the fit and was happy that Tanya was not in public, but exclusively his to ogle on the lounge area.

They headed west; the sun covered half the lounge area, Tanya came to him for some sun lotion help. Matt gleefully applied and smoothed SPF 30 on her lower back and upper thighs. Tanya returned to her towel, untied the top strings and relaxed in the 80-degree sunlight as the beautiful vessel moved through the smooth waters, establishing a slight rhythmic bouncing motion as its 70,000 pounds raced over the larger swells.

Matt beheld his perfect world: green water, low islands on his right, the Raymarine C120 graphically supplying a great deal of information with its GPS, radar and mapped channel markers all giving overlapping navigational security, no weather issues and everything highlighted by Tanya's beauty as she relaxed before him. No other pleasure vessels appeared in sight, several larger ships showed as blips on the radar screen to their south, hidden from eyesight by the sun's glare.

He knew that the various channel buoys, ending with marker 4 at the end of the breakwater protecting the Galleon Marina in Key West, would appear in a little over two hours.

11

Key West

The sun got hotter as noon turned into afternoon. Tanya, partially in her iridescent bikini, got too warm and went below to make some lunch.

Matt, at the wheel, had spent many minutes trying to find and work the secret compartment of the helm chair Webb had mentioned. Frustration and a broken fingernail were his only rewards until a little WD-40 and the screwdriver blade of his Swiss Army knife finally made a chrome bolt on the chair's back slide up a quarter inch. Matt had been trying to make it slide sidewise. This was clearly the key that should have opened the back pad on the front of the chair, but nothing opened. More careful inspection led Matt to figure out that the hinge of the back pad was at the top therefore the bottom should swing up. Prying and patience was finally rewarded when the back of the padded helm chair opened upward, exposing a space several inches deep and over a foot square—all padded with foam rubber. The edges were of hard rubber and had become sticky with time, salt air and heat. Matt found some silicone grease and applied a thin coating where the moving back formed a gasket with the chair. After working the system several times Matt was impressed with Webb's ingenuity and the overall craftsmanship of the hiding place. He would fit the new handgun into this space. The other firearm they carried was a black M16, secured in Webb's main smuggling hidey-hole under the master bed, accessible through the common bulkhead via a removable part of the tub in the shower area, exposing a lighted, casket-sized space.

Matt didn't feel safe without some weapons aboard. The Gulf and Caribbean were rife with opportunistic traffickers in dope, people smugglers and a mixture of some just plain psychotic killers. Matt had acquired the black rifle as a trophy in a war with Canadian hit men nearly a year earlier. Matt liked its accuracy, firepower and fully automatic selector that would make any pirate consider finding easier victims. On the open seas pistols and rifles were very accepted and legal equipment on yachts. The complexity and danger would come as they entered Mexican waters. The Mexican Government had zero tolerance for weapons aboard visiting yachts. Many stories circulated on the web about owners who were imprisoned and their boats impounded if the government inspectors found even a single bullet. Firearms could only be aboard legally with some very expensive and cumbersome permits—capriciously granted by generally corrupt administrative officials. Matt's answer was to use the concealed hiding places aboard the *Reefer*.

"Do you want this beer and lunch now or after you run over that little sailboat?" said Tanya, suddenly standing at the helm with a cork tray holding an insulated mug of beer and a plate with a sandwich and chips.

Switching off the autopilot, Matt brought the yacht to port, avoiding a tiny sailboat, apparently dead in the water, dead ahead and nearly invisible in the sun's glare. As they looked down, the sailboat's operator was shaking the sheet rope like a horse's reigns trying the get the boat to move forward.

Matt muttered, "He's in irons—no steerage, not enough speed to complete bring her about, now the sail is actually backing him up. He has to push the boom out until he gets some air in the sail. He'll learn if he isn't swamped by our wake. He shouldn't be so far from shore, but that may be because he is so inept."

Matt and Tanya watched as their wake actually helped the struggling line-puller by swinging his bow around, and the sail stopped its pointless luffing to fill and provide a solid, close-hauled tack toward Bahia Honda Key. Holding his rudder and securing his sheet rope, the intrepid sailor offered a one-finger salute toward the now distancing yacht.

"I'll have to be a helmsman again; I was concentrating too much on finding Webb's hiding place in this chair; looks like we are getting everyone out on a Sunday afternoon." Matt checked the waters ahead, dots of color and white vessels, some sail surfers near Spanish Harbor. A dozen craft could now be identified in front of them.

Tanya checked the horizon with binoculars and then reviewed the radar and multifunctional display of the Raymarine. "Let me know when we are off the Naval Air Base, I can take her in from there. I've already called the Harbor Master at the Galleon Marina—we're in slip five, just for tonight, right up by the buildings. Easy walk to all the doin's of the fair city."

Matt knew Tanya had made many charter trips to Key West captaining for her father's marina business. Matt was not her equal in boat handling, she had Master's papers, earned by far more experience and helm hours than his "Six-Pack" Captain's License.

Matt had been comfortably referencing the white line on his starboard horizon that was U.S. Highway 1, bridging the various keys. Now this guide disappeared as the highway went north and out of sight from the water. Their westerly course and speed did not vary, but some minor maneuvering accommodated sail craft and approaching boat traffic. Matt could finally see the towers and broad open space of the Naval Air Station, but before Matt could call Tanya, she came to the bridge.

Matt eased off the helm seat; Tanya took the wheel, standing next to him.

They kissed, Matt stepped back to admire the vision of beauty before him. Tanya had changed to white-canvas deck shoes, white shorts, a scoop-necked blue-stripped sailor's shirt topped with a white-billed visor. In her large, polarized sunglasses she looked like a model working on a photo shoot.

"You're looking mighty good," said Matt. "I'll go spruce up, too, seeing how we are soon going to be among the rich boating crowd."

Tanya touched Matt as he left the bridge. She felt she knew his thoughts. The community of rich boaters in a major marina was a far cry from the world Matt had known—people to whom money was something their accountants worried about, or their parents lectured them on. Their major problems seemed to be what house or fashionable diversion they would next visit.

Tanya checked all around the *Reefer*. There was plenty of sea room, with the exception of several jet boats that were wake-jumping the larger motor craft. They could be an issue, either by flying into a channel at fifty miles per hour, or by tipping over and floating, hard to spot among the wakes and chop.

Below in the main stateroom, Matt chose his outfit from a packed closet. He had about a third of its space. He had found a great clothes and sports shop in the Keys. The Islamorada Fish Company—really a multiple-story, barn-like store—large enough to have a replica of Hemingway's yacht from the '30s as a center piece, was the best sports/ clothing store he'd ever seen. To a Yooper, massive selections of top-notch summer clothing is as rare as being able to order pizza delivery. Matt was almost overwhelmed with the variety and quality of the shirts, shorts and swimsuits available to him; the icing on the cake: much of the Columbia products were on sale. Three hundred dollars later, Matt had shorts and fishing shirts with so many pockets they should have come with an instruction booklet. Matt picked a dark, blue-gray short-sleeved shirt, light tan shorts and Sperry TopSiders. Adding his sunglasses, he felt he was ready to take on Key West with his beautiful bride.

From the Main Ship Channel, Tanya passed Marker 24, slowly paralleling the long, white breakwater that ended with Marker 4 at its east end. Slowly turning into the large marina, she used channel 16 on the

VHF to contact John, the harbormaster, confirming slip 5 was clear and available.

Matt, looking sharp in his new clothes, stayed on deck below readying fenders and organizing lines.

The marina had room for about ninety vessels; it was nearly full.

Tanya reversed engines and held their position in the calm water with no wind as an impressive 70-footer, using both engines and bow thrusters, a crew of three and some awkward moments pulled from an along-dock mooring, swung across the channel, finally coming out on a port-to-port pass.

The harbormaster and his helper Suzy stood at the slip as Tanya expertly backed the 54-foot Hatteras in. The *Reefer* was quickly secured, shore electricity and water hooked up.

They went to the little harbormaster office, checked the Internet weather monitor on the counter, and used their new credit card for the $3.50 per foot, plus taxes, one-night charge—a total of over $200.

Locking the boat, now safely under the scrutiny of the harbormaster's office only a few feet away, they walked hand in hand to Duval Street.

Tanya and Matt had both spent many days in Key West. But now, as newlyweds, their mutual experiences took on more significance.

On rented Mopeds they cruised Duval Street from the harbor to the far south end, stopping at little art stores when they could find parking places. They waited in line to have their picture taken by the big buoy-like marker noting the most southern point in the US—only ninety miles from Cuba. Tanya had a small, digital Canon—it fit in one of Matt's many shirt pockets. As the afternoon passed, Tanya suggested they could eat an early dinner at a place her parents used to take her, several miles away but accessible by careful Moped driving on the back streets.

After many more shopping stops, checking out historical buildings and careful avoidance of the more difficult intersections, Tanya led them to Stock Island—and the Hogfish Bar and Grill.

Matt wondered how anyone could find this place without a guide.

They only waited a few minutes to get a table on the deck, looking over a busy, cluttered and working harbor—some rusty equipment on the shore, working shrimp boats, complete with occasional authentic fish and diesel fuel fumes.

Tanya watched Matt studying the menu, "I suggest the Hogfish sandwich on Cuban bread, in another hour or two they will be out of their namesake fish and you would wait an hour for a table. We could start with a cup of lobster bisque. I think I'll have the shrimp Caesar salad."

The waiter arrived, Matt ordered for them, adding two Mexican beers, and the waiter left. He appreciated Tanya knowing this territory like he knew the north woods. She wasn't being bossy, just wanting him to have the best experience.

As they were enjoying their soup, Tanya gestured toward an old dock area with rotting pilings. "That was where the ferry went back and forth to Cuba over fifty years ago. Also, a lot of the Bay of Pigs troops gathered and planned the invasion here. My folks built a lot of memories at this place. They would come here, just watching and thinking. I could never be sure if the thoughts were happy or sad— maybe a mixture."

A weekend band was tuning up or, maybe more accurately, amping up. Matt noticed the predicted line forming, the bar now standing room only with little room for the pool players to line up a shot.

They ate the excellent food, trading bites of hogfish and delicious pink shrimp.

They would have liked to stay longer, have coffee—maybe eat some key lime pie—but decided it would be smart to get back to the boat while they still had good light. As they were turning their Mopeds in the ally where they had parked them, Matt noticed a door with "Custom Firearms" newly painted on it. On a hunch, Matt had Tanya stay with his machine and he entered the shop. The owner was stocking glass-fronted shelves with ammunition. With very little chitchat, Matt purchased a fifty-round box of FN 5.7x28 ammo, paying $25. The man made change from his pocket, the shop having no counter or cash register. The black and white box joined several little items they had bought during the day, all rolled into a plastic bag and secured to Tanya's machine. They headed back.

Returning the two scooters to the rental shop, Matt happily walked Tanya back to the marina area—cutting in from a ramp off the street and crossing the covered bar area that fronted the harbor, they noticed a man waving at them from a table overlooking their boat.

It was Edward the DEA man: whom Tanya had reported to when she worked as an undercover agent for several years, the man who had given them the fancy spy glass for a wedding present.

Edward pulled out a chair for Tanya. "Can I get you some beers—Corona is only $2.25 here, real cold?"

Matt and Tanya agreed. Soon they were all sitting with cold bottles, watching the sun set.

Edward continued, "I thought you might be at Mallory Square with all the other tourists. But I'm glad I didn't need to keep drinking beer by myself.

"I understand you're bound for Isla Mujeres. Oh, and congratulations on your marriage, I hope you like the telescope—it's English—from the sailing-ship days."

Tanya broke in, "What do you want? We are on our honeymoon."

"I'm here to say hello, and ask you to keep your eyes open in Mexican waters. There is a lot of activity down there in almost every illegal area you can mention. The Texas and Arizona borders get all the headlines, but the underbelly of Mexico is no less a conduit for drugs, people smuggling, arms deals, extortion, kidnapping and gang warfare. It is just hard to equate that with the beautiful beaches, perfect waters, palm trees, happy *touristas* and a crime rate worse than most large cities."

Edward took out an envelope and slid it between Matt and Tanya. "In there is a dossier covering four people we have a particular interest in. I would appreciate it if you would inform us if you see or hear of them. That's all. Use your satellite radio, call my number and make a report. My number is on the envelope."

Neither Matt nor Tanya took the envelope.

Matt said, "Can we just give you back the spyglass?"

"Not really, besides the box has a locating device built into the wooden frame. You'd have to saw it in half to find it. It works when you open the case. So, if you see something interesting, just open the case, make your phone call, and *voilà,* you're making the world a safer place. What could be easier?"

Matt took the envelope, "What if some bad guys find this envelope?"

"That would be bad. Hide the material, or better yet, memorize it and destroy it. We work with some Mexican officials, but it is safe to say, the system is one of such corruption—an honest man has zero chance for a long life. That is why we need on-site information. You have a perfectly honest and acceptable cover, you may never report anything, but you are down there—amongst them—a possible source of help to us. Besides you can't honeymoon every minute."

Tanya got up, "We were going to try, thank you. I owe you a lot, so does Matt, but this is pushy even for you."

Edward got up, too. "Well, I don't want to keep you folks any longer. Have a safe and fun trip."

With those few words, Edward shook Matt's hand, hugged Tanya and left through the hotel walkway.

With a few seconds of eye contact between them, Tanya and Matt abandoned their half-full beers and went aboard the *Reefer*.

12

Dry Tortugas

Edward's envelope lay on the coffee table; ignoring it, Tanya and Matt took towels and toilet articles to the onshore shower area, saving their holding tank and the intrigue of a spying mission for the time being.

Matt commented, "For three hundred dollars, use lots of hot water."

Tanya flirted, "Our next shower can be on deck with whatever hot water is in the freshwater hose. I'll be glad to be alone with you. This trip has been in my dreams. We'll make it perfect."

After showering in the excellent facilities of the Galleon Marina, but passing up the other amenities available—such as a pool, lounge and even a fitness center, they returned to the *Reefer* just as the harbor lights came on.

Matt made drinks—bourbon and club soda—in the heavy glasses that gave perfect clinks when touched by the round ice cubes from their SubZero. Tanya took some white wine from a previously opened bottle she found in the back of the refrigerator. (Glass bottles were generally no-nos in a moving boat's fridge.) From the helm lounge, they overlooked the harbor filled with white boats.

Tanya had the envelope, unopened, in her hand and pointed at the marina to their right. "There's where we top our tank." An AB on a tall sign marked the marina next to theirs. "We won't be in a rush in the morning—tide's low, but the weather is good for the next several days.

"We could go southwest from here, but it would mean leaving in the dark and maybe getting to Mexico in the dark. Leaving from Ft. Jefferson will get us seventy miles west—three hours. We have 230 miles as the crow flies, but we need to figure closer to 280 miles taking into account our going closer to Cuba to reduce unfavorable Straight of Florida and Yucatan currents. The sun's up before 7:00 and sets at 8:00—thirteen hours, we should have no problem making our run in the daylight."

Tanya added, "A Canadian named Barnhart left this same marina in June, 2008 and made the run in 8 hours and 23 minutes in a fifty-foot ocean racer. We'll go a lot slower."

"You hungry?" asked Matt.

"Not really, we had a lot of lunch. How about some ice cream or other dessert? We can take this material along and look at it."

A short walk and they found an open-air restaurant serving ice cream and creamy desserts. They sat near the railing watching people flow by. Indulging in chocolate fudge layer cake and ice cream, they balanced the sweet with dark Cuban coffee.

The envelope contained four single-page sheets each with several pictures, on each a mug shot with inches or centimeters measured behind the unsmiling, cruel faces. Their histories, convictions, suspicions, known associates, aliases, outstanding scars, tattoos or features and at the end of the pages—highlighted with a yellow marker, obviously by Edward—an offering of a reward for arrest and/or conviction. Three were Mexican with million-dollar rewards for each, the fourth a Colombian with a five-million bounty.

Matt and Tanya looked at each other—this was not table-talk material. The gangsters' many names sounded made up for the musical *Guys and Dolls*. Tempted to say the names and laugh, the honeymoon couple knew too many eyes and ears were surrounding them, so the pages went back into the envelope, then Tanya's purse.

The second night of their married life was slow and comfortable, perfect for each. Dawn brought coffee and omelets, looks of love and happiness.

As a team they cast off and left the Galleon harbor.

After topping their diesel tank at the next marina and heading to the North Channel, bubbling along with nearly no wake, they passed several sail and fishing boats, soon clearing the anchored boat area, and the near islands. Kicking in the 2,400 horses put them above the light chop, the compass read 270 degrees, and the sun filled the helm area, making the instruments hard to read. With green channel markers parading on their starboard, Matt pushed the throttles forward.

The *Reefer*, as a thoroughbred Hatteras, knew what to do. Get on top of the waves, props digging into the water, push and glide across the seas, 70,000 pounds moving at over 20 knots, heavy-bottomed coffee cup not even vibrating on the helm ledge. Matt moved the speed to 38 knots, just for fun. He knew the rule, 'You can go fast, or you can go far, but you can't go fast, far. Matt enjoyed the pure joy of moving over water at speed—in command of a magnificent vessel, its mechanics preferring speed, its hull, props and balsa-stuffed design eager for speed.

The GPS, radar and chart information soon led Matt to the due west direction of Garden Key and Fort Jefferson. The morning chop turned to a sea swell from the northeast; after a few jarring bumps from overtaken waves, Matt slowed to a very easy 24 knots.

Tanya came to the helm. "I love being married to you. All of this has been in my thoughts from the time I first dreamt of men—really boys. I wanted a man to love, who loved me, who enjoyed my world and protected me. You've done all these things, no knight on a snorting steed could hold a candle to you, you took on hired killers, mob bosses, and beat them all."

"I'm just a lucky, retired teacher and coach, with a perfect bride. I dreamed of stalking big bucks, making the right call on third and long, what kid should start on the field or mat and every halftime pep talk and every single play of the games I lost. My dreams never got to making love on a million-dollar yacht with such a smart, sexy woman. You're all any man can wish for, even in his fantasies."

The honeymooners shared the helm chair. Snuggling and enjoying the morning. Low islands lay to port, shrimp boats worked some banks to the north, or were anchored to process the night's catch and work their nets, or maybe to get some sleep.

After two hours they finally spotted the low shape of Fort Jefferson off their port bow. The channel, spiraling around the fort from the north, brought them to a fine harbor on the south side of the massive structure. The *Yankee Freedom II* was docked, a 100-foot catamaran that carried tourists four or five times a week to and from Key West. They left harbor ahead of Matt and Tanya and at speeds equal to the Hatteras.

Tanya motored to the public dock area behind the ferry. Tourists were being issued snorkeling gear, some were going down the wooden dock area to the main gate of the fort that crossed a medieval moat surrounding the massive fort's forty-five-foot-high walls.

A girl in a National Park Service uniform helped with the docking. A sign on the only building around informed visitors they could only dock there for two hours and must check in. Ten dollars settled the park fee, and friendly park personnel provided free anchoring permits, a list of mooring and other park rules, three excellent park maps and colored brochures. Matt noted all the park's officers, men and women, carried semiautomatics on heavy belts with extra magazines, lights and radios. He asked them why they were armed. The vague, inconsistent answers led Matt to the conclusion that they were armed because they were told to be.

Matt and Tanya used an hour of their two to walk around and through the fort. Air conditioners cooled park offices, and large generators growled on the southwest side of the six-sided bastion. Matt remembered that they had been asked to keep their boat generator low or off after 10:00 pm.

They found construction activity at the beach on the east side. Weaving past Bobcats, piles of old bricks, port-a-potties, and a crew of men moving materials around, Matt paused to talk to a man wearing a white hardhat and non-sweaty shirt, learning this activity was part of the recent federal stimulus money, over $13 million to be spent on the fort's repair.

Matt and Tanya crossed the wooden bridge and entered the fort, where they learned the fort's history and viewed many pictures and military gear. Famous names came up—Ponce de Leon discovered and named the seven islands the Tortugas in 1513 after the turtles he saw there. "Dry" was added so everyone would know there was no water there. Dr. Samuel Mudd, accused of complacency in Lincoln's assassination, was mentioned as he later became a hero for treating soldiers and other prisoners during a yellow-fever outbreak and was later pardoned by President Andrew Johnson. The fort was started in 1846; its sixteen acres making it the largest masonry structure in the western hemisphere, but never finished as the military abandoned it in 1874.

After looking at a fair number of the sixteen million bricks that formed the fort, which was built to counter a possible threat that never developed, the newlyweds returned to their boat and moved to the far area of the anchorage. They set two anchors on the sand and gravel bottom in the designated area. With proper scope and no wind or weather issues, they decided to kick back, swim and snorkel around and under the *Reefer*, rather than find the many sunken ships doomed by the natural, ship trap formed by these low keys or going to the prize snorkeling area.

In the water only a half hour under their hoisted diving flag, and after seeing a variety of fish and some isolated corals in the fifty-foot-plus visibility, they showered on deck, got into dry suits, relotioned, and sipped gin–and–tonics while watching the angular frigate birds hover effortlessly in the light breeze. Matt, ever the biologist, observed, "Beautiful design in a bird, seven-foot wingspan and weighing just three and a half pounds."

Tanya proposed dividing a big steak, which she already had thawed and soaking in a soy, garlic, red wine and oil marinade for an early supper. Matt set up their Kuuma grill. After another round of drinks and some salty snacks, followed by an hour of bird and fort watching, as the shadow of their flying bridge covered a growing expanse of sea to their east, they were ready for dinner.

They ate a perfect steak-and-salad dinner, including buttered rolls and red wine, at their dinette, enjoying their view of the fort and Loggerhead Key as the shifting winds gently swung them.

At the end of the meal, Matt took out the Edward envelope and positioned the four papers on the table. "Let's memorize these and then hide them below with the rifle and ammo. I never realized how Old West our DEA has become—wanted posters, big money.

"I have the pistol and ammo in the hiding place now, National Parks aren't gun friendly. I'll get the pistol secured in the helm chair this evening while I still have day light."

Tanya added, "Put the silencer in there if you can, it's more damning than the pistol itself. Leave it locked and loaded. I learned from the DEA training, when you need a weapon, you might not have the time or a second hand to reef it."

While Tanya did the dishes, Matt got the pistol, its extra magazines and the box of shells they had bought in Key West. The afternoon ebb tide had turned the boat, hiding Matt's actions on the helm chair from anyone at the fort, leaving them visible only to the trackless water and sand islands. Matt cut the foam padding so it would hold the gun with its thin silencer. The result kept the pistol secure in the foam, with room for two magazines secured in notched spaces of their own. With the back closed, the foam-filled area would hold everything securely and quietly.

The anchor light attracted bugs, which drove Tanya and Matt below to the salon where they completed their plans for the next day. The National Ocean Survey chart 11438 spread on the coffee table showed the rather tricky exit out of the Garden Key harbor and the seven red buoys they needed to keep on their port side to navigate safely around Bird Key Bank and set up for the run past Loggerhead Key in the southwest channel. High tide would be just after 5:00 a.m., sunrise at 6:41 a.m.. They would be up, breakfasted and anchors up by

7:00am. Perfect weather was forecast with light southeast winds that would not rile the waves from the prevailing northwest current of the Straights of Florida. They had made notes of all the GPS coordinates they would need.

They went to bed early.

During the night their generator turned on twice, once more than Matt.

13

Crossing the Strait

The anchor lines snaked slack as Matt went forward to pull them in: the sky pink, turning to blue as he labored. The big diesels rumbled in a low duet. Tanya smiled from the helm as Matt looked up while securing the anchors and latching the rope locker. The sea was glassy, abnormal for this normally windswept group of sand islands. Four other anchored boats reflected mirror images in the becalmed waters of the large anchorage. Before Matt got back to the helm Tanya had the *Reefer* between the green and red channel markers numbered "11" and "12" on the chart and GPS. The white Hatteras wakelessly headed west, away from Garden Key and its huge fort. The time was 7:00 a.m., twenty minutes past sunrise.

At the helm beside Tanya, Matt pointed at the GPS screen, indicating a buoy that marked the southern limit of the Dry Tortugas National Park, "Before we go to cruising speed, let's stop outside the park for some pistol practice. I've rigged up some targets."

The *Reefer* slowly left the park area, coasted to a near stop in the calm waters. Matt deployed two empty half gallon plastic milk jugs

on twenty-foot lines. They went to the helm area, making their shooting distance about thirty feet. The helm seatback opened obediently
when Matt pushed the chrome bolt head upward on the back of the
chair. Matt took out the pistol, having replaced the special ammunition provided by Al with the Federal Hornady FN 5.7x28 shells they
had bought in Key West. "I just put fifteen in each magazine, you first."

Tanya slid the large magazine into the pistol's grip, easily worked
the slide to chamber a shell. "I can't believe how light this is, even with
the silencer. Let's see if I can miss the transom and hit the bottles."

She took her weaver stance and a deep breath and put three shots
into the right target.

As the bottle filled and started to sink, it fishtailed on its line. Tanya
fired three more nearly noiseless sets of shots, ending with the bottle
just a submerged froth of formless white plastic. With the magazine
empty, the receiver stayed locked back. The shell casings littered the
helm deck. "I think the silencer helps the balance. Nice trigger. Light
recoil, good sights, twenty in the magazine, very accurate."

She handed the pistol to Matt, who waited with another loaded
magazine. Matt ejected the empty magazine, slid in the new one, the
pistol now closed, loaded and ready to fire. Matt worked the safety,
noting the easy, finger-controlled levers on both sides of the pistol. A
red dot clearly indicated it was ready to fire, while moving the lever up
to cover the red dot meant the safety was on. In addition, a little pin
popped up on the left side of the slide when a round was chambered,
nice to know when picking up the pistol from a storage area—even
in the dark you could tell it was loaded and ready. Matt appreciated
these finer points of a very well-thought-out pistol.

Matt took his shooting position and fired several single shots then a
series of multiple shots, all of which hit the remaining bottle. "This is the
best designed and most accurate pistol I've ever shot. I wish we had more
play time, but we've got to travel and it won't stay this calm very long.

"We've got thirty casings to pick up, we can't even have one found
in Mexican waters."

Picking up casings, pulling in their bullet-riddled targets, they put
everything into a plastic grocery bag, weighted it with two water-filled
wine bottles and deep-sixed the shooting evidence.

Tanya pushed the throttles, and the Reefer came to plane, their south by southwest course showed like an arrow in the white wake behind them. Tanya took the boat to nearly thirty knots, saying, "Let's take advantage of the flat water."

Matt went below, spreading a towel on the dinette table and using the cleaning kit taken from the stock of the M16 to clean the Belgian pistol. He found little to clean, as the chromed barrel had minimal powder in it—the little 5.7 mm, 40 gram bullets, pushed out by a large powder charge at 2,150 feet per second, didn't leave much residue. The aluminum silencer had the most residue and took the most time to clean and lightly oil. Matt used graphite grease in a small tube to treat the fine threads. The rest of the pistol seemed to be plastic. Without a manual, Matt had no intention of breaking the pistol down any further.

He reloaded the magazines with Al's special cartridges, wondering what lethal qualities they held. Their points were a gray metal and they were marked FN Herstal and 5.7x28 sizing and two Xs. Pocketing the magazines and pistol, Matt one-handed two frosty Coronas and returned to the helm. Setting the safety, he repositioned the loaded and cocked pistol in the chair back and working the other two magazines into their padded areas, said, "I put eighteen shells in each magazine—they take twenty, but the last two were going in hard. All the extra ammo and the M16 will be in the hiding space."

Pistol secured, sipping ice-cold beer before noon and kissing at the helm, the honeymooners headed off for their Mexican adventure. There were ships on the radar, but nothing close. They held the thirty-knot speed until the afternoon, when a two-foot chop made twenty-two knots more comfortable for both the boat and passengers.

Lunch was sandwiches and more cold beer, the sun's heat dispelled by the boat's speed and the helm's shade.

All their gauges were in their comfort levels, fuel steadily being consumed. They had about a 600-mile range for their 300-mile trip. Given an acceptable 20% safety margin, their point of no return would be off the west coast of Cuba.

Matt reviewed all the GPS settings, the weather information, their charts of the Cuban coast. They would be getting close to Cuba—18 to 20 miles—before changing to a more westerly course. The current and eddies of the Straits of Florida and the Yucatan Channel made a direct line inadvisable.

Tanya left the helm lounge to take a short nap. The sun and glare, rhythm of the speeding boat and two beers had made her sleepy. Afterwards, she would organize their papers for Mexican Customs, including their Internet-purchased fishing licenses. With a fishing rod on board, a license for each person was required to avoid the wrath of severe Mexican laws. This fishing issue had been their first taste of a long list of complex, costly Mexican rules, laws and procedures.

While Matt had the helm, they passed several sailboats. They communicated via radio, exchanging names, destinations and weather information. Matt understood the efficiency and romance of being under sail, but moving at five or six knots in varying currents and then tacking to boot made for very long voyages, taking days to go where the *Reefer* can go in hours.

Matt could visually see rain clouds over Cuba. The radar—using line-of-sight limited by the curvature of the earth, nevertheless could easily search out more than forty miles—had picked up scattered reflections from hills and tall structures on the large island ahead. He had less than an hour before their planned westerly course change.

Matt scanned the empty sea with his binoculars just to feel like a captain. The sun was to the west and later would be an annoying glare for their last leg across the Yucatan Channel.

Matt's scanning moved to the east, easier to see. He noted a tiny white speck glowing in the sunlight to the southeast. As the boat got further south the white speck took shape. There was movement, but nothing showed clearly on the radar. Matt used the spyglass, mindful of the brief GPS signal it would send from its cleverly hidden DEA device. With the old, brass 25-power instrument, Matt could see a person, appearing to stand on the water, waving a piece of sail.

Matt switched off the autopilot, turning the helm toward the speck, now several miles away. Recognizing someone in trouble, he increased the speed. Even as Matt set his new course the speck came into and vanished from his sight. Then as the distance lessened, the object took form and stayed visible.

Tanya came to the helm, the course change having awakened her.

The speck had become a living person, not standing on water, but on some yellow wreckage around his feet.

Matt moved to the aft deck, Tanya took the helm and brought the boat off plane a hundred yards from the floating wreck, ensuring their wake would not wash the person off his or her precarious raft.

As the *Reefer* neared the wreckage the figure became a man, who waved then collapsed on the mess that served as his flotation. Tanya reversed engines, came to dead stop, then at no wake, expertly brought the boat slowly toward the wreckage.

While Tanya maneuvered, Matt was busy scanning the wreckage carefully with binoculars. He shouted, "There're sharks in the water, all around that raft. It looks like a beat-up catamaran. The sharks are aggressive, they're nosing at the guy."

Matt ran below, in less than a minute he had returned to the helm with the Colt Automatic Rifle known generally as an M16 and an extra magazine. Tanya circled the *Reefer* upwind of the twisted wreckage. Matt moved to starboard, ejected the magazine, tapped it to seat the shells, slamming in the thirty-shot magazine. He pulled and released the cocking mechanism, pushed the left side lever from its safe position to semiautomatic and fired six shots into the water. The sharks scattered in an instant. Matt could see blood dripping from a wound on the man's left leg.

Setting the safety, Matt left the rifle and extra magazine near Tanya at the helm. "I'll snag the wreck, you shark shoot if you see any. Just push the safety lever one click down and pull the trigger. It doesn't kick much, but it's loud."

At the main deck, Matt took the boat hook from its snaps on the port transom, twisted its locking mechanism and extended it to its full length. Hooking a float, he drew the man and wreckage to the stern of the *Reefer.*

It didn't take a crime-scene investigator's intelligence to realize the raft was a scene of slaughter—dried blood, bullet holes, tortured metal and catamaran pontoons that looked like they had been chopped to pieces.

Matt didn't know what to do next.

The man, really just a boy, lifted his head. His desperate eyes, sun-burned face and white, chapped lips softened to a grin. *"¿Estoy sonando?"*

Tanya answered his question in Spanish, "No, you are not dreaming."

"Can you get in our boat?" asked Matt. Tanya turned the question into Spanish. With no dive platform on the stern, there was over three feet of freeboard to cross to board the *Reefer.* Matt didn't want to try to step onto the bobbing mass of tangled lines, sail and broken pontoons. The man's leg showed blood seeping from under a crude bandage, his movement and standing disturbing his leg wound, he had dried blood all across his chest. Matt couldn't help him and maintain his pull on the boat hook.

Tanya, with the rifle, now stood at the transom beside Matt. She asked the man if he could stand, *"¿Te puedes parar?"*

The man tried to rise again, holding onto the broken piece of mast, but his legs and the conditions of the floating mass would not allow him to move toward the boat. Matt wouldn't be able to board the bobbing wreck to help him.

Giving the boat hook to Tanya, who had placed the rifle on the deck, Matt got the boat ladder that was folded and stored on the starboard side of the cabin. He secured it over the side. From a locker he got two life vests. He tossed one to the man, stripped to his boxer shorts and donned the other life vest.

Tanya looked at Matt in surprise, "You're not going into the water with blood and sharks in it?"

"I don't think there's an option. We can't maneuver around this mess very well, pulling on it very hard will tear it apart, and he'll fall in if he tries to stand again or even move. If he gets tangled in the lines and floats it will be hell getting him out while the sharks come up from underneath. Look, the wreck is coming apart just from our pulling it in. It's like ice chunks in a river that's breaking up, you can't step on them.

"Let's do this fast: fire into the water if you see anything."

Tanya, speaking in Spanish, told the man to put on the life jacket. She also tossed him a stern line, which she secured to the starboard cleat. The man just looked at the rope, not comprehending what to do with it.

Matt lowered himself into the water, and breast stroking around to the far side of the wrecked catamaran, motioned to the man to sit down and slide into the water. With pain, shaking from exhaustion, the man moved to the only stable part of the wreck—a yellow pontoon—and with Matt's help, allowed himself to slide into the sea.

Tanya released the boathook's hold on the wreck and brought the pole around to the starboard side where she offered it to Matt. With one hand on the man's jacket and the other on the boathook, he was quickly drawn to the base of the boarding ladder.

When Matt and the Cuban reached the ladder, Tanya dropped the pole and brought up the M16. Aiming into the water between the swimmers and the now-drifting wreckage, she pulled the trigger. Nothing happened. Quickly thumbing at the safety lever, she aimed again, the rifle fired a burst in full automatic. The sea erupted, the barrel kicked up, bullets pinged off the metal of the catamaran, shell casings rained into the sea and on the deck. Satisfied she had dispersed the prowling predators, acting like she knew all along she had put it on full automatic, she summed up her shooting with one word, "There…"

With Matt pushing and Tanya pulling, amid sighs of pain and gasps of effort, the wounded man finally got over the transom and rolled on to the *Reefer's* aft deck. Matt saw two sharks coming from under the wreck: six footers—lemons, he thought. His foot touched the ladder step, and he vaulted out of the water, glad nothing was hanging onto and chewing his leg. Tanya had a sunning mat under the Cuban and covered him with a beach towel. She offered him water, which he drank with restraint, even reverence.

The man looked around, sipped more water and said, "Thank you."

14

Alberto

The rescued man lay on the mat with multiple wounds, sunburn, dehydration and a fever. He was young, well-muscled and, even after suffering his ordeal at sea, still handsome.

Matt and Tanya debated their next action.

Tanya went to the storage area, returning with several bottles of Gatorade. "He needs liquids and electrolytes. This is warm, but it needs to get into him." She knelt and helped the man swallow nearly half a plastic bottle of the blue-green liquid full of magical metabolic chemicals developed by her alma mater—the University of Florida.

Matt looked at the wound on the leg. "This is bad, there is dried and infected flesh coming out of the wound, it's crusted with blood and sail cloth. We need to clean it up and get a good look. Anything we do is going to hurt."

Tanya left the man with the Gatorade, rushing into the salon, returning, arms filled with a first aid kit, sunburn ointment and various antibacterial sprays. She put the load down and went back for a large plastic bucket of warm soapy water and several wash cloths. Saying, "Let's clean him up out here and then get him to bed."

The man watched all their activity, his eyes gaining focus with the intake of liquids, and finally spoke in English. "I am Alberto, I have some English." Nodding toward Tanya, "You are Cuban?"

Tanya replied in Spanish, explaining they were Americans, her parents came from Cuba. She introduced Matt and herself, saying they were boating to Mexico.

Matt interrupted, saying he felt Alberto needed medical help as soon as possible, and they should be calling a U.S. Coast Guard helicopter.

Alberto, understanding the English but speaking in Spanish, said, "I'd rather be eaten by sharks than go back to Cuba. I have a waterproof bag tied to the mast. It has my papers. I have a Spanish passport and my Cuban papers."

Tanya translated this information to Matt, who went to the helm. Backing the *Reefer* to the wreck, careful of lines and sails in the water, he allowed Tanya to snag the bundle—a rubberized, waterproof fly-fishing pouch—with the boat hook. She skillfully maneuvered the bag and shoulder strap from its ties to the shattered mast.

Bag safely aboard, the man gratefully touched it as Tanya and Matt bathed him and tended to the sunburn and crusted salt. Using several buckets of warm water they exposed both wounds. After soapy water, they treated the chest wound, a foot-long shallowly ripped, scabbed-over flesh, with hydrogen peroxide, which bubbled and foamed, causing no pain, and hopefully flushing some material from the wound. Triple antibiotic salve was then applied to the gash and covered with several 4x4-inch gauze pads taped in place. The leg had a big-league wound, far outstripping the first aid lessons and experiences of Tanya and Matt. Washing, half a bottle of hydrogen peroxide, Bactine spray and antibiotic salve didn't seem to make anything look better. Finally bandaged, more for esthetics than real medical improvement, the patient was able to be moved from the sunny aft deck.

Alberto made no show of pain as he was worked on. Cleaned up, having consumed the second bottle of Gatorade and clothed in a pair of Matt's boxer shorts, he was helped to the port, guest room.

Matt made some chicken soup, buttered saltine crackers, cut a few little pieces of cheese, and brought it all to the small stateroom where Tanya was talking to their guest.

Alberto took and sipped the cup of soup, ate the cheese and crackers and smiled for the first time. In English he said, "I have much hunger. Thank you."

Tanya took away the empty tray, helped Alberto arrange himself on the clean white sheets and pillows. The room was comfortably dark with a single, small, shaded porthole, and the air conditioner kept it cool. Alberto relaxed, and quickly fell asleep.

Tanya and Matt went into the hallway leading to the salon. Keeping an eye on their patient, they talked about what to do with their honeymoon guest.

Tanya started, "We can't take him back to Cuba. He has been through torture so horrible he nearly panics when he talks about it. He even asked me to keep the door and porthole open to let light in. If we call the Coast Guard they will return him to Cuba. If we turn back to the States, we would need to smuggle him in and find a sympathetic Cuban doctor. If we follow U.S. law—he's foot-wet and goes back to the Cuban authorities. If we go on to Mexico we can get medical attention sooner, but who knows how they will treat him?"

Matt looked into the stateroom and came out, "I'd say go on, if we head back it would be at least eight hours against the winds and waves, which reports say are building, we would be marginal on fuel, and give him a long, rough ride. Mexico is less than four hours, smoother water. You said you knew the guy that runs the marina and he is a good man."

"Yes, Tomas and his helper Jose had managed and run the marina for many years, they know my father and will remember me as a young girl. It's been fifteen years since I've been there. Dad took many charters to Isla Mujeres as well as several vacations with mother. I can have Dad talk to them before we get there—they go way back, Dad talked to Tomas shortly before our wedding."

Tanya called her father on the satellite phone. He agreed with their decision to continue to Mexico. Also, he thought the marina at Isla Mujeres would be a more relaxed point of embarkation than going into Cancun, which was bigger and closer but more formal about regulations and custom procedures. George Vega noted there was a good naval hospital on Isla Mujeres. He also had known a doctor named Salas who worked at the base—whose mother was Cuban and who had studied medicine in the USA. He had treated one of George's early charter customers who had been stung by a Portuguese man-of-war and gone into shock. George and the doctor had become friends over the years. The doctor's office was close to town off the major road on the island. George told her that Dr. Salas was a sincere man and his medical code might mean he would keep a patient's nationality in confidence. George promised to try to contact the doctor and prepare him for the situation, maybe even to the point of making a house call—or rather a boat call at the marina.

While Tanya finished talking with her father, Matt thought about getting the *Reefer* underway. He felt bad leaving a hazard to navigation behind, but rationalized that the currents and tides would soon bring the floating mass into shallow coastal water, even to some beach. Technically, he should report the floating hazard with a *"securite"* announcement on the ship's VHF radio. Thinking about attaching some kind of radar reflector made him check his radar screen, where a large blip moved rapidly directly toward them from the south—Cuba.

The *Reefer* had been floating for nearly an hour eighteen miles off the Cuban coast, the current moved generally northeast but was eddying them toward shore. Matt scanned the southern horizon, he could clearly see a spike on the horizon that could be a patrol boat. After looking at the bullet-riddled catamaran bobbing twenty yards away, Matt knew he didn't want to have anything to do with Cuban patrol boats.

Matt quickly ran below to inform Tanya that they were going to be getting out of Dodge, riding their 2,400 horses. He would be going as fast as he could until they had no patrol boat following on the radar. Alberto understood the conversation and added his thoughts in Spanish—which Tanya translated. "He said the patrol boats aren't very fast and aren't given much fuel, they will not chase for long. Their guns can shoot several miles. They killed his friends."

Matt told them to hang on, it might be bumpy for the next hour or so.

The *Reefer* hit plane and accelerated to thirty-five knots. The two-to four-foot waves were well-spaced and no issue to speed, escaping gun boats made up for any discomfort.

After nearly an hour, the radar showed no pursuit or new blips vectoring toward them. Matt throttled back to twenty-four knots. He checked his GPS and scanned the sky, then he and Tanya laughed about including outrunning Cuban gunboats in their honeymoon adventure.

The westerly course and favorable winds made smooth travel until they came to the Yucatan Channel. Waves of four to six feet met them. They altered course to cut into them, proceeding southwest by west at 18 knots. They bounced and yawed some, but their Cuban patient slept on.

Tanya came to the bridge with the rubberized bag holding Alberto's papers. She showed Matt some papers, holding them securely against the wind, "His full name is Alberto Luis Perez Cárdenas. My mother is a Cárdenas. He comes from the same northern area that all her family either came from or still live. We're relatives. We've got to help him.

"We peeled off some scabbing, now his leg is draining; I changed the dressing and put on more ointment. I had Vicodin for him but he seems to be able to sleep without it. He said he had soaked his leg in sea water and it stopped bleeding after the first day or so. Bleeding started when he stood up. It is hot to the touch, he can move his toes and they are warm and healthy looking. I think it is all a muscle wound, with no major vessels or many nerves involved. But it is infected and will get worse without antibiotics and a doctor.

"His Spanish passport won't fool anyone looking real close. It is a color photo copy on typing paper inside a real Spanish Passport. It isn't laminated very well either."

Matt looked at the passport, "We could still use this as the basis for our crew list. Put it with ours, mixed with all our other papers for immigration. We've got several hours before we can call the Port Captain, hoist our Q flag and set up a Sanitation inspection."

Tanya closed the bag and started back to the salon. "I'll be happy to take the helm and get us to the marina after we get past the town. I'm sure I can remember the dock."

Looking over papers and Mexican rules taken from forms and internet documents, Matt said, "We've got running around to do, going to immigration with our passports and to a bank to pay immigration fees, or we might want to pay an 'agent' who will do this as a service for several hundred dollars. Also, your dad mentioned his *Importada* papers for the boat are still good for two more years. We can spread some money around and grease all these processes. With all the negative news about Mexican gangs and killings I bet they will be cooperative and appreciate our *gringo dinero*."

Tanya, hugging Matt, said, "Most honeymoons don't have a wounded escaping Cuban with them."

Matt, enjoying the hug, said, "We probably should have taken pictures of the shot-up catamaran, just to prove we are following one of the oldest laws of the sea: rescuing a sailor adrift and in danger. Let's get him patched up and hope we don't get into trouble for aiding him."

Over the next two hours, Tanya tended Alberto, spelling Matt for toilet and food breaks. The weather calmed in the afternoon, and as they shaded their eyes from the sun's glare, the low island's white sands and colorful town at the north end of the thin island came into view. They motored past an anchored Mexican frigate, looking ominous with its gray sides and decks sprouting antennae and guns. There were also fast, little jet-powered patrol boats buzzing between the island and Cancun. The presence of the Mexican military was very apparent.

The channel was well marked both on their GPS and by properly set buoys. Their marina was about a mile past the town, across from the airstrip. They passed several very luxurious new marinas. Now at the helm, Tanya remarked that many areas seemed changed and several of the docks and marinas weren't there just a few years ago. None of the marinas were full.

15

Mexican Paper Chase

The *Reefer*, properly outfitted with the yellow Q flag flying from the bow staff, the Mexican flag flying from a starboard bridge antenna and the U.S. flag snapping at the stern, motored past several naval patrol boats. Tanya at the helm looked businesslike, covering her beauty with sunglasses, a baggy flowered t-shirt and a large billed cap. Matt tried to look innocent, not showing the guilt of a person transporting an illegal passenger. Happily, none of the gray-brown military craft hailed them or sought to board them. They seemed more interested in getting out into the bay between Isla Mujeres and Cancun and showing how fast they could go.

Tanya brought the boat to a dock where three men waited with a wheelchair. They signaled her to back into a particular space halfway down the south side of the pier. There were only eight other yachts in a marina that could have taken forty boats.

Before Matt had all the fenders and lines secure, the three men stepped aboard and greeted Tanya, who came down from the bridge. After hugging two of the men while Matt finished securing the boat, she introduced the men to Matt.

"These are my friends Tomas and Jose, they make this marina the best and friendliest on the island, and this is Doctor Salas.

The doctor spoke in English. "Please, I need to see the wounded man."

Tanya conducted all present through the salon and into the bedroom where Alberto lay, awake. The doctor removed the bandage on the leg and gave it a quick inspection. Alberto took in several breaths as his leg was moved and lightly probed with the doctor's rubber-gloved fingers.

"This man must be in hospital immediately, he needs IV fluids and antibiotics. I will take the responsibility of removing him before all your papers are complete. Let us move quickly. Many of us have sympathy for the escaping Cubans. A few years ago this young man would be given a thirty-day visa, but not now, he is illegal without a Cuban visa and would be detained and sent back, or worse. Many have been victims of extortion and fallen into the hands of smugglers. Last year I treated a boatload that was put on a sandbar at night, told they were in Mexico, by the time they were found, two died of dehydration and many were in hospital for days. I'll register him under the name of a patient's son, Hugo Grova, you must pay his bills promptly in cash as soon as he is released. There may be months before the billing paperwork is sent out. I'll see to him and get you information about this Hugo through Tomas."

Matt and Jose hoisted Alberto from under his arms and quickly moved him to the waiting wheelchair, which Jose pushed to the doctor's vehicle.

To Tanya, Tomas said, "Many things have changed since you were here as a young girl. There are now more military. There are gangs and thieves everywhere, you can't leave anything lying around or unlocked now.

"As before, we will help you with your papers. I spoke at length with your father, you have all the many requirements. Such as many copies of your passports, the *Zarpe* and *Importata*. I would still suggest you pay our Miguel to help you. He will save you many hours of waiting and many kilometers of travel. He will be here soon and go over your papers with you, he can collect fees without your need to go to several banks."

Matt pointed at some of the forms and piles of copies, "We went through the Bahamas and the Dominican Republic with just passports, ship and crew information and one quick inspection. This process is like a scavenger hunt between offices and banks."

"I don't understand a scavenger hunt, however, I am sorry for these rules, they are a very great inconvenience to many boaters. I fear many of our open slips are the result of these rules, as well as the unrest with the drugs, smuggling and weapons. However, our sunsets are magnificent, the diving and beaches are still without equal, five hundred years of history is all around you and we will serve you like royalty."

Tanya spoke quietly, marinas, even empty ones, having many ears. "How do we handle our Cuban friend?"

"I'd say, do nothing for now, check in like he was never here. Wait for the doctor's opinion. The inspectors will be here within the hour, they prefer a docked boat rather than being rowed out in a little dinghy.

"We have magnificent dinners and cool drinks for you whenever you are cleared. It is wonderful to see you again: Matt, congratulation on your marriage."

Tomas left the boat and dock.

Tanya brought Matt into the salon and began spreading papers on the coffee table, saying, "Without dad's help and the experience of coming here several times, all this paperwork could have taken us a whole day and lots of frustration. Most people don't have enough copies of the passports—you need five each. The *Importata* is like a bill of sale for the boat, it costs money and is good for ten years, ours is still good. We have five copies. Otherwise we would need to go to a bank in Puerto Morelos to pay for it. Each fee seems to have a different bank and they seem to have their own business hours. The Port Captain uses a bank in Cancun: Immigration uses a bank here on Isla Mujeres. Miguel handles all these issues.

"We need to get our health forms certified at the clinic—Miguel will have the forms. We also have what they call a *Zarpe*, it is an old Spanish word for 'set sail' which documents our last port and later this port. The U.S. doesn't issue them for yachts—Homeland Security has CBP Form 1300 for commercial ships, Dad had us get a certified note from the Key West harbormaster, we need to get another from the Port Captain when we leave. Many boats come in without any documentation and are fined.

"Here is our list of all electronics on the boat, serial number of our outboard, and a certificate citing we have insurance, money and jobs so we won't be on Mexico's welfare lists."

Matt looked at the forms he had already completed, commenting, "This is a far cry from what we ask of Mexican visitors or immigrants—legal or otherwise—who fill our schools, hospitals and social programs. Not to mention our jails."

Just as Matt was thinking about adding more to the list of injustices, there was a tapping on the door frame. It was Miguel, neatly dressed holding a thick leather briefcase.

For 275 pesos, $23 US dollars, Miguel went through the cumbersome and confusing rules and picked up and organized the papers on the table. He was pleased to see all the copies, the boat customs permit and the paper that documented their last port.

In total, they needed ten different forms—with two to five copies each. Miguel collected various fees in U.S. dollars at the current exchange rate, gave Tanya a map to the clinic and immigration—with the hours they were open. He said he would return after the sanitation inspection was completed, the Q flag was lowered, health approval obtained and immigration had been cleared. He had a cell phone number on his card in case of a problem. To show he was a very busy man he turned down the offer of a cold beer and left the boat.

Tanya and Matt were halfway through their second beers when the inspectors came. They were quick and courteous, with questions asked in English from a checklist. Food, drink, guns, ammunition were no problems. Matt was thankful Tanya had very thoroughly picked up and disposed of the .223 brass that had fallen on the decks while they were shooting sharks. The Mexicans did take beers in the shade of the helm and seemed truly pleased to greet new boating tourists—who, with good humor, they called *Yatistas*, tourists from yachts.

The clinic was in the process of closing its barred doors thirty minutes early when Tanya and Matt found it. Their map was poorly proportioned and the street name and numbers didn't help because there were no street signs and no numbers on the houses. Tanya's Spanish and engaging smile saved the day and their forms were stamped by a male office worker.

Immigration stayed open late, and Miguel had armed them with all the necessary papers, in their proper order. Stampers stamped their passports and their visas were issued. They went to the local HSBC bank where over 438 pesos got their visas officially stamped and copied by a bank teller. Every stamp or form seemed to cost ten or fifteen US dollars. The copies surprisingly were free.

Returning to the *Reefer,* the honeymooners were hot and dusty. Miguel was waiting. He organized the completed stamped copies, taking what he needed to satisfy the Port Captain—who he would personally see the next day. In total, he had a package containing: five copies of the *Zarpe,* the original crew list with three copies, boat documentation (*Importata*) with five copies, two copies of their passports, two photocopies of their visas, and money for the boat fee—another several hundred pesos. He reminded the couple he had saved them a trip via ferry to Cancun, carfare to a bank there, another carfare to Puerto Morelos—a Custom Containers Inspection High-Security Area that needed several complicated ID checks and usually meant waiting in line and another bank visit.

Tanya reminded him they had the Puerto Morelos customs permit, then offered him a beer which now, at the end of his busy day, he took. He even chatted for a time about the complexity of the system and how it changed all the time. When he finished his beer, Matt thanked him again for his efforts, and gave him a handshake containing a folded twenty-dollar bill, and Miguel left.

With no more papers or visitors, the newlyweds took their time to clean up from the dusty streets and hot offices. Looking smart in colorful, tropical clothes they headed for the marina's bar and restaurant. At the bar Tomas, the omnipresent owner and operator of the complex, came to them, squeezing into their booth with news of Hugo, aka Alberto.

"Your friend will be staying overnight and another day. The antibiotics are working. He is going to be fine, just a weak leg, perhaps for some time. You can visit him tomorrow and he can leave the next day.

"The staff knew he is Cuban as soon as he spoke. They are mostly very professional and will say nothing, but this is a small island and word gets around."

Tomas left his last sentence hanging as information and possibly as a warning.

Tanya spoke, "We will take care of him. We will see him tomorrow and perhaps make some plans."

As he rose, Tomas said, "I will be happy to help you in any way I can. Have a good evening."

In a small, dark booth, they held hands while sipping superb frosty Margaritas made with Grand Marnier, the best tequila, cane sugar and fresh limes. Warm tortilla chips from a large clay bowl were dipped in another bowl of fresh spicy salsa. They toasted each other and ordered dinners of fish and *Poc Chuc*—a Mayan pork dish. When they weren't looking at each other, they took note that the restaurant was now nearly full, indicating that many people other than boaters came there, with most seeming to be locals—an indicator of the quality of the food and service.

A dozen people sat around a long table near them, mostly men, young and loud. Liquid from chilled bottles of the finest tequilas filled and refilled tall, thin shot glasses: limes, salt, beer chasers—all being enjoyed with Latino gusto. Several times the glasses were raised, toasting an older man at the head of the table. The name *Momo* kept coming up.

Tanya leaned forward, kissed Matt's cheek and whispered, "We need to check the wanted posters…I remember that nickname."

Matt had heard the name also, and he too remembered the wanted poster. He took his finger and printed MOMO in the thin film of tomato sauce on his nearly empty plate, turning it toward Tanya.

Looking at the name in the soft, flickering light of their table's candle, she nodded and quickly wiped the name clean with a small piece of bread. Leaning close to Matt's ear, she whispered, "Don't turn now, but be sure you take a good look at the man at the head of the party table. Don't be obvious, they can take offense quickly."

Their dinner enjoyment was complete: safe in port, having rescued a person in peril, now they dined on superb food, in an atmosphere spiced with the possibility of drama and danger.

16

Murderers in the Marina

S oft warm breezes made the sailboat halyard lines chime in the quiet marina as Matt and Tanya used the darkness to retrieve the DEA documents from their hiding place in the helm seat. Back in the salon, behind drawn shades and locked door, they went over the four pages they had been given by Edward the DEA investigator.

"Here he is," said Tanya, separating one page from the others, reading parts of the write-up below the several pictures: "*Mo-Mo*—nickname for Morgan Morales, top gangster in this state—Quintana Roo. Ties to the Zetas and the Beltran Leyva cartels, his enemies end up in caves with their hearts cut out. Controls drug trafficking from South America,—money laundering, owns or kills the public officials—mayors, police chiefs, even governors. A million-dollar reward for his capture and conviction."

Matt noted, "He makes Webb look like a Sunday School teacher."

"Well I wouldn't go that far. The Russians are very tough, many—like Webb—are well educated, they know bodies are a problem, many times a sudden disappearance with no clues or witnesses is a more terrifying message than a bloody corpse. I also think, underneath, the Russians can be as cruel as anyone on earth. You saw how Webb handled Cortada of the Venezuelan cartel."

Matt, looking over Tanya's shoulder, suggested, "Let's call Edward: we have no business messing with these men, particularly on their home turf. When I fought with Webb and his men it was on my own property in my own country. Here we have no power or rights. In fact, I think we should think about getting out of Dodge. We can celebrate our life together better and longer in safer places. All those gangsters at the table we passed this evening checked you out. I tried to look tough and controlled, but I felt like a parrot fish at a shark convention."

At the *Reefer's* dark helm, they activated the GPS beacon built into the telescope case. While they stood there looking north toward the next dock, they saw a big catamaran moored at the far side just as its mast and deck lights came on, flooding the area. The men from the restaurant were on board, still celebrating loudly, accompanied with music and several women in shorts and bikini tops. Matt, using the old telescope, scanned the thirty-meter craft.

"I see *Momo*, white shirt, in a chair by the cabin door."

Tanya took the telescope, closing it and securing it on the helm shelf. "No more peeking, let's go down and make our call."

The satellite phone transferred to Edward's phone mail. Tanya didn't give any names, referring to the page number and date of the wanted poster in a short message, followed by their number. An hour later, they hid the wanted posters, replaced the telescope and closed the case.

Before the honeymooners were ready for bed, the phone rang. Matt turned on the salon lights and they gathered around the satellite phone.

Edward sounded excited. "Good work, the GPS signal works perfectly, but the man you identified may be beyond our grasp at this time. We were able to extradite the governor last year for conspiring to import hundreds of tons of cocaine through Cancun, but your man is even more powerful and we have less documentation and government cooperation, plus a lack of living witnesses to his crimes.

"Keep reporting his activities and we will see what leverage and help we can get from the Mexican government. Keep a very low profile with these folks.

'I'll call you tomorrow late in the day with some thoughts and maybe some plans."

After some vacation chit-chat Edward hung up.

As Matt was about to turn off the lights again, there was a knock at their door. Turning on the outside, aft-deck floor light, he saw Tomas standing there blinking at the bright lights.

Matt invited Tomas in, where the man refused refreshment, apologizing for his late and intrusive presence. He had news. "The doctor called me, your passenger should stay another few days, the wound is draining well, responding to antibiotics and he has the attention of several young nurses who surround his bed most of the day. The doctor suggests you not visit the patient. It would cause too much talk and link you to an obvious Cuban refugee. He will be released day after tomorrow at noon. You should get some clothes for him when he can leave. You will need pesos to pay the bill, which the doctor will make sure is ready, plan on about 6,000 pesos. You may want me to bring him from the hospital to your boat with no involvement by yourselves. You would need to trust me with your cash. I will do whatever you think is best.

"I saw in the restaurant you were noticed by men at the party table as you left. They asked me who you were—I said newlyweds from Florida. These are not good men. Give them no offense, stay away from them."

Tanya changed the strained subject. "We want to just be tourists. Maybe tomorrow we will take the ferry to Cancun, rent a car and driver and see Tulum and snorkel at Xel-Ha on the way back. Can you suggest a good driver?"

Matt added, "Also, we want to be fueled and pumped out before... Hugo returns. We would like to be cleared by the port captain to leave in two days. Will Miguel help us on that?"

Moving toward the door, Tomas answered, "Jose and I will personally take care of the fueling and pumping tomorrow if you will trust
us to move your beautiful boat. I'll call this evening to find you a good
driver for the day. I'll have his name and number for you at breakfast. I
am sure Miguel, for a few of your dollars for himself and some money
for the captain, will take care of your exit papers.

"You should know, if you are going north, you will be boarded and
searched, if you are going south, there is usually no inspections—only
when you come north again. I wouldn't wish to explain your friend's
presence on board your boat. Many Cubans take buses or planes to
the Texas boarder where they walk across."

After glancing from Tanya to Matt with a stern, no-nonsense look,
Tomas left. Matt put out the lights and adjusted the AC to a good sleeping temperature.

In bed together, they kissed and touched. Tanya laughed, "It seems our
love life is usually heightened by the prospect of being arrested by the
authorities or shot by gangsters—in no particular order."

Throwing the covers off, Matt whispered, "I think its working."

Tourist Trap

Breakfast at the marina restaurant completed, Matt and Tanya got the name and number of a driver from Tomas. One call on Tomas's cell set up the meeting at the Cancun ferry dock. The pumping and fueling would be done at the marina's facilities. Tomas assured them the diesel was fresh and they could settle the bill when they returned from their trip. The bank was not open, but they withdrew $200 worth of pesos for the day from the ATM.

Back at the *Reefer*, they packed carry bags of snorkeling equipment, bottled water, camera, swimsuits, sun oils and towels.

Matt suggested they call the bank in Gibraltar and make sure that the credit card would be honored to pay for the fuel. The call took nearly fifteen minutes with many formalities, instructions, code numbers and code words being confirmed. When Webb's name was mentioned the level of cooperation increased and frosty tones quickly changed to kind professionalism. The European banker also agreed to call the local Isla Mujeres bank to establish the framework for a line of credit, should one be needed. The time was mid-afternoon in Gibraltar, but

the banker said he would gladly stay late to help his new clients. Matt finally hung up, happy with their newfound monies and international connections.

With their canvas day bags packed, they locked the boat and took the door and engine keys to the marina office for Tomas. As Matt and Tanya waited in the marina lobby for a taxi to take them to the ferry dock, two men approached them. Both were well-dressed in dark slacks and loose tropical shirts.

The taller, older man spoke. "We are in the service of Senor Morales. He would like the honor of taking dinner with you both this evening at the marina restaurant."

Tanya answered, "We have a day trip planned and are unsure of when we will return."

The man ignored Tanya and spoke only to Matt. "Time is not important, the dinner hour is late, ten o-clock, and dress is informal. He will have a boat awaiting you at the ferry dock when you return. Please say you will join him."

Neither Matt nor Tanya replied.

The man added, "He said to mention he can help you with the Cuban, he would not like to see you or the young man get into problems with the authorities. May I inform Senor Morales he can expect you? "

Matt responded, "Unless we are unexpectedly delayed, we will be pleased to join him for dinner. Thank Señor Morales for the invitation."

The men smiled, bowed slightly and left.

Sweat trickling down his back, Matt turned to Tanya who looked for a second like a little girl lost in a big department store.

Matt took her hand, "It looks like we are going to be closer to our wanted man than we expected."

The taxi drove up to the portico of the marina lobby. Matt took their bags to the cab, where the driver already had the trunk open.

No words were spoken until they were sitting on the side benches of the ferry's main deck. No one in ear shot.

Tanya spoke, "We may be drawn into something and we have little power to change or oppose their plans. I'm sorry I brought us here.

This is such a beautiful place, I wanted to share it with you. With my dad, we never had anything but fun and beautiful times here in the past. I was always working—helping with the boat and diving equipment, cooking, cleaning and being a babysitter at times. There are so many wonderful activities here. Being arrested or dead in a cave with our hearts cut out was never in my thoughts."

Matt took a water bottle out of his bag, and offering it to Tanya, said, "Let's hear them out, talk to Edward. We have Alberto to think about too. And I wonder how Morales would know when we get back from our trip, unless he has a boat at the dock most of the day."

Tanya took a drink of the warm water. "Let's call Webb, he's always been our protector, when he wasn't getting us nearly killed. I'd rather have a name to drop or at least let them know others know we are here and who we are with."

Matt took the water back, took a sip and concluded, "All our numbers are back on the boat. So is the pistol. Let's try to enjoy the day and not think about our dinner host."

They looked for their driver and the silver colored van they had been told would be waiting. A handsome, perfectly groomed and well-dressed, middle-aged woman came up to them. "I am Rosa, and I will be pleased to be your driver today. I believe you will find this vehicle more comfortable than the old van driven by the man you were expecting."

She led them to a Lincoln Town Car, several years old but gleaming black. Not dusty, even in a world of dusty streets and ocean mists.

Fighting thoughts of just going back to the *Reefer*, Tanya and Matt whispered to each other, without moving their bags, and debated if they should continue this outing.

Sensing their doubts, Rosa said, "I am a history teacher at the university, my husband is on the governor's board for Quintana Roo—our state. Please, prepare to enjoy the day. You will see many beautiful sights and I will be your guide."

She began moving their bags into the car's large trunk.

Matt asked, "Did Señor Morales have anything to do with your being here?

Rosa answered, "Yes, he did. He is a very important person in our state. He asked my husband if I had the time to be your guide. I agreed as a favor and because I know I will enjoy this outing."

Matt finally helped her with the bags. He and Tanya got in the clean and comfortable, air-conditioned vehicle.

Getting behind the wheel, Rosa turned to speak to her passengers. "I have put several guide books written in English in the seat pockets in front of you. Tulum and the ecological park at Xel-Ha are excellent areas to visit. I personally prefer Tulum to all the other temples. Its view of the ocean and white sand beaches is without equal."

Rosa was a careful and skilled driver. Her friendly and educated narration soon won over her passengers' previous trepidations.

The long drive went quickly. Rosa spoke perfect English. She knew a myriad of facts about the area—from its introduction of chewing gum to the mysteries of the Mayan culture.

Tanya looked at the guide books. She silently pointed out to Matt one little factoid from the *Cancun Guide* book, the Mayan for Cancun meant"snake's nest."

They looked at each other as the car raced through the single-lane road that cut through the heavy forest jungle.

They spent two hours at the ruins. It was hot and dry, but Rosa made the place come alive with fascinating information about the customs and people that built it. The cool car was a great relief as they drove back toward Cancun, stopping at the river park that was Xel-Ha.

Many people were picnicking there. Rosa stayed with the vehicle which she parked under the tall trees. After changing into swimsuits, Matt and Tanya took their gear to the rocks that made up the shore of the river that joined the sea. It was their first time to talk candidly about their situation. They talked about Momo, Alberto, their options—or more to the point—their lack of options. After weighing all the issues, they decided to enjoy the rest of the day.

Wading into the crystal clear, cool, fresh water, Tanya said, "This is a wonderful place, but Morales sure set us up with a day showing his power before we meet him for dinner.

"I want you to see all the fish and the turbidity currents from the salt and fresh water mixing. It makes you think your eyes are going. You can't focus."

They snorkeled for about an hour then dried off from the fresh water of the river, returned to the car, got their dry clothes and went to a changing building.

Rosa had cold drinks waiting for them from a local store, and they later had lunch at a small restaurant Rosa knew to be good, built around tall jungle trees at the edge of the highway. Then they continued their drive back north.

The sun was setting when the Lincoln approached the ferry dock. Rosa wouldn't take any money, saying she had given the tour as a favor for Senor Morales, and the day with them had been a total pleasure for her.

A powerboat at the Cancun dock with the two men they had met in the lobby took them back across the bay, directly to the *Reefer*.

In the back of the boat, Matt commented to Tanya, "Rosa had to have coordinated with the boat men. I think we should assume we are being constantly observed, maybe even having a bug on board the *Reefer*. Morales isn't doing all this for nothing."

On the *Reefer* they found a note from Tomas, noting the fuel tank was filled, the holding tank was empty, their bill was in his office.

With cold beers and salty chips on the table, Matt called Edward. Again, he got an answering machine. With the ship's stereo on, and speaking close to the mouthpiece, he reviewed and recorded the day's events and their coming dinner invitation.

Tanya called Webb and got him at his Dominican Republic villa. After pleasantries and updates from the time they had been together at the wedding, they discussed Morales.

Webb said, "I know him through mutual contacts. Not a man to fool with. They say he has no living enemies. The Mexican gangs go after whole families, ruthlessness not generally found with the Italian or Russian Mafia.

"Mention you are my godchild and have known me all of your life, that I was at your wedding. Be sure he knows we have just talked.

Chances are he is just curious and wants an interesting distraction by frightening you. You should get away from the Cuban as fast as possible. That is his leverage. Call me after your dinner—no matter the time.

"Carla just left, ending her spring break, and Karen wants to talk to you."

Tanya and Webb's wife, Karen, talked for over a half hour.

Tanya also called her parents, and just as she hung up, the phone rang. It was Edward, who said, "The best you can do is have dinner, see what they want. Don't commit to anything, but call me back as soon as you can.

"We need to get Morales out of this protected area: on the seas, a different country, in an illegal act with living witnesses."

Edward's call not being much help, Tanya and Matt disconnected, deciding to take naps before they had to clean up and dress for the late dinner.

18

Dinner Danger

The alarm buzzed aboard the darkened, cool yacht. Tanya and Matt checked the clock on the mahogany bulkhead of their master bedroom.

Matt kissed Tanya, saying, "Time to get up, clean up, dress up and have a nice Mexican dinner with a killer crime boss. Let's be a little early and have a drink at the bar, maybe get some information or a read from Tomas before we meet our host.

"I can't figure what use we could be to Señor Morgan—like the pirate—Morales. He moves drugs by the ship or plane load. They buy arms from Central America by the truckload—according to my NRA magazine. Money laundering, smuggling people, international embarrassment for the USA: we will just have to wait to see what he wants."

From the closet, Tanya said, "How about a nice short, low-cut yellow dress with a matching shawl. I'll put my hair up."

Matt took out dark tan slacks and a cream-colored, linen Guayabera shirt. "I think I'd like you in a Muumuu for Momo… but let them eat their hearts out. Maybe that's a bad thought in Mayan country."

The restaurant bar was cool and dimly lit. A very attentive bartender, particularly to Tanya, quickly sat a beer before Matt and a gin-and-tonic before Tanya. Tomas walked up to them from inside the bar, looking only at Tanya, "You both look wonderful this evening."

Matt thought, *Are you looking at us or down the front of Tanya's dress?*

Tomas leaned across to them. "I thought there could be trouble with Señor Morales, but from talks I have overheard, he is just interested in you as tourists. I was very worried. He can be dangerous. I only own this marina and restaurant, but he feels he owns the whole state. I would not wish to tell Señor Vega you had any problems on your honeymoon." Tomas looked up, changing from a conspirator's crouch and whisper to a broad grin and happy greeting for the Morales party as they entered from the other side of the room.

The seating was for eight: Morales and his wife, Rosa and her husband, a young couple—blond and European-looking, Matt and Tanya. Morales introduced Rosa's husband as a man responsible for local tourist information and publicity for the state of Quintana Roo, the young couple, from Denmark, photographers and writers working for the tourist council, were named Magnus and Anna Jensen. Morales introduced his wife, Lucy, a young Latin beauty with very little English.

After drinks were ordered and menus scanned, Morales began, "You are such an attractive couple we are hoping you will allow us to put you in some of our brochures and videos that we hope will attract more tourists to our lovely island and city. In our state we have had over five million tourists a year, seventy percent from the USA. Our recent problems have lowered that number. I would be very grateful if you would listen to the plans we are making."

Matt squeezed Tanya's hand, took a deep breath, a long drink of cold beer, before answering, "We would be very happy to help in any way we can." Thinking to himself, *Because we don't want to end up in a cave with our hearts cut out...*

Matt and Morales looked at each other across the length of the table. Even in the darkness of the restaurant, Matt detected a slight smirk and a gleam of satisfaction in his dark eyes—Morales knew he had scared them, making this request a relief, something they would be happy to accept.

The Danish couple explained to the whole table their campaign and photo schedule—looking for both video and still shots. Magnus, in accentless English, addressed Matt and Tanya. "You represent an age group we are very interested in attracting. We have used professional models, but real people are much more effective, couples can relate to them. You would be paid and we would only take a few hours of your vacation."

The discussion continued in English and included many of the locations and activities Tanya had planned to show Matt anyway. Tanya spoke to Lucy several times in Spanish, trying to draw her into the conversations; the answers came back brief, without opinions or any possibilities for ongoing banter. Lucy looked at Morales each time she spoke, trying to be sure she was expressing views he would approve.

The dinners were served and discussions ranged from personal histories, families, Denmark, the Upper Peninsula, to advice for the newlyweds.

Over coffee, Morales asked Matt to join him at the bar for a special brandy.

At the edge of the bar, over two snifters of golden amber liquor, Morales, spoke confidentially to Matt. "I will help you with your Cuban. It is my understanding he will leave the hospital tomorrow afternoon. He can stay on my boat for a few days, no one will be bothering him there. Then perhaps you can buy him an airline ticket to Matamoros. Once there he can walk, maybe using crutches, across to Brownsville and enjoy the freedom of your country."

Matt expressed his appreciation.

Morales continued, fixing Matt with a glare, "I know you were afraid of me. I am not so bad, I enjoy the respect people show me. In truth, I am just a business man in a very tough business."

Matt felt he was sharing a drink with a coiled, poisonous snake who had seen *The Godfather* too many times. He didn't like being the helpless victim of the intimidation that Morales was heaping on them.

After several seconds, Matt spoke. "We are grateful for your help. Tanya and her family are very close to a person you may know, a Russian known as Webb. He is her godfather, came to our wedding. We told him we were coming to dinner with you. He said to pay you his respects."

Absorbing Matt's information, Morales' arrogant demeanor changed only slightly. "It is a very small world, after all. I would like to talk to Senor Webb on some areas of mutual interest. Do you have his number?"

Matt saw this as a test, at least, and an uncomfortable involvement in international crime, at most. "We have a number to call, but I'll need to check to see if he wants it given to anyone else. I'm sure you understand. Is there a number I can give him so he can call you?"

Morales took an expensive fountain pen, slowly unscrewing it as he looked at Matt. The black ink blurred and ran on the soft bar napkin, but the large numbers were clear enough.

"This is my personal number. I am also very selective about who has it. Please destroy this paper when you have given it to Senor Webb. When can I expect his call?

Morales looked at Matt, all business now, no room for bluff or bull.

Matt folded the now dry napkin, "We'll call tonight. Usually he is very available to us. If there are any delays I'll call you on this number to give you a report."

Back at the table, Tanya and Anna were having an animated conversation about places and scenes to be filmed, Tanya seemed very happy about the prospect of being in a video and tourist brochures while on her honeymoon. Filming times, make-up and suggested clothes and swimsuits were discussed. Times during the next two days were outlined, all at the table ended their dinner in good spirits.

Morales announced the end of the evening with hugs and handshakes. Then he left the room.

Matt had to work at getting Tanya back to the *Reefer*. She would have liked to spend more time on the marina's patio with the two other couples now that Morales was gone. Matt finally made their excuses and led Tanya away.

Back on the *Reefer*, they turned on some music and moved to the middle of the salon, where Matt gave a word-for-word recitation of his conversation with Morales. Then he voiced his concerns. "We have to get Webb involved for credibility, but now if we tell Edward of Morales's movements, it could be a reflection on and be a danger to Webb."

Tanya took the bar napkin. "Webb can take care of himself. Edward can use this number—for sure a throwaway cell—to locate Morales. I think we can give Edward this number with his pledge to protect Webb.

"We may have a chance to rid the world of a very bloodthirsty criminal and maybe, if we have some luck, even get a reward."

Matt added, "I didn't miss the looks that Morales gave us. Even though his words and manner were charming, and his intensions seemed honest tonight, his life is one of foulness. I saw cruelty and arrogance in his eyes."

Webb answered their call on the third ring—even at the late hour. Webb and his wife were on their patio at their villa outside of Puerto Plata. They were enjoying the evening and the display of stars in the northern sky.

Webb ended the conversation with, "I'll call our Mexican friend right now. I don't intend getting involved with him, but I'll make it clear you are dear to me and I hold your ongoing health and fortunes as areas of importance to me.

"Have fun and enjoy every minute of your lives together."

Matt felt Webb's ending had a tone of the ominous, Tanya just smiled.

Tanya's next call was to Edward—who answered, even though it was after midnight in Washington D.C. Explaining Webb's situation, she gave the number Morales had written.

Edward didn't waste time with small talk. "This number may be good for days or even hours. We've got work to do. Be very careful.

Morales has no problem killing anyone he even remotely thinks is disloyal to him. Be careful when you call me."

Matt brought up his concern about listening devices aboard.

Edward replied, "I will try to get a bug sniffer to you, although that has a danger to it if you are being carefully watched. Let's use...your mother's first name as a code word. Good luck."

Matt and Tanya changed to shorts and t-shirts and went to the helm, enjoying the view of the harbor and the lights of the city across the bay. They cuddled on the lounge.

Tanya whispered, "I love you, we will have fun with the publicity work." She kissed Matt, who kissed back. They soon agreed the privacy and the air conditioning of their master bedroom would serve them better than the helm.

19

Picture Perfect

Tanya and Matt met with Magnus and Anna on the *Reefer* in the morning. They would be in two videos: one of them diving on a shallow wreck with tanks and the other a snorkel trip over a perfect reef. They would take still pictures of them walking on the cobblestones of the Isla Mujeres marketplace and at sunset walking along a lonely beach. Magnus also suggested some pictures on the yacht at the helm and as they were beginning their diving. They discussed several tomb visits, but the Danish couple had enough pictures of them.

Tanya and Matt signed releases and a contract for payment based upon what was published.

They would begin very early the next day on a reef. The sun and water would be best very early. They agreed to use the *Reefer* and would be on board at dawn. The sunset shots would be taken the next day if nature provided the spectacular visions the area was famous for.

The shopping scenes would be that morning, coinciding with the need to buy the Cuban some clothes. Makeup and clothes were covered and they agreed to meet in the heart of the island's cluster of little shops in an hour.

Alone on the *Reefer,* Tanya called her parents to tell them about the photo shoot. Then she called Webb to see how his talk with Morales had gone.

Webb reported, "The man was just checking if you knew me. We will never be friends or do business directly. He has an arrogance that will be his undoing. He thinks a few helpful civic actions will make up for a life of cruelty and crime. He knew all about Cortada and the Venezuelans.

"I'd strongly suggest you get away from him. Why don't you come and see us? It's a fine trip—stopping at the Caymans and Jamaica on the way. You've got enough money, no jobs to worry about and the weather is perfect for another month."

Matt jumped into the conversation. "I like the idea, this is a beautiful place, but I like the DR and Bahamas better: too many uniforms here. I don't think there are any honest officials. *La Mordida*—the bite, is expected for every official transaction. We'll call about extending our lease on the boat for a few more weeks—maybe a month."

Matt saw Tanya smiling and nodding agreement.

They ended the call and got their clothes for their photo shoot.

In the marketplace, the cameras on tripods drew crowds, destroying the ambience of the busy center of little shops. The Danish photographer switched to handheld shots both for still and video. The shoot was over in twenty minutes. Matt bought some clothes and sandals for Alberto. Then they went to the bank to exchange 700 U.S. dollars into pesos, just in case the medical bills were more than they expected.

They had lunch in a small shop with the Danish couple—where more pictures were shot. Then they returned to the boat, where some dock pictures rounded out the early afternoon. They agreed to meet on the boat at first light—with two dives scheduled.

A taxi took them to the hospital, which was clean and plain with ceiling fans but no air conditioning. They were guided to Alberto's room that he shared with three other patients. He was in a chair, drinking a fruit drink and chatting with two nurses. He was very glad to see and speak to Tanya. He stood with the help of old, wooden crutches.

Alberto introduced his white-uniformed friends and shook hands with both Tanya and Matt, adding in Spanish, "I am very well now. The leg is sore but healing. There is no infection. They took a tube out of it early this morning. I have been treated very well, but I will be glad to be out of this room."

Doctor Salas entered the room, looked at Alberto's chart, under his fictitious name, made a note and turned to the group. "He should take the antibiotics I have prescribed for ten more days—take all of them, even if you feel fine. Take plenty of liquids—mostly water. Stay out of the sun, your burns are still healing and antibiotics make your skin more sensitive to sunlight. An aloe lotion should still be applied several times a day. A little more rest and you will be fine. Your leg will be weak for some time, but you are young and will eventually be strong again."

After Alberto changed into shorts and a polo shirt, the doctor, Matt and Tanya all went to the hospital office, where the bills were paid. After converting the bill in pesos to dollars, Matt figured the room cost had been about $35 per night, and a bottle of antibiotics cost $15.00 US. The doctors' fees—and an operation—were in the hundreds instead of the thousands that would have been charged in the USA. The bills were all marked paid and they let him use the crutches, with the promise they would be sent back to them in a few days, when a cane could be purchased.

The taxi took them back to the marina. Alberto moved easily on the crutches. He was surprised when they went down the righthand dock to the large catamaran. Matt explained he would have more room and the kind protection of its wealthy and sympathetic owner.

The door to the main salon of the large vessel was opened by a man in a dark-olive uniform, wearing a military cap with gold braid. Matt and Tanya thought they had been betrayed but quickly saw it was the older man they had met in the marina's restaurant lobby, who had been sent by Morales. The man smiled at their surprised looks and invited them into the cool spaciousness of the salon, saying, "I am an officer of our civil guard. I have duties today that require me to wear my uniform. We will take good care of your Cuban friend. Also, tomorrow I have been asked to be with you when you take your vessel out. I will have my aide with me, and our uniforms will prevent inspections and we will provide you with protection also."

Alberto was clearly nervous in his new surroundings. The uniformed man with a pistol on a web belt made him very uncomfortable. Tanya explained they would help him get an airplane ticket and give him some money to get to Brownsville, Texas, and freedom. The uniformed man then showed Alberto to a fine stateroom, with a large window and its own bathroom. He turned down the bed, showed Alberto where toiletries were available in the bathroom. Alberto accepted his kindness, and seeming to tire, went to bed. He called Tanya over. "Thank you for all you are doing. I understand that staying here makes it better for you, but I will be very glad to get to the USA."

Tanya talked to him for a few minutes and left him so he could rest.

Back with Matt and the uniformed man, who had never given his name, she said, "If Alberto is strong enough, maybe he could come with us tomorrow. I feel he doesn't want to be alone."

The officer replied, "I'll try to bring him. We will see you with the dawn."

Matt and Tanya made a trip to two small grocery stores to stock up on fresh foods, breads and some beer. They also stopped by the port captain's office, explaining they would be leaving in two days and would like their papers prepared. The official treated them with respect and met their needs with no mention of extra expenses. He promised to have their papers in order and even delivered the next afternoon.

Matt figured Morales's influence had been felt at the port captain's office.

Matt and Tanya spent the rest of the afternoon checking their diving equipment and mounting the diving platform on the stern. They had thin, warm-water, diving suits ready, but didn't think they'd be needed in the 80 'F water. They would use diving vests and suits with the tanks and just swimsuits for the snorkel dive.

Matt had the locations for their dives—a fairly recent wreck with the tanks and a very pristine coral reef for the snorkeling. They would pass on the more popular areas that included many underwater statues and human artifacts.

They had a light supper and went to bed while the sunset was still in its glory.

20

Diver's Activity

The *Reefer* anchored over a superb diving area south of the island. There were reefs, arches and parts of old, wooden wrecks. The walls were festooned with living reef life: urchins, barnacles, corals, colorful fish—yellow tail, parrot and grouper joined uncountable numbers of silvery clouds of other schools. All this activity set against a background of red and dark-brown horned and scattered gray brain corals. Tanya and Matt, with tanks and short wetsuits posed in grottos with precocious parrot fish drawn by pieces of banana Tanya had broken up. Magnus, skillfully using the underwater digital camera, soon had all the shots needed, and they returned to the boat.

On the deck, Morales's two men stood in the helm area, uniformed, armed and imposing. Alberto sat in a shaded deck chair, happy to be in the open.

They repositioned the *Reefer* to a shallow part of the major reef they planned to use for the dive. Tanya, in a bright orange bikini brought an "Ah" from Magnus, who quickly drew a sharp look from Anna. Matt sucked in his stomach and they poised as they readied themselves on the diving platform with masks and flippers. The best pictures had Matt in the water helping Tanya with her flippers, when Matt happily allowed himself to breath normally again. The reef pictures went quickly and everyone was back aboard before 10:00 in the morning.

On the way back to the marina, they reviewed their next and last shoot. A taxi van, scheduled in late afternoon, would take them all to a secluded beach for the sunset pictures.

Alberto talked Matt and Tanya into allowing him to stay on the *Reefer* that night.

Back at the marina, with the Danish couple gone, the soldiers reluctantly left after Tanya explained they would keep Alberto out of sight, and if they had any problems, they would sound their boat's horn to summon assistance from the catamaran.

Tanya and Matt finally were able to spend time with a healthy Alberto. In Spanish translated by Tanya, and using some of his limited English, his tales of torture and confinement by Castro's communist minions sickened them. He had spent a month in a punishment cell one meter by two meters, only a little over a meter high. It was all bars and concrete with a hole for a toilet and a pipe that gushed water for a few minutes twice a day. His food was rotten vegetables and fish-parts stews. Flies, rats, mosquitoes and various crawling bugs his only visitors, a thin nylon sheet his only covering. Despite the summer heat, he sweat under the sheet all night to get some relief from the mosquitoes and biting flies. The soldiers wanted to know his contacts because he had US dollars sent by relatives in Miami, but couldn't spend them openly. An Italian diplomat friend and a few foreigners, living in Cuba, bought food and other articles he could use as barter to get meat and medicines for his family. When he would not give their names after weeks in a tiny punishment cell, he was put in a dark, steel box like a coffin, which was heated until his flesh blistered. Alberto showed them the scars on his knees and elbows. He finally broke. "I told them everything I knew, and then they dragged me to the prison gate, and threw me into the street. I lost my job, my apartment, and anyone that might help me was subject to arrest or at least harassment. I lived on the beach or in abandoned houses, sometimes overnight with some friends, coming and going only after dark. My family was watched by the Committee for Defending the Revolution—staunch communists—that lived in their apartment complex. Nearly every housing area has a CDR group, so wherever I went I had to hide and sneak in and out at night. I sold everything I owned of any value that had been moved to my parent's home: a motorbike, sound equipment, clothes. I once stole a tourist's camera—I took it back and he gave me twenty dollars Canadian. I begged money to live and to pay my part of the catamaran we put together to sail to Florida. I became like an animal, a wolf, stalking at night, without friends or family."

Tanya asked, "How did you meet your friends that were on the catamaran?"

"I met two in prison. Once a day we were put in a walled yard to exercise. It was the only time I could stand up and stretch. It made going into the small cell a nightmare during the day. We met and planned our escape. It cost us nearly four hundred US dollars to have a man use his truck to bring the catamaran to the beach. A fourth man helped and paid his part, but would not go at the last minute, when we were launching the sail boat. His wife was there to drive the car back, and he couldn't leave her." He stopped, jumping when he saw someone at the door.

A large man, dressed in all-white coveralls, knocked on the door frame and stood on the aft deck holding a large Styrofoam cooler.

They let the man in. Setting the box down, in Spanish-accented English he said, "These are the steaks and lobster tails you ordered. I think you will find them of excellent quality. Anita, at our store, said they are the best we have had in many months."

The code name Anita—Tanya's mother—changed the expression on Tanya and Matt.

Matt took Alberto's arm and helped him move to the aft deck. "Let's go check out your walking ability while Tanya tries to find room in the freezers."

When Matt and Alberto had gone, the man opened the cooler, took several small devices out and went to the satellite phone—attaching one box with cables between the set and the line to the satellite dish. He dialed a number, mumbled into the set and then removed his attachments. He scanned the salon and master bedroom with another device. "No bugs I can detect. We are now monitoring your sat phone. We have Morales's cell phone, and anyone he calls, covered. I'm not leaving any scanners with you, too dangerous. Edward said to tell Webb what we did.

He then put a dozen white-wrapped frozen packages on the galley counter. *"Bon appétit,"* his last words as he took his cooler and left.

Tanya joined the men on the aft deck, Alberto was hobbling back and forth, supporting himself with the railings.

"I am doing very well, it is more stiff than painful."

Matt brought the boat to the fueling dock, topping the tank, and settling their bills with Tomas, who was sad they were leaving so soon. He mentioned that the Morales catamaran was leaving also, very early. He would soon have a nearly empty marina.

Tanya and Matt inspected the vessel for their departure the next day.

Two sets of visitors interrupted their activity: the port captain had their departure clearance papers delivered and his minion asked for their tourist cards. Morales's two men stopped by—in casual clothes— to offer their help in getting Alberto to the airport in the morning. They suggested they could all ride over to Cancun in the *Reefer* and be free of the cost, walking and schedule constraints of the ferries. They agreed on a 10:00 a.m. departure.

Tanya, Matt and Alberto enjoyed a meal on the boat that night, watching the sunset with mugs of strong Cuban coffee and sweet, sticky coconut cookies.

21

Momo's Play

The morning was busy. A shower passed through at daylight, leaving the harbor with a slight chop and a gray sky. Matt worked the deck while Tanya backed the *Reefer* out of the slip. Alberto was in the fishing chair, happily watching all the activity. He had cash in his pocket and a small gym bag packed with an extra change of clothes courtesy of Matt's closet and drawers. He even had a lunch to eat at the airport while he waited for his flight. Morales's men hopped aboard in their uniforms, the aide carrying his M-16. They smiled and were very solicitous of Alberto's health. The older man helped with lines and then went to the helm with Tanya.

They worked carefully through the cut into the bay, dodging the many ferries that tended the three main island docks. About a half mile into the Isla Mujeres Bay, the officer drew his service pistol and, pointing it at Tanya, called Matt to the helm.

With cold eyes and authoritative voice he said, "We will not be going to the dock. Head out the south passage. Any resistance will be fatal. I am very able to run this vessel without you.

"I want the lady to go below. She and the Cuban will be under the control of my aide, he will shoot them if you do not do exactly what I tell you."

Matt took the wheel, he glanced at Tanya. They had been in this situation before.

Killers had them under their guns. They had looked at death delivered by armed men on another occasion and still triumphed.

As she went toward the ladder she spoke to the pistol-wielding officer. "We will do anything you ask, Carlos."

The officer corrected her, "My name is Ernesto, though it is of no matter to you."

He handed Matt a paper with coordinates and a bearing. "Steer this course, I am going to use your satellite phone. If I see the wake is anything but straight I will hurt your beautiful bride. My aide will soon join you up here. Cause us no problems and we will not have to tie you up or shoot you."

Ernesto unplugged the VHF's microphone and cable, jamming it into his pocket.

Matt watched them leave the helm, Tanya winked at him through Ernesto's legs as he waited for her to back down the ladder.

Matt remembered their encounter with Venezuelan hit men. Carlos had come to kill them and instead met a swift death at Matt's hand.

As Ernesto watched, partway down the ladder, Matt busied himself with course and autopilot adjustments. Their directions were almost exactly those he had plotted that previous evening for Grand Cayman. Matt turned the wheel, checked the course with compass and GPS readings. He held the wheel until Ernesto went below, then switched on the autopilot. He fumbled with the helm seat's secret button for several seconds until it moved, finally the front pad swung open, and Matt took the silenced FN pistol in his hand. Although the little pin was out, indicating a chambered round, Matt still drew the slide a half inch to make sure. The gleaming, copper shell exposed itself in the breach. Matt took a deep breath, moved the safety to the firing position, and tucked the pistol into his shorts. He turned as if working the wheel.

Matt thought, *Use the satellite phone asshole, better than me giving a report to the DEA. Tanya will know what you say, even in rapid*

Spanish, and I'm going to take away that M-16 from the guard, then settle with you, Ernesto.

Within a few minutes the helm ladder sounded with the scuff of military boots as the aide, with the rifle slung over his shoulder, climbed to the bridge. The aide came forward, holding onto the helm railing for support as the boat rocked at cruising speed. As he moved to bring the rifle into his hands, Matt turned, pistol leveled at the soldier's chest. Clearly the soldier had no chance. Matt extended his hand to take his rifle.

For some reason, maybe because the light-brown, plastic pistol with a mold-green silencer looked like a toy or because his honor dictated he would not be captured, the man continued to bring the rifle around, his finger on the trigger and the barrel moving from vertical down to firing position, when Matt fired from five feet. The single shell hit the man squarely in the upper left chest. He sagged against the helm rail like he had no bones. The pop of the silenced shot vanished in the twenty mile per hour wind surrounding the bridge. Matt grabbed the rifle barrel, twisting it away from the soldier's grip. The largest noise was the clatter of the rifle against the helm support before it came to rest on the carpeted helm floor. The man's eyes were open, his face looked surprised. Matt felt for a neck pulse, there was none. He leaned the man forward, there was no exit wound. The shell put all its energy into the man within the thickness of his chest. Webb's man Al truly had found a very deadly round.

Matt moved to the bridge edge, covering the helm ladder, lying on his stomach, pistol aimed at the salon door. He couldn't come down the ladder without being seen from the salon. He knew Ernesto would need to come to the bridge to check their bearings. Tanya would also know Matt would have gotten the pistol. She knew how to maneuver Ernesto to his defeat. Matt quickly checked the sea ahead and got back immediately into his shooting position. His legs touched those of the dead man. He waited in this position for nearly ten anxious minutes. A hunter must be patient. He would kill or capture Ernesto depending on a sub-second decision based on Tanya's safety. Matt's finger relaxed over the large trigger guard. The dead man made a gurgling sound. He slumped more toward Matt as the boat cut though some larger waves. Matt glanced sideways, the man was looking at him, his head now dangled nearly to the deck. Matt thought of moving him and closing the staring eyes, when the salon door began to open.

Tanya came out and turned toward the ladder, Ernesto came after her, his pistol in hand, but at his side. Tanya glanced at Matt peeking below the helm's plastic weather shield, Ernesto followed her eyes and saw Matt's silencer pointing at his head from two feet away.

Matt said, "Drop the pistol or die—now."

Ernesto paused for a count of two, Matt started his trigger squeeze, the pistol's break point was a tenth of a pound away when the officer's pistol clattered on the plastic deck.

Tanya bent to pick up the pistol by its barrel, and in her move to stand, drove it fast and hard into Ernesto's groin. She followed with a downward blow to his now exposed neck as he doubled over in crippling pain. Ernesto crumpled at her feet.

"He touched me," she said.

She then went into the small bedroom and untied Alberto, whom Ernesto had tightly bound, causing his injured leg great pain. Alberto asked many questions in Spanish. Tanya explained their situation. Alberto pledged his help in any way they wished.

Matt and Alberto hoisted the barely conscious Ernesto into the salon, tying his hands and feet. Alberto extracted a little payback as he fiercely bound the legs. Tanya went to the helm, glanced at the dead man, then checked the horizon and radar, confirmed their course and lowered their speed. There were freighters to the west, heading toward Cozumel. The seas had a light chop with some well-separated swells. She returned to the salon.

Ernesto was on the floor, his back against the largest salon couch, he had an ice pack between his legs and on his neck. He looked sick under his suntan.

Tanya looked at Ernesto then, with a raised eyebrow, at Matt.

"He needs to be able to talk, I got him ice," said Matt.

Matt was reaching for the satellite phone to call Edward when it rang. He jumped away, then relaxed a bit and answered it. It was Momo, speaking in Spanish—believing he was talking to Ernesto.

Matt spoke, "Your man is right here, I'll get him for you."

Momo switched to English, "Ah, Mr. Hunter, I wish to thank you and your lovely wife for helping our tourist business, soon your boat will bring more people to our fair country. I have people that make a very handsome business bringing tourists and Cubans to Cancun.

"You will be brought to us, we have a new crew for your boat. I look forward to seeing you again. Don't worry, we have no caves for you. Let me speak to Ernesto."

Matt brought the phone to the length of its coiled cord. Tanya helped Matt drag Ernesto closer. The three were all close to the earpiece as Matt held the phone to Ernesto's head. Matt's pistol was positioned over Ernesto's knee.

In Spanish Momo told Ernesto not to kill the pair, but to deliver them to his waiting catamaran, which they would overtake within some hours. Momo asked for their speed, Tanya whispered in Spanish into Ernesto's other ear, "Eighteen knots."

He responded to Momo, who said in Spanish, "Good, we are at eight knots, we should see you by early afternoon. Stay on our agreed bearing; let us know if you change speed."

Tanya brought ice tea in large plastic glasses. Ernesto didn't get any. She wouldn't have given him the ice either, and said as much. She jerked the bag from between his legs and slapped it across his face, then looked at Matt as she threw the ice into the sink.

Matt changed the unspoken subject. "We need to plan. Let's coordinate with Edward, slow up Momo and get him captured. We are in international waters, he has committed piracy with his men and his directions. If we get near him and he prepares to take our boat— and Edward has that last conversation recorded, and maybe good old Ernesto here will see some profit in talking about his boss—we might even get ourselves a reward."

Tanya suggested, "What if we stay away from him or just follow from a safe distance?"

Matt answered, "I'm thinking Momo will smell a rat, figure something is wrong, make for shallow and or Mexican waters with full sails and both engines—he might make thirty knots with a broad reach and engines. Our navy won't touch him. We will have a very free and powerful enemy."

Matt picked up the phone set, which had been on the deck, to replace it on the counter, but not before hitting Ernesto on the back of the head with the handset, just for fun, and said, "Let's get that uniform off of the man on the bridge, it may fit Alberto, we can stand Ernesto up like a scarecrow near the helm and get very close to their vessel. We shoot the shit out of them, trying to cripple their outboards and sails, then get away before they know what's happening: leave 'em for the navy. We have surprise, speed, maneuvering and, hopefully, firepower on our side. Besides, I really enjoy shooting at folks that want to kill me and mine."

Alberto, seeming to understand Matt, said, "I will do anything to help. I can shoot a rifle, I trained at school, and for a little time, on the rifle team. We used small bore weapons, but shooting is shooting."

Tanya, making no objections to Matt's plan, helped him take the uniform off the dead soldier, only one small hole and very little blood showed on the dark material. Alberto soon looked like a uniformed civil guard. Even the boots fit well. He inspected and worked with the Mexican M16. Soon, he was very comfortable loading, cocking, aiming and dry firing. It had a full twenty-shell magazine.

They rolled the dead man in a plastic tarp and put him in the dinghy, replacing the white cover.

Matt commented, "I wouldn't want to be the person to unwrap him after hours in this sun. But if things go the way I figure, we can turn him over to some authorities at some point. But he's for sure not going all the way to Grand Cayman with us."

When Matt was getting the tarp he had found the extra anchor chain—white with a rubber coating, but its weight and rattle were still impressive. Matt took it to the salon and wrapped it around Ernesto's waist, securing it with plastic ties.

Ernesto looked questioningly, Matt anticipated his question, "That is in case we need to make you go away, we won't need to use a firearm. What was Momo going to do with us?"

Matt opened the secret compartment. There was his M16 wrapped in a storage sock with three magazines, two holding twenty and one holding thirty cartridges, plus four boxes holding fifty shells each stored in Ziploc bags. As he pulled the rifle from the gray storage bag he saw the maple leaf logo on the receiver and remembered this wasn't a true M16 but a Canadian version called a C7, made in Canada for their armed forces. He had claimed it from Canadian mercenaries that had tried to kill him. The main difference in the two black rifles he now had were slightly different peep sights and selectors—the Canadian Colt had an "S" for safe and by moving the lever all the way forward it pointed to "Auto," but halfway it pointed to an "R." This baffled Matt until he researched the weapon—in Canada semi-automatic is defined as Repetition. *Go figure*, thought Matt. The Mexican M16 was also a Colt-designed weapon, but its selector very clearly was stamped SAFE, SEMI and BURST. It didn't go to full automatic, but fired three shells in a burst. Not a bad system, full auto was very hard to aim, but could be a life saver in an alley or jungle.

Back on deck, Matt had Alberto fire a few shells through the Mexican rifle.

After Alberto commented in Spanish, Tanya translated. "The noise is worse than the recoil. He says he will have no difficulty with this weapon."

They ate some lunch, drank more ice tea, and even fed Ernesto. The waves decreased and the sun got hotter, without a cloud visible. Several ships could be seen to the west. A radar blip came up on their bearing. They were rapidly overtaking it. Tanya figured it would be visible in less than an hour, their radar was picking up its hundred-foot mast—they would catch it another hour.

Matt and Alberto took up their shooting positions on the bow and helm. They practiced changing magazines. Their targets were agreed upon—Matt would shoot at the two large outboards attached and raised from the water at each pontoon. Alberto would shoot at the helm, mast and boom, hoping to cut steering cables or crack the carbon fiber material that formed the structure of the high-tech vessel. His shots should also provide suppressing fire, forcing the people on board to keep their heads down.

They agreed they would get to within fifty yards if they could. The Mac-10, Uzis and 9mm caliber weapons the Mexicans favored were not very useful at longer distances.

The blip on the radar moved closer to the radar screen's center as the *Reefer* plunged across the gently rolling sea.

22

Shootout

The satellite phone buzzed. It was Edward. "We've heard everything. There will be a plane overhead in minutes. It will be high and you may not see it. There are naval vessels vectoring your way. Best guess—several hours. We want this phone clear in case our man calls you again. You've done great work. Don't get too close. We just hope we can stop them while they are in international waters."

Tanya spoke. "We have a dead Mexican and one tied up, both had us at gunpoint and had hijacked our boat. We acted only in self-defense. We intend to go in close to their ship and mark it or cripple it with gunfire. We would like to turn over the body and our prisoner—both of whom, by the way, we would be glad to throw overboard."

Ernesto missed none of the conversation. He shook his head and said, "I will answer any questions."

"Could you hear that?" asked Tanya.

Edward said yes, told them to be careful and broke the connection.

Matt and Tanya went to the helm, leaving Alberto guarding Ernesto. On the couch with his loaded M16, the Cuban seemed to be concentrating on working the fire selector, every several clicks of the selector the barrel casually tracked across the very nervous, bound man.

After some time, they could see the large catamaran. They were quickly closing on it. Its sail had to be 100 feet or more, the multicolored jib made it easy to pick it out of the bright ocean and sky.

Tanya suggested, "Shouldn't we get Ernesto up here so they can see him?"

"No, let's leave him tied up and gagged in the salon, it might get them to call us again with instructions," replied Matt.

He continued, "If they call, you can run down there until we get near our firing range—about fifty yards. They should be busy taking in sails, they will come into the wind, bring us up on their stern. If you put on Ernesto's shirt, cap and sunglasses, I think we can fool them until we get very close. All their vulnerable targets will be exposed and we will be at our smallest exposure, showing just a lot of white fiberglass. One good firing pass, exit at full throttle and we will lay off waiting for the Navy to get here. With their sail and outboards they could really move, without them they should be an easy capture. Alberto and I will also try for their antenna and satellite cone as we pull away, I don't figure them getting much help from the Mexican Navy. And one more thing, if you see a .50 cal being mounted or someone with an RPG, all bets are off, get us away and pray as you duck and weave…"

An hour later, the Morales's craft was less than a half mile in front of the *Reefer*. The wind wasn't the best for them, but they were making good time. The big ship turned into the wind, which was from the south southeast, and it quickly settled in the wave troughs. Matt brought the Hatteras to port and swung wide, seemingly to set up an approach to the catamaran's port side. Alberto sat on the Boston Whaler dinghy, in uniform, waving a greeting. Tanya, wearing a dark shirt, Ernesto's

military cap, and sunglasses, called Matt to the bridge. He had been
making sure Ernesto was well secured.

They sounded several blasts of greeting from their air horn.

Matt swept the large, white sailboat with his binoculars, count-
ing four men working the sails and two at the helm. Momo wasn't on
deck. The jib was self-furling and most of the controls allowed for a
very small crew. The phone below buzzed, Tanya left the shirt and hat
and raced back down to the salon to answer it.

It was Momo. Assuming he was talking to Ernesto, he shouted in
Spanish, "Be careful, I don't want any paint scraped, or marks to show
another ship has touched us. I've got a crew of four to takeover. They
will clean all traces of the original owners on their way to our dock in
Cuba. You've done very well."

Tanya thought, *A smarter man would know who he's talking to.*

Tanya hung up and ran to the helm, where she put on her disguise
and took the wheel as Matt ducked down, preparing his rifle and extra
magazines.

At slightly more than fifty yards, Tanya brought the *Reefer* directly
behind the catamaran, came off plane, then increased her speed slightly.
The distance closed quickly on the nearly motionless craft.

Matt stood in the helm's lounge, and took careful aim through the
peep sight, his front sight bobbing up and down across the large Yamaha
motor on the left. He aimed low on the tilted motor, then touched the
trigger, the selector set on AUTO. The outboard shattered in a spray of
shiny gray and silver plastic. He changed the sight to the right motor,
missed with a burst of five or six shots, followed his water hits back left
until the shots hit the motor and held on it until the magazine emptied. As he slapped in the other, smaller magazine, he heard and saw
Alberto's efforts chewing into crew, mast, bunched sails and boom. With
his primary targets badly damaged Matt aimed at the wheel house—
totally exposed from this angle. He saw a crewman appear with an AK
machine pistol. Matt's shots forced him back down into the salon. He
then shot at the satellite and radar domes until his weapon locked open
and empty. They were now only thirty yards from the stern of the catamaran, at least eighty to one hundred shells had hit Momo's boat—his
engines now gone, his sails and crew screwed up.

Matt yelled, "Let's get out of here."

Tanya cranked the wheel, shoving the throttles to their stops. The *Reefer* spun on its stern, dug into the water, its bow came up and it shot away from the well-holed Mexican vessel.

Several bullets hit their stern, one came through the helm windscreen, close to Tanya, who had ducked as soon as she had set the course and speed.

Matt watched Alberto almost roll off the smooth forward deck, but he managed to just save himself and his rifle. Holding tight to a rail support, legs spread wide, with the rifle under him, he flashed a grin up to Matt.

There were many shots fired as they put seawater between them and Momo's craft, but none were hits.

Matt began reloading the magazines from the boxes of shells, commenting, "I wonder how long it has been since Momo was given some of his own medicine?

"Do you see any ships coming our way on the radar?"

Tanya, changing the gain on their radar, said, "I see two fast-moving vessels from the east. They are maybe thirty miles away."

The phone buzzed below them. Matt left the helm. He gave Ernesto his cap back, checked the ropes and picked up the phone. Expecting Edward, he said, "We're waiting for the Navy."

Momo interrupted him, "You stinking piece of…I'll cut out…heart and feed it to dogs, I'll…"

The line went dead. Matt thought, *Must be something wrong with your dish.*

Up on the bridge, Tanya used the telescope to watch the activity on the catamaran. The mainsail started to go up, but seemed caught after ten feet, then she saw the boom was sagging more than just because it had folds of sail. Then the jib was hoisted, went up and was secured. The catamaran got under way, moving toward Mexican waters. They had a whisker pole out, but the jib wasn't the most efficient sail with a following wind. There was no sign of a spinnaker, which would have been a good sail for them.

Tanya called down to Matt on the ship's hailer, "Call Edward, let him know they are under way with only a jib, heading northwest at maybe three or four knots.

"I can see the two ships coming our way—they are really moving, maybe thirty knots or more. I see nothing from the west, not even freighters."

After nearly an hour of slowly following Momo, Tanya heard a hailing horn and the sound of a shell ripping the air overhead, and then a boom that could be both heard and felt. She saw a splash rise a hundred feet in the air across the catamaran's bow. She looked back to see a U.S. Navy frigate knifing through the blue-green water. Their approach speed was awesome. The catamaran tried a sloppy jibe and only accomplished getting the whisker pole caught in the lines, while the damaged boom with a few yards of sail swung back and forth knocking men to the deck. Momo's crew finally turned into the wind with what little forward momentum they had left and put up their hands when the second shell hit fifty feet from their vessel.

Matt captured most of the action from the helm with his digital camera, its 300 mm zoom getting good shots of the second shell plume and of a small arsenal of weapons being dumped fast and furiously into the sea. He mumbled as he shot dozens of digital pictures, "There's gun control in action, Pelosi and Feinstein would be proud. I'm waiting for Momo to issue fishing rods or start a Sea Scout class."

With the big, gray naval vessel screening the catamaran, Tanya brought the *Reefer* to its other side. They approached within a hundred feet. She plugged in her VHF microphone and hailed the huge vessel. A naval officer said they would bring a boat to them to get their statements and prisoners, after the Mexicans had been secured.

They asked if anyone was wounded or if they needed assistance. Tanya said no one was wounded, but one pirate was dead and the other tied up, ready to talk, particularly if they left the anchor chains on him as they were transferring him to their jolly boat. The officer got the picture, fought to keep his professional tone and said it would be some minutes before they could get a boat to them.

Edward called, totally happy. He even commented that the Mexican government wouldn't cause a problem at this time. He wished them Godspeed on their voyage and said the check might be in the mail sometime in their lifetime.

The Navy crew took the body and Ernesto into their thirty-foot craft. Matt explained the gun battle, not mentioning who started it, while talking them out of two foil sealed, USN-issue boxes of M16 ammunition that they had stored aboard. He explained he had tried to scare Ernesto with the threat of walking the plank with twenty pounds of chain around him. Matt started a trend when he broke into a smile and said, "Har, the lubber almost pissed himself!"

The sailors and officers, flush with the taking of a pirate ship on the high seas, were all talking pirate when they roughly moved Ernesto into their boat. They slowly unwrapped the chain from around his waist and gave it back to Matt. Mentioning between "Hars" that a plank and a victim bobbing up and down for a while is better than just a quick one-way dive to Davy Jones. They also said the passengers and crew of the catamaran were being transferred to the frigate, and another smaller craft would repair or tow the impounded vessel, eventually getting it to Guantanamo Bay, the closest Navy facility.

Matt and Tanya signed complaints and dictated a detailed account of the incident into a Navy digital movie camera. Matt gave them his digital camera flash card of the weapons going overboard, he added they would have a bonus of Tanya in various shorts and bikinis plus many Key West pictures in some of the earlier photos. Tanya, as captain during the battle, couldn't remember who fired the first shots. Matt showed the pistol he used, minus the silencer. They took the Mexican M16 and Ernesto's pistol.

By late afternoon Tanya turned the *Reefer* toward the island of Grand Cayman, several hundred miles away. The sunset saw them cruising on a peaceful sea. Matt cleaned his pistol and rifle with Alberto's help. They enjoyed several beers while establishing a system of four-hour helm watches.

The honeymooners, plus one ex-Cuban, motored east by southeast through a beautiful sea.

23

The Wings of the Morning

The Caribbean was calm and friendly as the Hatteras moved through it at twenty-two knots. Their almost easterly course basically ignored the slow two-knot flow of the Caribbean Current which ran west because of the earth's rotation and then was forced northwest when it hit South America, then funneled through the Yucatan Channel. The light, easterly breeze didn't build waves. Their passage was even helped slightly by the eddy effect of isolated currents curling off Cuba.

The sun had gone down over their stern a little past 8:00. As the western sky went through its spectacular display of yellows and oranges, Matt could just make out the moon that would peek over the bow standard in another half hour.

Matt looked at the helm wall where the soldier had died. He found he didn't feel any great emotional dilemma over his actions. The Mexicans would have killed them all, perhaps after having their pleasure with Tanya. He leaned back into the helm seat, feeling the slight lump of the pistol. It felt good.

Tanya and Alberto joined Matt on the bridge. They didn't talk for some time, just enjoyed the rhythm of the speeding boat, the expanse of calm water and the increasing moonlight that seemed to be guiding them toward their destination.

The three-quarter moon was low enough for them to see the southern sky full of stars. Tanya pointed out the Southern Cross just at the horizon. There was a cruise ship to their north, moving faster then the *Reefer*, its lights washing out the northern stars on that horizon. They couldn't find Polaris—the North Star.

The three eventually spent hours talking about the shooting, their actions and their situation with regard to Alberto's international status, or really lack of status. They had decided going back to Mexico wasn't wise. Momo had a lot of friends—including nearly every official on the peninsula. Alberto was pleased he had finally been able to fight back at cruelty and injustice. They all agreed they liked watching their wake putting distance between them and Mexico and further questions from the Navy. The perfect weather made the Grand Cayman run attractive.

Matt summed up the next problem, "We have to refuel in the Caymans. Tanya and I are fine with our passports; the guide book says no visas are needed for a short stay—up to thirty days. Alberto's Spanish passport doesn't need a visa either, but the passport looks phony. I think it's better to hide him rather than risk a conscientious official questioning him. His Spanish is Cuban, and wouldn't hold up in an interrogation. So we need to hide Alberto while we clear customs, get a mosquito control visit and refuel: actually just while we are boarded—which may be just a few minutes. They have a couple of cruise ships come in every day—they can't dock—so there are little boats carrying tourists to and from the island by the thousands. No one is going to count noses on every boat in their harbors."

After Tanya translated for Alberto, he asked in English, "Where do I hide?"

Matt spoke, "I'll show you, Alberto. Come with me.

"Tanya has the helm."

In the master bedroom's bathroom, Matt removed the bottom of the little tub, exposing a well-lit and ventilated, white-painted hiding area. He turned to Alberto for approval of the cleverness this space offered.

Alberto was ashen, his face reflected fear, near panic. "Little spaces bad for me. Is there another way? Please."

Matt said, "Stay here and look how it was made, you can get out by yourself. I'll talk to Tanya and she will be down in a few minutes."

Matt saw Alberto didn't understand all of his words.

Back on the bridge with Tanya, Matt explained their problem. "We have to make the hidey hole work or we are in deep doo-doo. I can appreciate claustrophobia and his background, but you need to convince him he must do this now, and again in Jamaica. We should be fine in the Dominican Republic with Webb's help and in Puerto Rico he is foot dry. Otherwise, we can give him some money and let him swim ashore and take his chances. I don't want our honeymoon to be spent in separate cells."

"Maybe we can give him some tranquilizers—I've got some we used on seasick passengers—they're old, but should still work. If he takes them with some rum he'll be relaxed. I understood Webb used a hypo sometimes with people that couldn't stand tight places. I'll go talk to him: appeal to his macho side."

Matt paced the helm area, frustrated. Thinking, *Why do I get into situations like this, maybe it will be funny someday. On a perfect honeymoon cruise, finding an adrift Cuban with no papers, having our first meal in Mexico next to a gangster—one of four we had papers on, fighting for our lives, now smuggling a young man through three or four ports...*

Checking radar, scanning the sea with binoculars, listening to the occasional static crackle on the VHF set and checking all the instruments passed the time until Tanya returned with Alberto more than an hour later.

Tanya patted Alberto on the shoulder, "He can do it. We did a quick practice, I showed him he can get out by using the metal rod, kept in there to pull out items that slip to the back, to move the tub up. We agreed to have a little hand radio in there—we tested it, so we can talk.

He also will take the pills and drink the rum. The lights and fans help. Also, I gave him swimming as an option."

Alberto looked at Matt, "I can hide in the box, it is not so bad." His words were brave, his eyes still showing some fear and doubt.

Tanya suggested that Alberto should go below and get some sleep. She would remake his bed at dawn when they neared Grand Cayman. They couldn't be honeymooners with two beds being used. Alberto laughed at this, a nervous laugh. He was steeling himself to crawl into the hiding place. But he also understood Tanya wanted to be alone with Matt on this beautiful night.

Alone on the bridge, Tanya moved to Matt's side, putting her head on his arm.

They kissed, and soon moved to the lounge area. The autopilot kept their secret as it guided the boat through water glistening with moonlight. They wore just beach towels as they snuggled together, watching the bow move through the calm water.

Matt held Tanya in his arms, leaning back against the helm wall, and said, "The sea is so big, but I don't feel lonely, we can't see ships or land in any directions. Look at the stars around us, like a halo, most washed out by the moonlight, putting us in a special place. We are moving, the stars and moon move, everything has a pattern and, it seems, a purpose, a plan. I don't feel all frustrated now. I think about the words I saw on Lindberg's grave on Maui—*If I take the wings of the morning, and dwell in the uttermost parts of the sea; Even there shall Thy hand lead me, and Thy right hand shall hold me.*

"I can picture Lindberg flying over water—like us. I understand why he took those words from Psalms 139 as his own."

Tanya kissed him, "You're wonderful. You need sleep; I'll wake you in four hours, we'll watch the sunrise together, maybe it will have wings.

24

Caymans

etting in and out of Grand Cayman went perfectly. The *Reefer*, fueled up and pumped out, moved through a slight chop into a five to ten mph breeze out of Grand Cayman Bay, their collective worries disappearing in the straight white wake behind them.

Several hours previously, Matt and Tanya had watched the sunrise. Tanya called the Cayman Port Authority on the VHF Channel 16. After the Caymans understood the type and size of their boat and their wishes for a quick fueling, the *Reefer* was directed to a marina on the north side of the claw-shaped island. George Town on the south side was expecting two huge cruise ships within a few hours. For an extra 75 Cayman Dollars, 80% of US Dollars, the security and health inspectors were happy to come early and get the small yacht off their duty list, they would meet them at the fueling dock of the Barcadere Marina. The hardest part of the landfall was navigating the shallow bay that formed the whole northern grip of the pincer-like peninsulas. The tide was two hours from full, still the depth in the channel got down to eight and nine feet over several sand bars, only three feet from the *Reefer's* props.

The marina personnel noted with pride they provided premium diesel containing a good biocide to control the microorganisms that seemed to thrive in diesel tanks, living between the fuel and water molecules. Their dead remains sink to the bottom of the tanks, waiting to clog fuel filters with a black sludge, if a yachtsman was not vigilant and proactive.

The fueling came with a complementary pump out.

Alberto spent only ten minutes in his hiding place, when the mosquito-patrol man did a quick spray in the lower areas of the yacht. They never entered the bathroom. The papers were dealt with on the dock while the fueling was underway. Passports, their Mexican port papers and inventory lists were all in order. The usual scrutiny over food and liquor was waved because they were heading out immediately after fueling.

The officials did a selling job about their islands, encouraging Tanya and Matt to stay a few days. They pointed out the best beaches and shopping areas and the fact that leaving around noon would put them in Jamaican waters in the small hours of the next morning, running all night. Matt noted the fine weather forecast for the next twenty-four hours and said they planned to stay many days in Ocho Rios, on Jamaica's north coast. They also discussed diving locations, and both officials talked at once about great diving areas, suggesting that to miss Little Cayman's colorful walls when they were going right by them would be indeed unfortunate, and the stop would break up the long voyage.

In the marina office, Matt paid their bill—enough for a good secondhand car, he pointed out. The smiling Cayman owner shrugged and pointed out a rack of brochures advertising the many activities they would be missing by heading immediately to Jamaica.

While Matt was ashore, Tanya got Alberto free, but told him to stay below deck until they were far into the bay.

On the bridge, Matt and Tanya looked at the beautiful island they were leaving as they worked the channel north, leaving the bay. They would have liked to explore it, maybe do some duty-free shopping, or at least stock up on fresh bread and sandwich meats, their standard diet while the yacht was under way.

Tanya said, "Let's find an anchorage on Little Cayman, drop the hook, take a swim, cook a good meal. We don't need to work so hard to use up our honeymoon so quickly."

Alberto remained out of sight while there was boat traffic around them.

Matt grinned as he produced a colorful folded pamphlet about Little Cayman Island. The pictures, maps and write-up noted locations for the "Quintessential island escape…spectacular diving…Bloody Wall Bay," and several typed columns of suggestions and rules. Handing the material to Tanya, Matt said, "I'll call the port authority and let them know we would like to anchor overnight off Little Cayman."

As luck would have it, Matt was switched to one of the officers that had been at the dock, who was happy they were staying longer and suggested several sites for anchoring safely on the island, which was about 70 miles east. He pointed out there were many free public moorings identified by their white color with a blue strip and yellow pick-up lines. Most were found over excellent snorkeling areas—there to save the coral from anchor damage. He emphasized the rules protecting the coral gardens and marine parks—even the rule about not wearing gloves when they dive. The most popular moorings were limited to three hours of use, but the man gave directions to several, less frequented but well protected, that would allow them undisturbed, if not officially sanctioned, overnight use.

Four hours later, secured to a mooring, Matt and Tanya dropped into the water and enjoyed the sights of beautiful living coral, schools of varied fish and easy snorkeling in fifteen to twenty feet of crystal clear water. Alberto, beer in hand, kept the anchor watch from the helm. He would sound the ship's horn if any boat approached. They had anchored in a small cove, protected from the wind on three sides, a half mile from an uninhabited, palm-lined shore.

With steaks and lobster tails thawing in the sink, wine chilling in the fridge, the grill connected and waiting on the aft deck, the beautiful setting lacked nothing for easy and affluent living. And the prospect of a well-cooked dinner, a great improvement over the sandwiches and finger food they ate while underway.

The bright sun soon brought the temperature to over 85° F. The water wasn't much cooler, and the lure of a freshwater shower and the shade and air conditioning of the salon brought the swimmers back aboard.

They prepared and ate a feast: besides the surf-and-turf, they enjoyed previously frozen vegetables, steamy and delicious from the microwave, Cuban rice and a plate of various fruits that had to be eaten. Red and white wine flowed liberally. Alberto ate as much as Tanya and Matt together. He told stories of dreaming of so much food, and how families would save and barter for weeks just to have a decent meat to go with their usual staples of rice, beans and potatoes. With his second glass of wine, he spoke of his family and how they knew nothing of his fate.

Matt suggested they phone some of Alberto's relatives in the U.S. He also suggested they call to Edward and Webb to learn the fate of Momo and his gang. Their usual call to Tanya's parents would complete their phone use.

After cleaning up the late lunch, or early dinner, they used the satellite phone to call Miami information and soon located Alberto's uncle. The excitement crackled from the handset, Alberto told of the gangsters, his rifle shooting, his wounds and the care he had been given. He emphasized he was very happy and healthy now. They agreed to meet in San Juan, with more specific timetables and meeting location to come later when the *Reefer* arrived in the Dominican Republic. His uncle said he would relay the sad fate of Alberto's two companions to their families in Cuba. After several minutes of sad and serious reflections about living and dying, the subject gratefully changed to other areas. With comic relief, the uncle laughed when Alberto told of the meal he had just finished and that he was the third person on a honeymoon yacht.

Matt took the handset back from Alberto, hoping the DEA was not listening or not interested in the Cuban.

Edward was not available. Webb was out also. Tonya's parents were brought up to date with Tanya's travels, although she left out the adventure with Momo. They spoke to Alberto with warm wishes for his future in the USA. Anita talked at great length about Cárdenas relatives. George Vega finally brought the conversation to a "good-by."

After nearly twenty hours at sea , when the sun went down in the peaceful cove they were all ready for their beds. The anchor light on and GPS alarm set, the salon door locked, the pistol on the table beside his bed, Matt turned off the bedroom light. Everyone was too tired to stand an anchor watch; however, Alberto volunteered to sleep on the bridge lounge. The light breeze blew towards the sandy shore, rocking everyone to sleep.

Two hours later the phone buzzed. Matt, deep in sleep and holding Tanya, woke to the noise filtered through the padded Hatteras walls, an irritant calling him from the comfort of a very needed rest. Matt padded out to the salon. It was Edward. Tanya also came out of the bedroom wrapped in a sheet. Matt pushed the speaker button.

"I'm calling from Guantanamo. Momo and his gang are officially charged with piracy—defined as a war-like act by a non-state group, in this case at sea. They were apprehended by military personnel and will be tried by a military tribunal. I'm here because he may confess to criminal charges under the jurisdiction of Mexico and/or the US. His gang is talking very freely, they have been informed that piracy is still a hanging offense. Along with gang member confessions, we have voice tapes, spy plane pictures and your photos and testimony.

"Mexico is comfortable with the piracy charge, it gets them off the hook in several ways. But I'm here in case he elects to confess to criminal charges for dope and people smuggling, assorted charges of coercion and collusion, even some levels of murder convictions may be more appealing to Señor Morales than dancing at the end of a short rope."

Matt asked, "Do we get the reward money?"

Edward paused for a few seconds, "Maybe. Governments make lots of promises, but don't like to pay if they can wiggle out through a technicality or the small print. The piracy charge isn't a DEA issue or crime. It actually falls under international law—the UN Convention on the law of the sea. Momo has one lawyer here already, and two more coming, and probably more after that.

"He is talking vengeance on everyone around him. I'm afraid you both are at the top of his list. We are doing what we can to protect you, but he has a right to confidential talks with his lawyers. I have a scheduled meeting with him tomorrow, I'll point out he has family members who may be vulnerable if he starts a bloodbath among the Mexican cartels."

Matt broke in, "It's a nice mess you've gotten us into... What should we do?"

"We just have to see how things shake out. Morales has many enemies. These gangsters will feed on each other if they see weakness. I'll keep you posted."

They discussed their travel plans for the next week, and at the end of the call, Matt asked if their sat phone was still being tapped. Edward said no, it was not.

Matt and Tanya went back to bed, each lay there, awake with their own worries, hoping the other would finally go to sleep. After some time, Matt knew Tanya wasn't sleeping. He moved to her, gently hugging her, rubbing his free hand over her back and hip.

"It will be alright, we aren't dumb or helpless."

"I love you," she whispered, nestling against him.

Their breathing deepened, and soon they slept.

25

Jamaica

After a fitful night, worrying about being on Momo's hit list, Tanya got up before dawn to make breakfast. The smell of toast, eggs and ham brought Matt into the salon. Alberto was already awake, little bugs from the near shore had bothered him on the helm lounge and sometime during the night he had returned to his bedroom.

The three talked about the thirteen-hour run to Jamaica. Alberto was excited about getting closer to his dream of freedom. The weather would be getting worse as they neared the island, but the whole trip would be in daylight, if they could pull out within the next half hour or so.

Alberto and Tanya cleaned up the galley while Matt started the diesels and winched the *Reefer* to the mooring float. No anchor had to be raised, just a simple unhooking from the yellow, plastic pick-up line. Slowly moving from the anchorage, Matt brought the boat northeast, avoiding several sand shallows. With four fishing boats going north, Matt stayed off plane until well clear of the little fleet, then he pushed the twin throttles forward, shot to a smooth plane and headed several degrees south of east into a rising sun, bound for the north shore of Jamaica at twenty-two knots, their best cruising speed.

The GPS, radar, depth finder, autopilot and a rhumb line Tanya had drawn on a Mercator projection map she brought up from the navigation desk in the salon all, happily, agreed with each other. Tanya came to the helm and, after kissing Matt and handing him an insulated mug of coffee, rechecked all the instruments. Increasing the range on the radar showed a few ships, blips of the several islands they were leaving behind, but no bad weather. Tanya said, "I called the Caribbean weatherman—scattered showers north of Jamaica late this afternoon. Ten to twenty mile-per-hour winds from the northeast later, it could get a little rough for a few hours before we dock."

The *Reefer* plunged along all day, the wheel making little movements that the autopilot felt necessary. The only distractions were several VHF chats with sailboats plying their nautical craft between Caribbean ports of call. One 41-footer they neared asked for some water, theirs had become unfit when they put in too large a dose of water purification chemical. Tanya brought the Reefer alongside their trim craft, luffing into the light breeze, and Matt took two of the sailboat's five-gallon, plastic jerry cans, filling them from the *Reefer's* water tank, kept filled by a desalinization system that could produce 600 gallons a day if it had to. The grateful sailors gave Matt half a fruit cake, in a Ziploc bag, padded in newspaper, bound in a shoebox.

Matt spent part of the afternoon munching delicious fruitcake, reading its padding—a four-day-old Montego Bay newspaper and a sales slip from a man who had bought size 12 Sperry Top Siders in Jacksonville, Florida on December 28th.

The waves they sliced through began to include swells, well spaced but occasionally jarring at their regular cruising speed. Slowing the *Reefer* to sixteen knots made the porpoising tolerable. The depth finder indicated they were leaving the Bartlett Deep, which calmed wave action, and were now in relative shallower waters. The recalculation of speed and distance would put them into port, assuming no further delays, between 8:30 and 9:00 p.m. Jamaican time.

Tanya refreshed her suntan on the aft deck, out of the wind. At the helm, Alberto worked on his English with Matt, more than occasionally looking down at Tanya to make sure she wasn't burning.

Matt thought, *Eat your heart out, she's mine.*

Matt made eye contact with Alberto after one of his more lingering Tanya inspections; Alberto blushed and stammered with some Cuban phrase Matt didn't understand. Matt laughed and gave Alberto a high five, but Alberto ducked away. So Matt started over, explaining a high five and that he understood a young man taking a few looks at a beautiful woman. Matt had the feeling Tanya was awake and was enjoying his fatherly efforts to explain cross-cultural and generational male behavior differences.

The coast of Jamaica came up on the radar about the same time as storm clouds formed in the north—coming right at them. They didn't change course or speed as they went through two squalls, water pelting the sea so hard it actually flattened the waves. For the next two hours the air was freshened and cooled, the sky gray. With the green coast to port, they called the Ocho Rios port authority and hoisted their Q flag.

The Jamaican officials directed them to a marina just off the curving white beach that is a highlight of the city. One cruise ship was in the Cruise Terminal, 1000 feet of white plastic and windows looming more than a hundred feet above the water, looking like it would tip over and crush the little *Reefer* as Tanya piloted it through the increasingly rough water into the nearly waveless lee of the gigantic ship and toward the peninsula dock area that pushed out into the bay. The dock master greeted them, helped them moor and offered them the coolness of his office while they filled out his forms and he explained the accommodations, fees and rules of the port. The customs inspectors would be there within the hour. They would need to wait on board. He gave them two forms to have ready for the government folk.

Alberto disappeared into hiding as the two officials came down the brick and cobblestone dock. He seemed to have overcome his initial fears of the small space—no longer needing pills or rum.

The inspection was quick and cursory. Fees were paid in US dollars, their papers and passports stamped, and a pamphlet of national rules for yachts in Jamaican waters was reviewed and handed to them.

Tanya clicked on her two-way handheld radio and gave Alberto the all clear, even as Matt went down to open the tub area.

The wide roadway dock area was crowded with people, vehicles and vendors. A ship carrying over 3,000 tourists was in its final boarding stages. The *Reefer* was squeezed between an old barge-like, wooden hulled, glass-bottomed boat whose only appealing feature was its paint, crudely brushed in blue and greens and, in great contrast, a sixty-foot Viking whose sign in front advertised fishing charters, diving and sightseeing. Security and customs had a small office in a large complex consisting of a low, brick building with an atrium filled with information booths, souvenir vendors, hotel and property sales people, and tour sign-up areas. There would be no way anyone would note Alberto coming or going from the boat. The Ocho Rios Marina was a marina in name only, little more than a small area of dock on the north side of the huge peninsula that was home to the cruise ship terminal.

With the yacht mooring very exposed to the north and east, Matt and Alberto spent time carefully adding more spring lines and doubling their bow lines, in anticipation of northerly winds that were blowing and would get worse when the wall formed by the cruise ship pulled out. Crewmen on the Viking were doing the same thing.

After chatting about how wonderful each other's vessel was, the two charter sailors accepted Matt's offer of cold beer on the aft deck of the *Reefer*. The captain was from Detroit, then Miami and, after wedding a Jamaican stewardess, had settled in Ocho Rios to raise their three children.

The Viking captain gave them advice about the port and Jamaica in general.

He suggested a good dinner could be found at Jimmy Buffet's Margaritaville—within walking distance but they should absolutely hire a taxi to come back after dark. Begging children, drug peddlers, and some very intimidating Bob Marley look-alikes roamed the dock and shop areas after dark. After suggesting they keep someone on the boat at all times, he said, "You can lose lines, an outboard, GPS, radio gear and anything else not locked up in just a few minutes on a dark night."

Tanya fixed Alberto a microwaved supper. She and Matt walked to a busy area at the end of the peninsula with many stores and shops beautifully set amid palm trees and interspersed with stone-paved patios. Finding Buffet's restaurant, in the middle of the complex, they ate a fine dinner of freshly caught fish and jerked chicken under a palm-covered veranda, watching tourists and natives enjoying shopping and sightseeing.

Tanya leaned toward Matt, "You ever notice how many people look like Mexican hit men?" Matt choked on the unimpressive $6.00-a-glass, wine.

With the last cruise ship pulling out of port, the complex was no longer crowded with white-legged tourists. The locals thinned out as store after store closed. Matt and Tanya walked hand in hand toward the entrance that fronted the highway. Near the gate there was a general store still open and filled with people. They went in.

A half hour later, each carrying two plastic bags of groceries, they walked by many groups of men loitering along the walk, leaning against palms with dark eyes that scanned the newlyweds. Tanya eased closer to Matt and moved her diamond to the inside of her hand, while Matt put his Rolex into his pocket...the band of white, untanned skin easily giving away his action. Several of the men moved more into their way as they passed. Matt looked at them, they smelled of smoke and sweat, some still had on sunglasses, some had uncovered eyes that said..."Nobody home..." With no little relief, they found a driver who seemed non-threatening and hired a ride right to the stern of the *Reefer*.

Alberto was glad to see them, excitedly informing them, "Here we have many vendors, selling many… products." Wanting to explain more, he switched to rapid-fire Spanish.

While she put away items from the bags, Tanya translated for Matt.. "Alberto said that some came right on the boat. He finally had to sit outside and order them away. He could have bought drugs, watches, shirts, even knives…but of course, he had no money or wish to do business with them. Two police or army men, in jungle uniforms and heavy boots, walked by, both with machine guns strapped on their shoulders, and the groups left quickly."

Matt kept three items on the counter: a bottle of fresh, locally produced, lime juice, a two pound bag of the island's cane sugar and a liter bottle of light rum.

As Matt produced a gallon plastic jug, he said, "Watch and learn a technique I picked up on the beach in Nassau." He poured in the lime juice, a little over half of the sugar, the whole bottle of rum, and filled the jug with water. Then he put on the top and shook the plastic jug. Getting three heavy, ship's rock glasses, putting in the round ice cubes from the automatic icemaker, he poured the mixture over the ice. Giving a glass to Tanya and then to Alberto, he lifted his glass in a toast. "Here's to Jamaica and daiquiris by the gallon."

The three moved to the helm to observe the town and harbor lights, then the northeast stars, and drank most of the jug, going down for more ice several times. Alberto talked about his two friends that had been killed. He seemed to feel guilty for living and having a good time on a yacht.

Tanya had translated the Spanish, but Matt had understood the sadness and turmoil within the young man as he waited to express more of his feelings. One friend had only said, *Abajo Fidel*—down with Fidel—to a friend in the car as they were stopped at a crosswalk. He was overheard, the vehicle license number allowed the police to track him down. He was confined until he admitted his action. He lost his job and apartment, and his already meager and controlled life went from hard to impossible. The third man had stolen aspirin from a

Pharmacia for his child, who had cried for a whole day with a fever. It seemed the vaunted Cuban healthcare was nothing but a propaganda ploy, in reality all the little neighborhood clinics were never stocked with professional help or drugs, most were not even open regularly. He had been informed upon by someone in his apartment complex. He had gone to prison for three months. He also lost his job and had to report to authorities each week.

Matt saw Alberto was not only morose but getting sleepy as he drank hard liquor hidden in the sugary liquid. He told story after story of life in a socialist society. Workers being paid by a hotel or European business the equivalent of several hundreds of dollars a week, although the money went directly to the government, who then issued Cuban checks equal to fifteen or twenty US dollars a week.

Finally Tanya changed the conversation to happier subjects—attractions they might want to see and things they might want to do the next day.

Matt felt Alberto would need reminding of any later conversations from that evening and escorted the young man down the ladder and into the smaller bedroom.

Matt closed up the boat and, heeding his neighbor's advice, brought in or locked up all items that could be removed overnight: bumpers, life rings, boarding ladder, boathook, and flags. He checked the chain and lock on the outboard and dinghy, encased the instrument panels in their locking covers. He looked at the big Danforth anchor—which could be removed from its shackle—but decided he had had too much of his gallon-jug special to solve that problem tonight. Besides, if someone could run with that anchor, Matt didn't want to catch him anyway.

Leaving the anchor and aft-deck lights on, Matt left the lovely evening breezes and harbor waves to enter the salon. He found a trail of Tanya's sandals and clothes leading to the master bedroom. Her halter top looped over the master bedroom door.

By the limited light coming from the slightly opened bathroom door, he saw Tanya on the bed, hugging his pillow to her chest, her tanned leg over it, her less-tanned bottom a breathtaking invitation.

She sighed. "Rum drinks make me feel sexy..."

26

Jamaica Farewell

Tanya's blue-green bikini bottom filled with the water careening off the right side of the rock walls as they climbed the Dunn's River Falls. The thin, ballooning fabric moved lower and lower, exposing more and more of her less-tanned bottom, until Matt gave her a supportive push up to the next ledge. Their Jamaican guide stood on the middle of the ledge, part Sherpa—with multiple cameras and sunglasses strung around his neck—and part mountain goat, herded the unwitting tourists up the rocks, against the rushing tumble of roaring water. He didn't miss any opportunity to view what he could of the lovely ladies that the climb and the force of the water happened to expose.

Tanya, was strong and an expert diver, at times she even was submerged by the torrent. Other climbers, less athletic, even frightened, had a rough time; the fun of climbing falls became an exercise in terror and survival. Matt watched several couples exchange heated words about the wisdom of this tourist-must when in Ocho Rios.

When Matt and Tanya finally made it to the top, they found their driver and his van, all the doors open, with Alberto in the front seat guarding their cameras, towels, sunglasses, money and dry clothes. Matt had been warned by his mooring neighbor—the charter captain—that valuables were often stolen from the tourist buses while their owners were paying for the privilege of having a near-drowning or bone-breaking experience. Often the whole bus would be driven away, to be found along a jungle road empty of all valuables.

As they dried off and put t-shirts over their swimsuits, they surveyed the falls and groups of tourists shuffling off the moss-covered upper ledge, getting to dry land with smiles of satisfaction, and for many, relief.

This would be their last day in Jamaica, they had spent the two previous days enjoying tours of coffee plantations, river rafting, eating out, shopping in straw markets and listening to a lot of Bob Marley tunes in scores of craft shops. Alberto had joined them during the day trips, his leg quite healed but still weak. The metal staples showed clearly against his tanned skin.

Back at the *Reefer* in early afternoon, the three travelers prepared their vessel for the next lengthy sea run. They sanded and waxed the gel coat Matt had applied to the three bullet holes found on the stern. They were now noticeable more by the newness of color and wax than by the chips that had been there. They made a grocery run later in the day after they had topped off their fuel. The captain in the next slip had recommended a fueling dock down the bay. He said their costs were less and they sold more diesel than anyone in the area. He had used them for many years with complete satisfaction. The alternative would have been fuel trucks coming to the *Reefer*. The run across the bay and the fueling took only about an hour, Tanya was satisfied with the quality and professionalism of the fuel-dock workers.

Tanya had been in daily contact with her parents. Edward had called, pleased to inform them that Momo was plea-bargaining for multiple criminal counts of smuggling, collusion, coercion, attempted murder, kidnapping, and more—all to avoid the piracy charge. The legal wrangling could go on for a year or more, piracy being in a military court while the other charges came under civilian jurisdiction. Matt had called Webb with their plans to visit him. Their conversation had been very guarded because Webb was not convinced that the DEA, NSA, CIA and CNN weren't listening.

Alberto stayed with the boat while Matt and Tanya ate an early dinner back at Margaritaville and once again bought fresh bread, milk and eggs at the local store.

They brought Alberto a to-go meal.

After watching the sun set over a third huge cruise ship tied up at the dock that fronted the old bauxite plant—which had been featured in an early James Bond film along with Dunn's Falls—they felt that they had done justice to the local sights and happily turned in early, expecting to leave port at dawn and make a long voyage to the Dominican Republic via the Windward Passage.

27

Gunk and Gunboat

Matt and Tanya, both at the helm, fought the twelve-foot waves that pounded the *Reefer*. Matt yelled above the wind and spray blowing through the bridge, "Great weather forecasting, we paid good money for two services and our taxes pay for satellites and national weather services—this sure as hell isn't isolated showers and seas three to four feet."

Tanya scanned the radar, wiping the spray off the screen. "It's better to the north, the storm is moving west southwest. It came right over the eastern tip of Cuba. Even the Havana radar we checked in Jamaica said *lluvies dispersas*…scattered showers. I just checked—the marine radio is saying small craft advisories and isolated severe winds in the Windward Passage moving toward the west coast of Haiti."

Matt turned them a few degrees to port, trying to work north against the wall of wind and waves, the result crashed the bow deeper into the green frothy water, followed quickly by the boat climbing steeply into the next wave. He moved the throttles back to counter the jarring and rolling. They were down to eight knots. Two forward fenders had popped from their chrome holders and flopped wildly back and forth, held by their lines. The waves increased by the minute, Matt couldn't see over them from the bridge when they went into a trough. The dark sky gave no clue of a clearing or a future letup of the sudden, intense storm. The radar showed the center of the storm to their southeast; they couldn't go directly north, their only choice was to angle north, fighting each army of increasing waves.

They were in the beginning of the Windward Passage between Cuba and Haiti—a very busy shipping channel with eleven major routes converging in these waters. Matt could see several large blips on the radar screen. They had planned to go through the passage near Cuba, out of the major shipping traffic, using the lee of the land mass to mitigate the prevailing northeast winds.

Matt was tired. They had had smooth cruising for six hours after leaving Ocho Rios, but he had worked hard at the helm for the last three hours, standing at the wheel, jamming his back against the helm chair to keep his balance against the pitching and yawing of their 54-foot vessel. The boat felt heavier, he knew water was entering at the engine air baffles as he saw the engine room bilge pump lights go on and off. The other instruments were reading normally, but he felt the engines were not as efficient as usual. The oil pressure gauges bounced erratically but stayed in the green. He had changed the large fuel filters in Ocho Rios, they hadn't been very bad for over 1,000 miles at sea. He could imagine the black gunk, made of dead microorganisms that sank and coated the bottom of the fuel tank, being bounced into suspension by the violent wave action, their greasy sludge stopped only by the two progressively finer filters that guarded each engine. Each filter would slowly become clogged, restricting the flow of diesel fuel to the ever-hungry 1,200 hp MAN engines. The multiple fuel pumps and the appetite of the engines' would cement the black gunk to the copper-coated folds that made up the filters.

Tanya came to his side, took the throttles, moving them back and forth. She watched the tachometers and noted the lag in response. She turned toward Matt, her voice nervous and loud against the sounds of the storm. "Filters clogging up, we could be in trouble."

Matt yelled, "Let's take one engine down at a time to change filters. They might clog up again but maybe we can work our way out of this storm."

Tanya shook her head. "Don't think it will work in this sea...it would be hell down there."

Matt moved from the wheel. "You got the helm, I'll change the filters, starting with the starboard. I'll stop and start it down there."

Matt went below, and Alberto followed him to hold the engine hatch open. The heat hit them like a blow as Matt moved into the engine compartment. Two huge engines flanked the centered catwalk: roaring noises, diesel and exhaust fumes, water spray, hot metal sounds and smells, constant unexpected movement up and down and side to side and—unlike watching the water and waves from the helm—no stable horizon and no ability to anticipate a climb or dip, a yaw to the right or left. There were two filters per engine, easily accessible from the catwalk, each a metal cylinder over two feet in height, eight inches in diameter—holding over a gallon of diesel fuel. Matt moved on hands and knees, bracing where he could against supports or non-heated parts. The air temperature had to be over 150 degrees F. A sauna had nothing on this engine room—and it held still.

Matt yelled back at Alberto, "Keep the hatch open, I can hardly breathe down here."

Matt put on noise-suppressing earmuffs, their rubber and everything in the room was painfully hot to the touch, as he moved awkwardly forward carrying a plastic oil pan he took from a bulkhead hook. When he shut the stopcock in the fuel line to the starboard engine, the 1,200 horses snorted and grew silent. The port engine still painfully loud, the heat and fumes almost unbearable, the disorienting effect of the moving boat made the bile move up in his throat. He positioned the pan to catch the fuel oil that would drain into the aluminum bowl positioned below each filter. With jerking efforts like those of a drunk, he opened the drain of the first filter, and diesel fuel started to pour out. Strong diesel fumes filled his lungs and sickened Matt instantly. Fuel splashed from the drain bowl. He tried to move the pan to catch the sloshing liquid but pitched forward, hitting his forearm, shoulder and forehead on the metal catwalk. The oil spilled from the low-walled pan and the bowl below the filter, splashing Matt and letting diesel fuel pool along and under the catwalk. The heat and fuel smell, the movement and noise were too much for Matt. He threw up while spilling more fuel. In defeat, he closed the plug, spilling more fuel on his hands, clothing and the deck. He gave the valve an extra twist to make sure it was secure: dizzy, sick and feeling he could lose consciousness at any time, he turned on the fuel line, and slipped to the deck, his muscles feeling like putty.

Alberto dropped down beside him, wounded leg in pain from bending, helping and almost dragging Matt from the engine room.

Back on the aft deck, Matt took in deep breaths. The diesel fumes still filled his lungs, his stomach heaved again. His throat burned, he reeked of fuel, sweat and vomit. He pulled off his shirt and, throwing it overboard, crawled along the bouncing deck to the outside freshwater valve where he drank, spit, and rinsed himself off. The clinging diesel fuel would not come off, but the smell seemed to decrease. As he sucked good air into his lungs, he tried to climb the helm ladder, but didn't feel he had the strength or balance to make it.

Alberto gave him a towel, Matt wiped his hands and face. "Tell Tanya I couldn't do it, she can start the starboard engine—for what good it will do. I've got to just lay here for a few minutes."

The minutes passed, Matt heard the engine restart. The *Reefer* fought the waves.

Matt closed his eyes for a few more minutes, grateful for the clean air, the rain, even the cool, salt water spray that blew across the aft deck.

On the bridge, Tanya felt the second engine help thrust the vessel from the wave troughs. The frequency of the mountainous waves was decreasing, as was the wind. She shot a look at the radar—they were almost out of the worst of the northern edge of the storm. The engines were losing power every minute, but those 2,400 horses could lose a lot of power and still have authority.

Alberto made his report about Matt and his difficulty in the engine room. Tanya wanted to go to him, but her work at the helm took all her experience and ability. The bilge lights blinked on and off, the RPMs dropped more and more—even as she added throttle. She had steerage, and every moment took them out of the storm. She could see reflections from the coast of Cuba on the radar; they were over twenty miles out, international waters. Although the storm winds here lessened, rain came down harder, she couldn't see a hundred yards.

After battling the waves for another half hour, she saw Matt's head appear on the ladder. He crawled across the bridge toward her, supporting himself on the helm chair to get to his feet. He wore only his boxer shorts, blood ran down his face from a cut on his eyebrow.

Matt mustered a weak grin as he looked at Tanya skillfully maneuvering the boat. "I fought the engine room. It won…"

Tanya turned to him, wiped the blood from his cut, patted his shoulder and, with one hand, helped him into the helm chair, where he could absorb the wave action with less effort.

"You have very little chance of getting lucky tonight," Tanya yelled. "Put some ice on the bump, have Alberto get it. I'd say we will be alright if we can get a little farther north and stay out of Cuban waters. I had the mic in my hand twice to call for help, but I think we will limp along until it gets calmer. We can turn on the fans, get more air down there. We've got to change the filters."

Alberto brought Matt a towel full of ice, moving well despite his bad leg and the bouncing of the boat. The three huddled at the helm, watching the radar and the lights on the control panels. Minutes turned into nearly an hour.

The rain stayed steady, heavy and vertical, the waves slackened to four feet. And then the engines stopped. The world became very quiet. Rain hissed on the deck and water—the red lights on the console indicating the engines should be working, but weren't.

The *Reefer* wallowed in the troughs, blowing west and north as the wind shifted while the center of the storm went to their south and west.

Matt felt better, his strength returning and his head clearing. "Do we have a sea anchor? We need to turn into the waves. I don't really look forward to breathing more diesel fumes, but…"

There was no reason to man the helm without engine power, so Matt and Tanya searched the forward areas and anchor locker for a sea anchor. No luck.

Matt took two empty and open five-gallon, plastic pales from the engine room—used to store the old filters—lashed their handles to a life ring, and tied the assembly off at the bow with fifty feet of line.

As the buckets filled and bit into the water, the line jerked, the *Reefer* immediately came into the wind and waves. The effect was immediate and welcome.

They tied open the engine hatch, turned on the engine room blowers, replacing as much hot, stinky air as possible with clean, cool air.

Matt heard the generator come on. Normally, it was too quiet to be a distraction above the main engines and normal sounds of a powerboat.

Matt commented, "At least the generator hasn't clogged its filters yet. We have electricity."

Tanya added, "Yes, and many hours of battery power, too. The engines have their own batteries, with the ability to cross over and start each other if they have to. I think I'll make a VHF call to the Coast Guard to let them know our position and status, and we'll have Alberto keep an eye on the radar to make sure we don't get run over by a freighter."

While Matt put on long pants and an old shirt, Tanya put out a call to the Coast Guard—figuring a cutter might be in the channel or they might have a monitoring station at Guantanamo. She called three times before the Coast Guard replied, its signal strength caused Tanya to turn down the volume. She reported their position and situation, turned down the need for immediate assistance. The return call had come from a ship in the Windward passage, their patrol run would bring them toward the *Reefer*. If help was needed, they could be on station in a few hours, or their helicopter could be over them in less than a half hour.

Happy to have help available, Tanya dressed in old Levis and a long-sleeved, cotton shirt and went below to help Matt in the engine room.

The job of changing filters was messy even in a calm marina. All boaters have their own formula for keeping the diesel fuel under control. Tanya and Matt were schooled by George Vega—an exAir Force sergeant who had worked on almost every internal combustion engine still used to fly planes or helicopters. His method used multiple garbage bags, careful draining of the filter cylinders and very careful disposal techniques—all followed by degreasing sprays, oil absorbent powders and lots of paper towels. Matt and Tanya tried to follow his procedure—but the diesel fuel was already on the deck, the smell was strong, the room still hot. It took them an hour to do one engine, stopping three times to move to the aft deck to breathe fresh air. They used a large, stainless steel salad bowl to dump the dirty fuel over the side many times. With their plastic buckets being used as sea anchors, the process was slow and messy. They were soon both covered with oil, sweat and grease. The second engine went faster, under thirty minutes including two fresh-air breaks. The sea had become nearly calm, flattened by heavy sheets of rain. Already as dirty as two mechanics could possibly get, they started to clean up the messy engine room with a spray degreaser, absorbent powders and paper towels when Alberto, who had helped by dumping oil and other environmentally unsavory materials overboard, yelled down to them, "A boat is here."

Matt and Tanya popped up to the aft deck beside Alberto. Not fifty yards away, sliding out of the sheets of rain and mist of the dark afternoon, came a gray Cuban patrol boat.

28

Boarded

The Cuban patrol craft swiftly came up on the *Reefer's* stern. Covered with canvas, the twin barrels of its deck machine gun pointed forward, not down at them. The light gray, upper deck with windows and portholes sat gracelessly atop a dark gray hull. The red letters TGF were prominently displayed on its bridgework. Five crewmen, two armed with machine rifles, stood at the rail, sinister looking in military rain ponchos. The vessel, only some twenty feet longer than the *Reefer*, slid alongside, no fenders out, its engines reversing, the sharply slanting hull of the gunboat touched the *Reefer*. Matt noted some white paint streaks from the *Reefer* on the gunboat's flaking, dark gray paint as three uniformed Cubans with boathooks pulled the two craft together.

A loudspeaker tucked under the bridge awning blared in English, "You are in Cuban waters, prepare to be boarded."

Matt looked at Alberto. "It's too late to hide, let's try to talk our way out of this."

Two men jumped aboard the *Reefer*, both wearing hooded rain ponchos over their billed caps so no rank could be seen. The older of the two seemed to be in his mid-thirties, the younger should have been in high school.

Matt addressed them both, "We have had engine trouble which we have repaired, we will be glad to leave your waters. We believed we were and still are in international waters. Let us look at our radar and GPS on the bridge."

"That is not necessary; our instruments show you clearly in Cuban waters. We must see your papers, and inspect your vessel."

"May we contact our Coast Guard?" Matt asked. "They can verify our position and that we had contacted them when we had engine trouble."

The two Cubans were joined by the other two armed men with rifles now leveled at the three wet, oily and beginning to be frightened yacht crew.

The leader, in English, commanded the three to sit on the deck with their hands behind their heads.

Matt stepped forward. "This is an insult and you are acting like pirates, I will protest to my government. We have done nothing wrong."

The Cuban, seemingly in charge, took a step back, and motioned his men forward. They pushed Matt to the deck. The Cuban in charge then rattled off several commands in Spanish, and one man went to the helm, another into the salon. Several minutes passed, the rain began to let up.

Tanya had said nothing, watching and listening. Alberto looked sick, and sat close to Tanya.

Matt moved closer to Tanya and Alberto, his action brought the muzzle of an AK-47 to within a few feet of his head with the Cuban's finger on the trigger.

When the armed man saw the three were not trying to move any further, he backed to the far side of the deck. The leader went to the helm; he wore regular shoes, while the rest wore combat boots. Matt figured he was the officer in charge.

Ten minutes passed. Their single guard spoke to the crewman holding the vessels together. Matt looked at Tanya to translate, she lowered her eyes and gave a slight negative shake of her head. She did not want them to know she spoke Spanish, and Cuban Spanish at that.

Alberto whispered to Matt, "They insult your wife and call this boat a fat chicken to pluck."

Their guard took no notice of the talk between his prisoners. The crewman who had been inside the boat came out with two bulging pillow cases. As they became rain soaked, they apparently were cans of food and the frozen packages of steaks and lobsters. The man had Matt's old Rolex in his hand. Matt had put it on the coffee table before going into the engine room.

"You are thieves," said Matt.

The Cubans ignored him.

The officer came down the ladder and took the Rolex, which he put into his pocket. He turned to Matt. "We will now look at your papers. Let the woman get them."

He looked at Tanya, who still had her hands over her head, the rain plastering her shirt to her chest, making a very interesting view for the smiling sailors.

Matt understood the meaning if not the words of the crewman's comments, he wanted to get his pistol and shoot the grins away, but knew he would have to wait.

Tanya was escorted into the salon, then Matt and Alberto were ordered in.

The officer had removed his rain cape, exposing a khaki uniform with a round shoulder patch that read *Guarda Fronteras Cuba* and the same TGF initials that were on their vessel. He took their passports, identified each by their pictures. He asked Alberto several questions in Spanish, then pushed him into the master stateroom accompanied by another sailor. Shouts and thuds could be heard through the closed door. After five or six minutes of beating noise, struggling movements and groans, the sailor came out dragging Alberto by his arms—his face bloody, his shirt ripped—and tossed him to the carpeted deck.

The Cuban officer spoke English to Matt and Tanya. "This man is a Cuban, he has no emigration papers, he has a false passport. You are smugglers and are now under our arrest. We will take you to port and you will be interrogated, and charged with several crimes against the people of Cuba.

Matt relaxed his voice and demeanor and said, "We rescued this man from the sea. Given a fair hearing, we can explain all our actions. Would you like us to try to start our engines or do you intend to tow us to your port?"

"If you can make your engines work, we will escort you to port. Go to your helm and see if your mechanical efforts have worked."

Matt thought a moment, then replied, "You must have been listening to our radio conversations with the Coast Guard."

"Yes, our duties include search and rescue, we work closely with your Coast Guard." The officer grinned, happy he had been so smart as to locate them by their own VHF conversations.

The officer remained behind to question Tanya. As Matt moved to the ladder he heard Tanya say that she spoke only a little Spanish, to which the officer grinned, and said, "You will speak very good Spanish after several years in our prisons."

At the helm, two Cubans, one with an AK at the ready, guarded Matt. There was no chance of getting at his pistol. When he hit the starters, both engines started and idled smoothly.

The Cubans took Tanya, now wearing a clean, dry shirt, and Alberto to their vessel. Matt mentally damned them. He might have been able to defeat the guards and escape, but without Tanya it was pointless.

Matt checked the radar and GPS. If they were in Cuban waters it had to be by inches. He opened the spyglass case and put the opened case in a storage locker, securing the glass itself on a helm shelf, looking like he was getting it ready for later use. The two guards just watched. He hoped the DEA was awake and noting their movement. The guard reached up to the VHF radio, switched to an unused channel and communicated with the Cuban gunboat. He had the gain turned low, so the signal carried only a few miles.

The officer's voice came over the VHF speaker. "Steer due north until I give you other instructions: fifteen knots, no more. We follow in your wake, with your woman, our deck guns manned and sighted on you."

Matt's mind seethed with killing hatred and plans for revenge, but there was nothing he could do with two guards watching him and Tanya at the mercy of Cubans on their gunboat.

Hopelessness and fatigue swept over Matt as he watched his compass and speed. The guards moved to comfortable positions on the bridge. The one with the AK went forward to the lounge, safe from any sudden tricks or attack from Matt. The other guard leaned against the chart table, watching the instruments. The Cubans were young but not sloppy or dumb as they controlled their prisoner.

The rain finally stopped, the gray sky merged with gray water as the white bow plunged toward Cuba. Each turn of the screws and successions of spray generated as the boat cut through the waves increased Matt's depression. He moved to the helm chair, trying to relax, saving what energy he still had for the challenges he knew were yet to come.

29

Santiago de Cuba

Tanya sat on a hard, metal bench, her back wedged between the cool, damp wall and a bulkhead of the Cuban vessel's rusting main cabin. Alberto was on the other side of the small, cluttered room, bound with rope and curled in pain, wedged under a metal table. The helm was on an open bridge, above her, but she could see and hear the radio operator—they were bound for Santiago de Cuba, Cuba's second largest city.

She looked at her unbound hands. Less than two weeks ago she had the perfectly prepared nails of a bride. Now the gloss was gone, grease and dirt were on her cuticles and knuckles, the nail edges rough and broken. She smelled of diesel fuel, sweat, and maybe of fear. She had been given time on the *Reefer* to put on a clean, dry shirt, she had also quickly put on a sports bra, her Levis were the ones she had had on in the engine room, dirty and reeking of oil and cleaning compounds. She saw the Cubans take Matt's diving Rolex—and look around the main cabin for more easy booty—so she took her rings and dropped them behind the bottom drawer of the small nightstand by the bed.

Her Cuban guard stood in the master bedroom door courteously, with his back turned, while she changed her wet, dirty blouse. A final inspection of her hands showed the tan line of her rings; she rubbed grease over the pail skin.

The patrol boat's salon was their mess area, communication center, radar station, and navigation desk, and somewhere forward was a head and maybe bunks. Everything looked in ill repair. The bulkhead clock didn't work and the engines ran rough with a vibration on the starboard side that fluctuated like it could be a shaft, packing, or prop—or all of the above.

From her seat, Tanya could see out the front windows. She got glimpses of the *Reefer* as they followed her through the swells. There was no one manning the twin bow guns, but they were uncovered, elevated and looked ominous.

As anxious as she was, she could not fight the sleep that overtook her as the vessel rode the comfortable swells toward Cuba.

Tanya awoke to the sound of the radio speakers. She had been covered with a thin gray blanket. It smelled of tobacco and mold, but showed an act of kindness toward her. The captain was giving Matt instructions for entering the harbor of Santiago de Cuba. He spoke from the bridge, but the radio operator's speakers allowed her to hear Matt's voice as he asked about a channel marker. He also asked them to lead him in. Request denied, the patrol boat would follow. Its only large weapon was in the bow, and they apparently would take no chances of Matt making a run for it.

It was early evening when the two vessels passed under the imposing fort on the right bank of the harbor entrance—*Castillo del Morro,* also called *San Pedro de la Roca*—the massive fortifications went from the water's edge to the hilltop, over 200 feet: a very imposing system of defenses built into or looking down from steep cliffs. Her father had shown her pictures and she had friends who had told stories about it and the city it guarded. When she was a little girl and the family watched *I Love Lucy,* her father would say, "Desi Arnez came from Santiago de Cuba." The channel curved past islands and peninsulas then opened into a well-protected harbor, with extensive dock facilities and, in the distance, a large city surrounding the bay, impressive by the glow of its lights.

Alberto had been awake for some time but hadn't moved, lest he receive another kick or blow from the passing crewmen. Tanya said nothing, she was offered a cup of water—which she accepted with thanks. She spoke in halting Spanish to the attentive crewman, who was also the radioman. She learned the vessel was a Soviet Zhuk, made in the 1970s, and currently had six men on board with two more on the *Reefer* for a total crew of eight. Tanya stood and, leaning against the mess table, could see the Hatteras tying up at a large dock jutting into the bay in front of massive, red-roofed warehouses. The large initials TGF on a building that fronted a warehouse, she learned, stood for *Tropas Guarda Fronteras*—part of the ministry of the interior, not army or navy. The crewman took some pride in explaining they were an independent unit of the government and had captured many drug boats and foolish people attempting escape.

After the crew secured the Zhuk to the dock, Tanya and Alberto were escorted over a gangplank, across the wide, wood and stone dock to the TGF building. It was the only structure that had been painted in the last decade, also the only structure along the pier with any lights on.

Inside, Matt sat between two guards on another gray-green, metal bench. He rose to greet her but a guard pushed him back onto the bench. She saw his hands were not tied, he looked very tired and dirty. Tanya knew he had only slept three hours in the last twenty-four, and his face looked pasty and drawn. He looked at her, his smile quickly followed by a wistful look that she interpreted as both love and an apology for not being able to defend her.

A matron met Tanya who, escorted by a male guard, led her to a small room. She was given no opportunity to talk to Matt.

The room's floor was painted gray, its walls light green, the tables wood with scratches and cigarette burns on the edges. The stench of tobacco, sweat, and some kind of disinfectant filled her nostrils. The matron pushed Tanya down into the single, metal chair on the far side of the room, behind a small table. Her guards left, the door slammed shut and the lock clicked firmly into place.

She was alone.

Matt watched the matron and guard take Tanya down the hallway. The guard returned to his desk behind a low, room divider. Alberto sat at the far end of the row of benches against the long wall of the main room. Matt could see he had been beaten. Alberto looked at Matt, his eyes red, puffy and showing none of the sparkle and humor Matt had come to enjoy so much.

Matt spoke to Alberto, "Stay strong, we will come through this."

A guard immediately stepped between the two men, in Spanish and English ordering them to be silent and to keep their eyes downward.

He ordered two men to take Alberto out of the room. Matt heard their footsteps receding down the long hallway, then a metal door creaking open and slamming shut. The guards didn't return.

An hour passed. Matt asked to use the bathroom and was taken to a small, smelly room with a sink and toilet; he was able to wash his hands and face, scraping some residue from the empty soap dish. There was no paper in the *banyu*…just a filthy towel on a wooden dowel. Matt dried his hands on his pants.

No one talked to Matt, and soon there was a shift change. The new personnel took Matt to a holding cell far down another hallway. The room was large and well lit and had benches wide enough to sleep on along the walls, a toilet area in a far corner, just a four-foot-high wall that divided the waste hole from the rest of the room. Nearby was a large, low sink with a single tap. The cell held three other, dispirited men.

A guard informed Matt in Spanish with sign language subtitles that he had missed the evening meal and breakfast would be his next food. He was given a threadbare blanket and pushed through the cell door. Inside, he exchanged looks with the other men slumped on the benches as the lock clinked and key rattled behind him.

He was now a prisoner in Cuba.

⚓

Down the hall, Tanya sat across from three smiling officers, each making smoke clouds from their Cuban cigars. On the table, their passports, ship's papers and the thick package of Mexican permits and certificates were spread out.

Tanya sipped strong coffee, in a very nice china cup served with a matching saucer. She reiterated her story for the fourth time, "We found Alberto on a shot-up raft, he was hurt. Mexico was the closest help, so we took him to the hospital there—you can see his wounds were professionally treated—we encountered Mexican gangsters in our marina, who then highjacked us when we tried to leave. They were going to steal our boat, maybe kill us. We overpowered the two men and called the Coast Guard. The ship they were taking us to was intercepted by our Navy vessels and the Mexicans were arrested. This matter had to be on the news; the boss of the gangsters was Momo—Morgan Morales, a very powerful and very bad man."

The short, fat officer, seemingly in charge, spoke. "You tell a great story, but you could have gotten much of this from the news yourself. Your papers are not in order—your father owns the vessel in part of the papers and yet you are renting it for this trip from another parson—which is truth?"

"My father owned the *Reefer* when he ran a marina and a charter business. He traveled in Mexican waters many times and his *Importata* is valid for the vessel for ten years, so we used it. The boat is owned by the new marina owner, from whom we leased it for our honeymoon trip."

The word honeymoon was questioned then quickly translated into Spanish, to the delight and added wistful stares of the three men.

The man on the left opened Tanya's passport then handed it to the man speaking. It listed her as Tanya Cárdenas Vega. He must have known the U.S. naming conventions: three names ending with the male surname, unlike the Cuban system that normally had four names, ending with the female parent.

"Your mother came from Cuba?" asked one man.

"Yes, so did my father," answered Tanya—wishing she had not given so much information. *Too much caffeine...*

"Why don't you have better Spanish?"

"My parents worked hard at learning English, so that is all we spoke at home—I learned most of my Spanish in high school and from friends," Tanya lied smoothly. Without really knowing why she wanted them not to know she spoke and understood Cuban Spanish. It gave her a little sense of power in an otherwise powerless situation.

"Why did they leave Cuba?" Asked the leader, while all three men took a draw on their large cigars, slowly exhaling, waiting for Tanya's sure-to-be-incriminating answer.

"They felt there were more opportunities for them in the USA."

"Did they plot against Fidel Castro?"

"I was not born then, but I don't believe so—they never spoke about Cuba, except of the good times and beautiful places.

"We have done nothing wrong, rescuing a person at sea is always the right action.

"If you could contact our government they would tell you all I've said is the truth. Also, your people stole from our boat." As the words came from her month, she knew they were a mistake. The eyes of the three men changed from friendly-lecherous to defensive-angry in an instant.

After a moment, the littlest man said in perfect English, "We will look into your charges. You will be our guest for a time. We will talk to you again."

The three left the room. Tanya waited an hour, cursing herself for so strongly voicing her accusations. She left the last of the coffee, cursing it for loosening her tongue and unleashing her combative nature.

Two large, strong women came to the room and escorted Tanya to one of a group of small individual cells, with a metal bed, a porcelain toilet with a low wall providing some privacy, a small sink and a single, caged light high in the ceiling. She was given a gray dress and cloth sandals. She was told to put her clothes near the door, that they would be washed and returned.

One guard took a small comb from her uniform pocket. "Here, you may have this; a woman must keep her hair beautiful." Looking into Tanya's eyes, she presented the comb with one hand and caressed Tanya's hair and shoulder with the other.

Tanya took the comb, thinking, *Damn, just what I need on my honeymoon, a girlfriend!*

30

In Cuban Cells

Matt turned to watch the guard walk away. He touched the cell's bars—or more accurately a grid of flat metal strips held together with rivets at each junction. The metal felt old, many layers of paint giving a smooth appearance, but closer inspection showing hammer work on the rivets and at the multiple hinges on the door. The grid of steel was very old, the work of smiths not welders. The smell of the cell came in waves: human excrement, mold, fried food, sweat, tobacco smoke. Matt also noticed the heat—he had been in a cooled office, now the heat was oppressive, the humidity equal to the temperature in the mid 80s. His shirt had soaked through in the few minutes he stood inside the cell. A mosquito enjoyed a good pull of Matt's blood, before he slapped it, smearing his wrist with mashed mosquito and a streak of red.

The slap broke the staring session within the cell. A small man rose from the group of three, wearing thin cutoff dungarees, no shirt. "Hello, gringo, welcome to our little party—now we can play bridge before cocktail hour. There is your bed, fresh blankets maybe every three months, a pillow will cost you some money. You got anyone that can get you money? I am called Lupe. *Mucho gusto.*"

Lupe escorted Matt to the group, seated on the beds near a small table, and formally introducing him to his cell mates. A well-muscled large man of indeterminate age—35 to 55—called Camilo shook Matt's hand. The other man—sporting a beard and pony tail, young, mid or late 20s, thin with mean eyes—mumbled a hello. His name was Mario—he did not offer his hand, just a brief wave of recognition.

Lupe offered Matt a cigarette—which he refused—then a small brown box with a Swiss Red Cross label that contained sweet crackers—which Matt accepted, eating two—realizing he was very hungry. Lupe explained they would have no more food until morning. During hot weather, the cooks often served lunch and followed it an hour or so later with dinner to save reheating their ovens and getting them out of the hot kitchens. The dry crackers and the heat made Matt thirsty, and he drank from a communal cup tied to a large metal bucket. The water was warm, but looked clean. Matt learned the water was turned on twice a day for about an hour in the morning and afternoon. They kept the valve open, so the water announced itself when it came. During the time the water flowed, they had to do all their washing and flushing and save enough for drinking.

Lupe explained how lucky they were to have only four in the cell—sometimes there are over a dozen men. They had to buy soap, pillows, bug repellent, tobacco, candy bars—even pills—from the guards. A man without money was in sorry straights.

They got a newspaper every day—it was a few days old and all Castro-cleared information and editorials, but it was a link to the outside world. All were read and reread by everyone in the cell.

The lights went out as they finished the instructions for cell life. Matt moved to his bunk—a canvas mattress, stuffed with rag-like material and with urine, sweat and dirt staining it in all the expected places. With no pillow, Matt rolled up his shoes in his pants, laid out his shirt to avoid as much mattress contact as possible, and lay on his back, tired to the bone. He considered the large stones that made up the wall, the high ceiling formed by timbers and metal beams, and the lack of windows in the cell, although there were several large, open windows in the hallway. The weak, bare lights from the hallway drew clouds of bugs and provided enough light for Matt to locate the sleeping forms of his cellmates—each with mosquito nets over their bunks, stretched across a thin wooden bow and tucked under their mattresses. Matt soon understood why, as the buzzing of the bloodthirsty insects swarmed around him. He finally had to put on his pants and socks, sleeping under his shirt, his face on his shoes—preferable to being on the foul canvas. The insects droned and bit, coming in swarms, drawn by his slapping and exhaled CO_2.

Lupe finally brought over a towel and sprayed repellent on it and over Matt. "This will help you a little, I hope. You will want to negotiate for a net...and you will need money."

Matt relaxed on the bunk: his worries about Tanya, the sounds and smells of the cell, and the drone of insects finally fading from his awareness as he fell into a deep sleep.

Fifty yards away from Matt, in a newer wing of the jail, Tanya had covered herself with a thin blanket to ward off the mosquitoes. The light outside her cell was off, drawing no bugs. Two male guards patrolled the hall outside her cell. They tapped the bars with wooden batons just to annoy her. The patrol went by every half hour. The noises of other prisoners slowly decreased as sleep finally gave them some escape from the awful environment of captivity. Tanya went to sleep, thinking of Matt, her family and even poor Alberto.

She awoke when strong hands pinned her arms above her head. Other hands pulled her dress up and partially over her head. She kicked out and started a scream that was instantly muffled by a hard, callused hand. She felt the weight of someone straddling her, pinning down her flailing legs, hands grabbed and stroked her breasts. A hoarse voice in Spanish whispered, "Don't fight, this will not be so bad."

Tanya shook her head free from the restraining hand and lunged at an arm that held her wrists, getting in what she hoped was a painful bite. The man cried out, hissed, "*Yanke puta*"—Yankee whore—and pulled her arms wider and painfully over the head of the bed. The other man returned his hand to covering and controlling her mouth and chin while working on her panties, trying to bring them down while he controlled her potentially dangerous knees and legs. The struggle continued for several minutes, the hand across her mouth occasionally covering her nose—her breathing came in gasps. Tanya began to weaken, the pain in her shoulders and arms increased as she lost strength and they were pulled farther back and levered against the metal bed frame. She made sounds from her throat, not her mouth, hoping to draw attention to the rape from others in the cells down the hall.

Soon, her strength almost used up, she could not breath, her head pounded with the rapid beat of her heart, she was sinking into unconsciousness. Then she heard the cell door clank open. The hall light was on and the tall woman that had given her the comb stood outlined in the door way.

"Bastards, cowardly beasts, dogs…" she spat in Spanish. The men released Tanya, thinking she was unconscious, and rushed past the woman and down the hall. Tanya, taking her first good breath in several minutes, was able to hear the last man whisper to the matron in rapid Cuban Spanish, *"Companera, ya esta pa' ti"*

Comrade, she is (ready) for you.

The woman came to Tanya, now in a sitting position and trying to adjust her clothing. She sat down and hugged Tanya. "You must not be afraid, I will protect you. This will not happen again."

Tanya smelled the woman's perfume, her clean clothes and hair. She felt relief and gratitude—but as the woman's hug turned into a caress, her body pressing against Tanya's and her breathing becoming deeper, Tanya realized the rape had been a setup, and a planned procedure carefully choreographed to aid in the seduction of female inmates.

Tanya's mind raced—she was trapped between awful and rotten choices. She let herself relax against the guard, whose caresses continued along with soothing words.

Tanya fought the desire to grab the woman's hair and slam her head against the massive stones of the cell wall. However sweet the moment of revenge, the aftermath would be swift punishment and injury, maybe even death.

Desperately, Tanya went through ideas to escape from this woman and the awful power she possessed: fainting, sexual diseases, being violently sick, going crazy—maybe catatonic. Actions came to mind, played out, and were rejected. While Tanya thought, the woman's soothing voice droned on, one of her hands massaged Tanya's lower back, making slow circles near the base of her backbone, a light and warm touch, the other hand slowly working up the outside of Tanya's leg.

Taking a deep breath, Tanya hugged the woman and began to cry, sob and shake. It was part acting and part a real outlet of emotions for the hopeless situation in which she found herself. Tanya buried her face in the neck of the guard, sobbing, "You saved me from those men, I will always be in your debt, I will thank you in my prayers every day for the rest of my life." Tanya repeated the words in halting Spanish, getting verbs and pronouns wrong and out of place. The woman began kissing Tanya's forehead. Tanya moved off the bed and knelt before the woman, taking her hands—so they couldn't keep touching her— and looked into the woman's eyes. "My husband has much money, if you help me I will pay you a great deal. Thousands of U.S. dollars are nothing for what you have done for me this night. I promise you, on the Holy Virgin Mary, your action tonight will be remembered."

Tanya read disappointment, followed by cunning satisfaction, in the woman's eyes and face. She helped Tanya up, got her into the bed, covered her and gave her another kiss on the forehead and, touching Tanya's face, said in English, "I will be here for you tonight and also tomorrow—now sleep."

The woman looked at Tanya as she closed and locked the cell door.

Tanya waited until her steps faded and another metal door was heard closing, then got up and washed from a water bucket until the smell and touch of the men was gone.

She went back to bed and fell into an exhausted sleep, unmindful of the few mosquitoes that buzzed in the room.

31

Minutes in Court

The room looked like an under-equipped classroom: large desk, three old high-backed leather chairs behind it, on which were ash trays, a water container, and glasses. Four metal chairs positioned a respectable distance in front of the desk, then more cheap wooden chairs in rows in the rear of the room. Dull greens and muddy browns made up the walls. A Cuban flag and a picture of Fidel dominated the wall behind the three padded chairs.

Matt was seated with a young female interpreter when Tanya was led in. She wore a gray, shapeless cotton dress with her own jogging shoes, her hair was combed and she wore a touch of makeup and lipstick. She lit the room with her smile when she saw Matt. They hugged, kissed and hugged again, their first meeting in six days. The matron with Tanya pulled her away, putting Tanya in the fourth chair, the interpreter and the matron separating them. Matt's interpreter told him this was very unusual to have both charged individuals in the same courtroom, and he must not touch or talk to his wife.

Tanya felt in her dress pocket—Matt had put something in it. She felt paper. Peeking at her hand that held the bundle in the pocket, she saw a note around a roll of US bills. She glanced at Matt—got a wink from tired eyes. She noticed he had a bruised swelling above his left eye and a scrape on his forehead.

Matt looked across the two women toward Tanya, she looked thinner in the baggy dress. His stomach rumbled, having suffered the cramping pains and humiliation of diarrhea for the last several days. He was on the mend, good enough to get out of bed and not in immediate need of a toilet or the hole in the cell floor that served as one.

Just being near Tanya helped his overall mood, but he hoped she had better conditions than his. He reflected on his last few days in the communist hellhole. The cell conditions he experienced were designed to break him down. The food was disgusting, nearly poisonous, prepared and served in ways to make it worse than the awful ingredients within it. Matt grudgingly acknowledged the skill that had gone into the preparation of spoiled or marginal food to make it even less palatable or nutritious. Tripe that was undercooked in rancid grease, rotten plantain soup—watered and unsalted, a pig's ear with the hair still on it floating in cold oily gravy, milk products left in the sun to sour, potatoes—usually hard to ruin—with some soft and mushy and some half green and undercooked and all piled in the same *jaba*—the food basket. Yellow, hard beef fat still clung to the metal, divided plates they had to eat off of. Matt once thought his college freshman year dorm food was the bottom of the culinary barrel, until he experienced this total mastery of bad food that the Cuban prison system had perfected.

His life had begun to improve on his second day of captivity. In the yard, where the prisoners were taken for an hour a day, he met a young guard who knew Matt had arrived on a yacht. They discussed boats in English. Matt suggested he would give money to be taken aboard his yacht to get clean clothes and toilet articles. That same afternoon he had a two-guard escort back to the *Reefer*. One guard stayed on the deck, the young guard went inside with Matt.

The boat looked the same from the outside, but inside it looked like a fire sale had taken place. Blankets, pillows, food, drinks, a wall clock, pictures, soaps, clothes were gone. Matt mainly wanted soap, a pillow, sheets and some crackers and candy—all were gone. Matt checked the engine room; his tools were still in their places. This was confusing. But his next area of interest was the large wall safe in the master bedroom.

There were scratches on its edge, but it was unopened. He had given the original boarding group their ship's papers and their passports as they had watched him open it. They had seen no money inside. Now Matt reopened it, a false bottom yielded two bundles—twenties and fifties. Matt paid his guard several hundred. Matt silently thanked Webb—who had refitted the stateroom—for the quality and design of the safe. The young guard was so happy with his reward he made no move to take it all. Matt thought that a higher-ranking official would have acted differently. Matt found some small soap bars, a disposable razor, a hard throw pillow from the guest stateroom, two sheets from the back of a forward linen closet and bug spray and a small personal packet of Kleenex in a helm drawer. He noted nothing seemed to be missing from the helm. All the very expensive navigation and communication gear was still in place. He made one last trip through the master head—stripped to the bone—the medicine chest empty, the toilet paper gone. After fifteen minutes of inspection, with his limited booty and the comfort of money in his pockets, he was escorted back to the smelly confines of his cell.

His cell mates seemed pleased that he had gotten items to make him more comfortable. They were interested in how and why the guard helped him. Trouble started when Matt told Lupe he had some money and could buy mosquito netting and perhaps bribe the food servers to get them better food or at least better delivery. Mario overheard the conversation and came to Matt suggesting he—Mario—should hold Matt's money to keep it safe. Matt knew there would be a fight sooner or later. If he gave the man a little money, Mario would just demand more and more. The lessons of bullies and history were not wasted on Matt. Matt moved toward Mario saying, "I'll give you nothing!"

Mario's right fist shot like a snake strike at Matt, hitting him on the left ear as Matt tried to duck. Matt gave ground as each of three right jabs came toward him. He knew Mario was left-handed from watching him eat and from the untanned band around his right wrist from a wristwatch that was no longer there. Matt circled left; Lupe tried hard to stop the fight but was pushed to the floor by Mario. Mario moved in, trying to set up what would be a powerful left-handed blow. After three retreats, Matt charged in under a pawing right punch, pushing the arm up and locking Mario's arm and neck in a tight headlock.

Matt's head pressed just behind and under Mario's now upward and useless right arm. The two combatants stood for a few seconds. Mario confused by what this maneuver would do. It finally dawned on Mario he couldn't breathe very well. Next, Matt twisted; Mario went down, thrown over Matt's extended leg and hip. On the dusty cell floor, in silence, Mario's struggles got weaker and weaker as Matt squeezed with all his considerable strength, aided by the added pressure of his weight on Mario's neck and chest. Matt finally released the limp Mario, who took his first full breath in some minutes. Matt tasted his own blood from a cut lip, he felt his ear throb and touched a swelling over his left eye. Pissed off by being hit and marked, but not leaving a mark on the man he had beaten, Matt brought his right elbow into Mario's face followed by a short backswing into the jaw. Blood spurted from Mario's nose and Matt knew the blow on the jaw would certainly swell. Feeling like he was back in 5th grade, on a playground fighting with Roger Tyler, Matt got up and turned to a smiling Lupe. "Tell Mario I can take care of my own money…thank him for his concern."

Matt's thoughts jerked back to the now as uniformed officials came into the room. There were three that sat in the main chairs, another man wheeled in a cart with a large reel-to-reel tape recorder—which he plugged into a wall socket—and brought up a chair to sit in next to the large machine as he adjusted a small microphone. The recorder had Sony 550 in silver on its black finish. Matt noted that the court of the People's Paradise of Castro's Cuba was three generations behind in recording technology.

The middle man, without badges or rank on his neatly pressed uniform, began the trial. In rapid Spanish, followed by the interpreter's translation, he explained Matt and Tanya Hunter were guilty of illegally transporting a Cuban national from his homeland. He held up a paper which he said was a signed confession by Alberto Luis Perez Cárdenas admitting his escape was aided by the defendants, the female being a relative.

He listed other various charges that included anti-Castro activities, activities counter to the revolution, and a long list of crimes by the USA that went back nearly to the charge up nearby San Juan hill—which to him was probably the last time Cubans and Americans fought on the same side.

Finally, in excellent English, he said, "Your vessel is confiscated; you will be taken to Boniato Prison for an indeterminate time. Your country's officials have contacted us. We may, at some time, negotiate with them for your bail and time of confinement."

Matt took in a lungful of air, having mentally prepared a rebuttal, but no opportunity was given to him or to Tanya before the group got up and left, the recorder unplugged and rolled out.

The whole, so-called trial hadn't taken twenty minutes.

32

Bank or Boniato

T anya and Matt were not taken back to their cells. They were led to a small room off the main receiving area. In the room, the man who had passed sentence on them sat alone, drinking coffee and smoking a small, dark cigar.

"Sit, please, I am Colonel Manuel Grosa," he said in English. "You have heard the official judgment of the Cuban People's Government, now we can talk about alternative futures. Our time to talk is limited, once you are sent to Boniato Prison I have no control over your fates.

"Have you heard about Boniato? It is called the sweet potato—because its great walls are a yellow color. It makes our humble jail seem a vacation resort by comparison. You will not see each other—if you are lucky enough to live for a few years, you may be transferred to a work farm—we have two hundred of them. There you will help in the sugar fields or the mines or clearing swamps."

Matt interrupted, "What do you want to change our future?"

"Money…sent to a person in your country. This money will allow you to stay with us, your conditions will be made more pleasant, you will eat the same food as the guards, you will be allowed to be together a few times each week. You will still be prisoners. I can't put you together in the same cell, but you will have many comforts while your country and mine slowly work out terms for your freedom. I'm afraid your fine vessel will be lost to you. The TGF has need of it. However, it will not be moved until all our negotiations are complete. I am sure your planes and satellites have identified it, even under the roof over the dock.

"I will let you two talk. When I come back I want you to have a number for me. If it is acceptable I will arrange for you to have a telephone, your credit cards, and official documents. I can even show you your personal property—such as your watch and the lovely lady's beautiful rings we found when we carefully searched your boat.

"You have fifteen minutes."

The colonel left, the door was locked.

Matt made a pantomime that indicated the room had to be bugged. Tanya nodded her understanding. They both looked for microphones and cameras. Matt found a mic located in the ceiling, hidden in the old, stained acoustical tile above the room's table.

Hoping they weren't on camera, Tanya spoke as she looked at the money roll and note she took from her pocket. "I'd say pay the man a lot, keep us healthy and together until we can get out of this latrine with bars."

While she talked, she silently read Matt's note: "I love you, money from boat should help, careful they don't take it away from you. I had to fight to keep mine. We will live thru this. Your loving husband, Matt."

Tanya read the note while Matt talked about the condition of the *Reefer*.

Tanya continued, "I had a visitor—Alberto's mother, all the way from northern Cuba. She brought me candy and breads she had baked. She was very grateful for what we did for her son. He is in another area, they hurt him to make him sign the paper about our helping him escape. His leg is worse, they hung him by it, but he is young and they allow his mother to bring him food and clothes." Tanya moved to Matt, whispering in his ear, "Edward sent her—somehow paid her bus fare, told her to tell us he is working to help us."

Matt began talking even while Tanya whispered. "That was a fine thing she did, that's a long trip. I'm afraid we are on our own here. Now, we need to come up with a number for the colonel."

Tanya and Matt looked at each other—Tanya spoke, "I really want my rings back. I bet you he'll want double of whatever number we say—so let's start at $50,000 and see what he does."

Matt said, "We wouldn't be wise to give him a lump sum, he could take it and still send us away, how about $10,000 a week to stay in this five-star shithole, eating boiled cabbage and fish heads." Matt leaned closer to Tanya and whispered, "We need to get this information to Edward—maybe get some leverage on our jailor—taking bribes is not good communist doctrine."

They held hands and looked at each other. Tanya was softly touching Matt's bruised eyebrow when the lock turned and Colonel Grosa came back into the room.

After a little discussion so Grosa understood they were talking U.S. dollars not Cuban pesos, a $10,000 a week payment was agreed upon. Grosa seemed almost lightheaded over the amount of money involved. He left and returned in a minute with a large envelope he emptied on the table—Matt's watch and wallet, Tanya's purse, their passports, ship's papers and finally, tied together with string, her two rings—the wedding ring and her diamond. A secretary brought in an old, black dial phone, trailing its cord into the office area.

Matt found the business card for his Gibraltar banker. Grosa produced a notepad with the name and address of a man in Dallas, Texas. He also got up and closed the door, careful of the phone cord. As the door closed, Matt noted that the office was empty—official government lunch hours.

Matt said, "I am sure you have turned off your microphone—you would not want these transactions to be recorded. I am also going to ask you to cover your ears when I give my banker some security codes. You can listen to my mailing instructions—they will mail cashier checks unless you have direct deposit numbers."

"Checks will be fine," said Grosa, his voice higher than before, his mouth seemed filled with saliva.

Matt added, "We can send a check immediately—and one every week from today. We would like to have our time together starting today also."

"I can arrange your time together in a pleasant place, your new cells will take a few days to be prepared."

"How many days is a few" asked Matt, gaining more control as the officer stared at the black credit card Matt held in his hand.

"I can have new, clean cells—with a flush toilet and a good bed, in two maybe three days. They are in our newest wing—screens on the windows—few bugs, there are trees to be seen from your windows."

Matt made the call, got quick and competent service from the banker. While the officer had his ears covered, Matt, with his hand cupped over the mouth piece, told the banker to inform his head teller, Mr. Webb, of this transaction and give him the number of the phone Matt was calling from. Then, as he motioned that the officer could listen, Matt said, "We will call you each week to approve sending the next check—either I or my wife will have the security information."

The bank officer asked to speak to Tanya. She was asked to say several common words. Matt figured they were being recorded or some type of voice recognition was being initiated.

The colonel took the phone away and returned. He put everything on the table back into the envelope. Tanya looked surprised and hurt. The colonel said, "I assure you these will be in my safekeeping for you. My office and desk are sacrosanct. You would have great difficulty keeping these on your own. I also want to warn you about talking about our agreement—some people will be surprised with your new treatment, but no one will say much—such arrangements have happened before. A prison is a dangerous place, there is too much time for talking and thinking—you must not speak even to yourselves, except to thank your God for the favors someone has given you. If I become threatened by this action, I warn you, you both will just disappear. I will have a fine watch and my wife will enjoy your beautiful ring—if only inside our home."

Then he stood up, opened the door and, standing in the doorway smiling, in a loud and authoritative voice said, "You will be taken to a courtyard—for an hour to consider your crimes against the people. We hope you will use your time wisely."

Tanya and Matt sat together on a stone bench in the middle of a pleasant atrium, grass underfoot and trees to one side, all surrounded by the massive stone walls of the oldest part of the building. Matt had learned some of the structure dated back to the 17th century.

Matt asked, "How will you protect your money?"

"I have guards that can take anything, they come in the cell every night just to show me they can. I'm protected by a woman jailer that wants me for herself. I promised her money from you. She is now trying to charm me into bed after she had men do a fake rape."

Tanya told Matt the whole story.

Matt's face hardened. "We'll get out of here. We seem to have improved our situation short term. We have people worried about us. Let's just play each day as it comes."

They kissed as their guards came to take them back. They left on separate paths, back to their own cells, their own hells.

33

Cell Life

The cell door clinked and its lock snapped into place behind Matt, each time the sounds tore at his mind and stomach. Moving into the large cell area, he saw Camilo was gone. Lupe was reading a newspaper sitting on his bed. Mario had tissue in his swollen nose, his left jaw puffy, eyes like a raccoon's with dark rings under them. He glared at Matt.

Lupe continued looking at the thin paper, but spoke. "Mario says you didn't fight like a man."

"Tell Mario he slept through the best part," replied Matt.

Lupe rattled off the translation. Mario's glare increased. Matt prepared for an attack.

"Tell Mario if he comes at me again, I will not be so kind to him. I will kick his *cojones* up into his throat, he will have to open his mouth to scratch himself."

Lupe translated, Mario tried to look even meaner. Matt mimed scratching himself through his opened mouth. Mario smirked, snorted, then couldn't hold back a laugh. Lupe laughed. Matt laughed. A new relationship had begun. There was no handshake but Matt saw a glint of friendship or maybe just a glimpse of a little boy who never had a chance to laugh and trust on the tough, dusty streets of his Mexican village.

While they were still laughing, a guard wheeled the food cart up and passed the *jabas* through the cell slits. Each man took his basket to his bed. The stew actually smelled good, the bread rolls— thin crusted, yeasty and delicious—could actually be bitten into without being dunked in some liquid. The stew was spiced with salt and peppers. There was white rice—actually warm.

The men ate, expressing their surprise and appreciation.

Lupe added, "This is guard food—it has fresh meat, good bread, clean rice. I didn't pay anyone yet. I just talked to the server in general terms—getting him ready for some favors for cash."

While they were eating, guards escorted Camilo down the hallway. His sad face and shuffling gate meant bad news from his meeting with a lawyer.

Camilo noted he had missed dinner, just another bad break on top of more problems. He announced, "We go to Boniato next week. There is no help for us. They are moving all the convicted smugglers."

Matt had learned the Cuban system segregated its criminals by their crime category. Each wing or floor contained jailbirds of a feather: killers, thieves, smugglers, pimps, prostitutes, political dissidents always grouped by their worst crime.

Matt offered Camilo half his bread roll and then put his remaining rice into what was left of his stew, offering the tray to Camilo.

Camilo looked as if it must be a trick; he smelled the bread, then the food, tasted it with his finger, nibbled the bread, got his spoon, sat down and ate. After he had swallowed three large spoonfuls he finally said in English, "Thank you Matt." Then he added, "Maybe in morning we are shot!"

After dinner, the prospect of Boniato dominated the conversations. Matt didn't understand all the Spanish and felt an impediment to the group by always asking for a translation. He knew enough Spanish to understand the place was the worst prison in Cuba. Men wasted away and welcomed death. The guards were cruel and food even worse than at the TGF facility. Matt had learned that Lupe and Mario were Mexican and Camilo was Colombian. Lupe and Camilo supported wives and children. They smuggled Cubans to Mexico or sometimes Puerto Rico. They had a fast boat and a good business with Cuba's 3,500 miles of coast line, over 4,000 coves and only six or eight working, armed TGF patrol boats as interceptor threats. They had been caught because of an informer who infiltrated their pipeline. They had friends in Cuba and access to some gang money, but their land-based operation had been broken and the authorities were going to make an example of them.

His cellmates had never talked about smuggling when Matt could hear, or at least never in English, but their fates now seemed sealed and they figured Matt wasn't a plant to rat on them—a common jail technique. Some prisoners would testify to anything for a few of the delicious bread rolls they were now eating.

Soon, with bread-polished plates and bowls before them, they all agreed that they had eaten the best food since their captures.

Lupe, Mario and Camilo talked late into the night—after lights out. As Matt lay under his new mosquito net, on a clean pillow between clean sheets, he felt grateful for his relative good fortune, sickened by his cellmates' despondency, understanding that Tanya and he would be facing the same terror sometime in the future. He also silently reflected upon how depravity and awful conditions can make a bit of decent stew seem so wonderful. He vowed to appreciate his blessings more if he ever got out of Cuba.

Tanya was in trouble. Earlier she had given five $20 bills to the matron who wanted to be more than a friend. She again thanked her for the protection she offered. Hours went by, the lights went out. Just as she began to sleep the lights came on, two guards and the matron came in and threw Tanya from the bed. Grabbing a sheet, she huddled in a corner as every part of her cell was ransacked. They found all the money she had hidden in cracks in the wall, in the metal tubing of the bed, in the tongues of her jogging shoes, and finally the men ripped her panties off and found the two bills she had rolled into the elastic of the waist.

The largest of the male guards held the bills and, in Spanish, spit, "This is all you have?" Leaning over her, trapping her in the corner, he hissed in broken English, "You say a thousand dollars is nothing for saving your honor. We maybe get money from men who would come to your cell in the night. You must get more money, unless you wish to be a friend to many men—and maybe some women also."

The men left, the matron closed and locked the cell door, blowing Tanya a kiss as she turned off the cell lights.

Tanya fought panic and tears. While reorganizing the room and remaking her bed, she gritted her teeth and promised herself that she would survive no matter what. She hated being powerless and a victim of these foul people. She rolled up into a ball on the narrow bed, vowing to get some measure of revenge, wishing she was with Matt. She finally fell asleep.

34

Freedom's Call

lank-clank-CLANK...

      Tanya shot bolt upright in bed, confusion and bewilderment were quickly replaced by the hideous smells and the filth of the cell surrounding her.

Clank-clank-clank...

Suddenly, reality overwhelmed her like a terrible waking nightmare—a hostile country, predatory guards, her isolation, hunger, exhaustion.

Clank- clank-clank...

A guard was coming, dragging a club across the metal bars as he walked.

She slowly got to her feet, wincing at the pain in her muscles that protested as she slowly moved to the water bucket. She desperately needed to wash away as much grime as possible, something she had been too upset to tackle the evening before. She fought back the despair that threatened to overwhelm her.

Don't give up. She scolded herself. *Survive, beat these bastards!*

She felt herself overcoming the despair that would have been easy to accept and let conquer her. Instead of allowing defeat to be an option, she knew she had to contact Matt, maybe get word to Colonel Grosa about her treatment, plan some way to fight and live through this ordeal.

When her breakfast gruel and cold bitter coffee arrived she asked to see the matron.

It was mid-morning when the matron came to the cell door. Her smile made Tanya's skin crawl, or maybe it was the little cell insects that had appreciated her warmth overnight.

Tanya moved close to the cell door and whispered in high school Spanish, "I know you want more money, if I could meet with my husband I could get more."

"You will stay in this cell until you become more agreeable. You are not to be trusted—you hid money from me. The men may want to come to you tonight…"

Tanya broke in, "What if I send a note? It may get you money and reward you for keeping the men away from me. I thought you said you liked me and would protect me?"

The matron smiled again, put her arm through the bars, touching Tanya's hair, "You need to use your comb, my pretty one. I'll bring you paper and a pencil. Also, I have a clean dress for you. If you are nice to me you will find your time here can be very pleasant."

Tanya fought the urge to grab her arm and break it against the cross bars, but instead, leaned toward her and said, "I will be grateful for your help. I will write a note as soon as I have the paper."

A few minutes later, Tanya had the paper and a pen. While she printed out a note, the matron left her alone, returning shortly with a clean dress—a blue smock with a gathered waist, newer than the one Tanya now wore.

"Put it on, it will look good on you," said the matron as she took the note and passed the dress through the bars.

The matron unfolded the note, which was in English. She began to read, working to understand the English words she knew.

Tanya slowly took off her dirty, gray dress and, taking her time to inspect the new one, stood in her ripped panties and bra. The matron's attention shifted from the note to Tanya. Just the reaction Tanya had hoped for. Tanya put on the new dress and, as she adjusted her hair, smiled at the guard. "This is very nice, it is soft and fits very well. Thank you.

"You will get that note to my husband?"

The matron refolded the note. "He will have it with his noon meal."

Matt talked all morning with his cellmates. They now spoke freely about their lives, laughed about close calls, bad weather, getting stuck on sand bars, hitting rocks, boats overloaded, engine trouble and spending hours under plastic tarps to avoid airplanes or patrol boats— Matt really didn't want to know them so well. He wanted to think of human traffickers as the ones that took all their money and then left passengers at night on waterless sand islands, with the dawn whole families had to face a hopeless and horrible death.

Lupe seemed to read Matt's mind, or maybe just the disgust in his eyes. "We were raised as Catholics, we have souls, we never abandoned our passengers. A few times they had to swim or float longer than they expected, but we counted heads until they were walking up the beach. In Mexico, we had guides that kept them from the corrupt authorities. A few were caught, but we did the best we could. Word got back, our business was always good."

The lunch was as good as the breakfast that preceded it. There were confused questions about their change of fortune. But their stomachs overcame their curiosity.

Matt's basket was handed to him by a large guard not seen before, who stood silently near the cell, watching Matt.

Matt found the note tucked under his bread. It read:

> Matt
> Have need of more money.
> Everything is fine.
> Love you,
> Put money with big guard—he knows me.
> Tanya

The structure, phrases were strange. Matt read it twice before he saw the HELP.

He also understood the big guard line—"he knows me" meant he messed with me. Matt got his roll of $50 bills, took six and folded them into a piece of newspaper. No one had a pencil or pen. Matt used the handle of his spoon and some tomato soup to print on the newspaper:

FOR YOUR HELP, LOVE. M.

He took the folded paper with the note and bills to the cell door. The big guard came over, Matt studied him, memorizing his eyes, face, hair, hands, and stature, thinking, *I'll see you again and you might not live through the meeting!*

Matt was too upset to finish his meal. He gave it to the others—who were concerned. Matt explained his wife was in trouble. The three ate their meals—saddened but silent, speculation would only make the reality worse. Anyway, they were powerless to help.

Matt called out for the head guard of his wing, demanding to see the Colonel. He had a fistful of money to go with the request. The guard looked at the money, took only two bills and, shrugging his shoulders, said, "I am sorry, but Colonel Grosa is away for sometime, I will tell him of your request when he returns."

Later, Matt's cellmates had to force him from the cell to take the exercise hour in the yard area. He went to a corner of the open area, found a large rock, sat on the ground, his back against it. He had to think.

A shadow fell across Matt. It was the young guard with whom Matt had discussed boats earlier. He said, "Stand up please, follow me, I want to talk to you."

Matt and the guard walked to the yard's gate, it was opened and they went to the courtyard where Matt had last been with Tanya. They sat on the same bench. The guard, nervous with sweat staining his uniform, looked at his hands for several moments, then said in English, "My brother is the radio operator on the patrol boat. They will be at our dock this evening. Your boat is still fueled. They will take most of your fuel tomorrow afternoon for the Zhuk and to store. Your fuel has been approved for use by our mechanics. One of my jobs is to move prisoners. You and your wife are scheduled to be transferred to new cells. I have the forms, all filled out and signed by the Colonel's hand, before he left for a week or so." The guard took in several breaths. He let Matt absorb the litany of facts he had presented.

The guard continued, "My name is Luis. I can take you to your boat instead of the cells. We can leave the harbor and be out of Cuban waters in a half hour. My brother and I want to go to the United States."

Matt felt the rush of hope fill his body like some powerful drug. "I will do anything to get Tanya and me out of this hell on earth."

Luis continued, "There are issues—problems. We move prisoners always with two or more guards. I can trust no one. I cannot use my brother—he is known in the jail and also looks like a schoolboy. You do not have much Spanish, and you do not look like a guard, but you will need to try. We must do this tonight, tomorrow your boat will be useless for an escape. The Zhuk is only fueled for short patrols—so they are not tempted to escape Cuba. What is left, except for a little, will go into storage drums. I thought I had more time—I just learned about the fuel plans."

Matt, hardly believing his ears, asked, "Can you get uniforms for three men? My cell mates are going to Boniato—they would be happy to be guards, they are not Cuban, but would pass for guards—they are fit and of a good age."

Luis thought, then said, "Point them out to me when we go back to the yard. If they are informers…"

Matt broke in, "They are smugglers, in great fear of Boniato. They have families, I will risk my life with them."

Luis stood up, again taking a deep breath. "Let's return, this is not planned out as I would have wished, but my brother will disable the patrol boat. The only other boat that could pursue us is at the docks at Santiago de Cuba—over fifteen kilometers away. Also there will be radio problems my brother can cause. There should not be any airplanes or helicopters available for maybe hours. I am assured your vessel is seaworthy. The orders were to not touch anything mechanical or electric. I am sorry all of your food is gone—we didn't want it to spoil. Your air conditioning is not on."

Matt saw a little grin from Luis when he tried to justify their theft. Matt added, returning the grin, "Your people must be storing our medicine, pillows and bed linen also—very thoughtful!"

Luis's face became serious again. "We may have to overcome the guards at the boat and on the pier—if they are even awake or on duty."

As they walked back, Matt asked, "Could we get a Cuban prisoner out? Alberto came with us, he has been tortured. I don't know where he is."

Luis whispered back, as they approached the yard gate, "I know where he would be—we may be able to sweep him up as we gather transfers—I'll make up papers and sign the Colonel's name—I've done it before when he has been gone. It will be the most dangerous part of the plan. We will get you aboard your boat first, then I get your wife, then we will try for your Cuban friend. We will try, but for now, I don't know.

"Be ready sometime before dawn. That is the usual time when we take people from their cells. Pray if you can."

Back in the yard, Matt paused to chat with each of his cellmates as Luis watched from outside the fence, judging their size compared to Matt.

Back in the cell Matt signaled for a huddle, a useless gesture for Latinos only familiar with soccer. He still got them together near the far wall. He could hardly wait between Lupe's translations. He watched their eyes get large, their breathing get shallow—just like his own.

Lupe fired back problems: their shoes were wrong, their hair was wrong, they were dirty.

Lupe talked to a guard and, for some of Matt's money, managed to rent some scissors—tips broken off—and combs and bought flea powder to help explain their need to clean up.

The rest of the afternoon the cell could have been a scene from the main dressing room of a Miss America pageant: haircuts, shaves, shoes darkened to look less worn, shampoos, hands and necks washed until they were red from scrubbing.

Mario, looking very young without his beard and ponytail, approached Matt. *"¿Por que?"*

Matt had Lupe translate the rather difficult answer: "Freedom should be a right. I could not enjoy my freedom thinking about you in Boniato. I cannot turn my back on you. Besides, I am sure there are a lot of beautiful women that will thank me for bringing you to them. Also, we need you to be a guard—to act like a guard.

"You have seen how the guards act: their walk, how they look at you, their arrogance. You need to be a guard for a few minutes. Think how you must act."

Mario extended his hand. Matt shook it.

In the women's cellblock, Tanya read Matt's note on the newspaper, the money already confiscated. No one had come to her with more threats or demands. She knew Matt knew she needed help: folding the paper, tucking it into her dress, its presence a good omen. She would keep her faith and keep alive.

35

Under The Guns

I n Matt's cell no one slept after the lights went out. They gathered in a far corner, whispering about posing as guards, their chances of success, what punishment could follow if they failed. Failure, even death by gunfire or the guards' clubs, they always balanced against the prospect of Boniato Prison.

Camilo—the Colombian—told of a cousin who had been there for many years, who finally crippled his own hands to get a release. Lupe translated for Matt—Cuba allowed no prison inspections by outside organizations. Cuba camouflaged some of the world's worst prisons with propaganda films of happy inmates in newly painted rooms, enjoying good food, served by a smiling kitchen staff. Camilo waited for Lupe to finish then, scoffing, went on to say, "Bugs crawl all over, many cell blocks get no sun, the windows have metal over them, everything is damp, scorpions and rats crawl over the sleeping men. Some prisoners catch the scorpions; they trade to the guards for tiny pieces of meat or bread. The venom is used in medicines. It is living in hell, he swears this is true...*verdad*."

The four finally went to their bunks, but Matt could tell by their breathing that no one slept.

A door clanged in a far hall. Guards marched through, stepping hard to make their passing a disturbance to the sleeping prisoners.

The night dragged slowly on. They had no way of telling time, no guards came through on regular intervals.

Just when Matt was finally falling asleep, a quiet shuffle in the hall-way and a key turning slowly in the cell door's lock jarred him awake.

"*Silencio*," whispered Luis, who moved into the cell with a large sack on his back. He had a small flashlight he shined around, locating Matt. Moving to Matt's bunk, he laid out three sets of guard's clothes, three pair of boots, three batons—two wooden and one metal, the ones nor-mally carried by the guards—and very carefully he took from the bag some handcuffs and a wide leather belt with a metal ring on it.

After he identified the three other men in the cell he handed out a pile of clothes and shoes to each. Whispering in Spanish, then in English for Matt's understanding, "Dress carefully, look neat, stuff your beds to look like someone is sleeping, and come to me when you are finished."

He left the light on the floor, so they could see what they were doing. Turning to Matt, he brought out the leather belt. "Put this on, then turn it around so the ring is in the front, the handcuffs go through the ring when they are open. I filed the teeth off one cuff—it was very difficult, put that one on your right wrist, practice getting out of it, use both hands and it opens easily. Do not make noise."

In a few minutes the four stood ready for inspection. Luis went around each with his flashlight, adjusting the uniforms, hiking up pants, adjusting belts, putting the batons correctly in their carrying rings. He watched as Matt practiced freeing himself several times.

With some degree of pleasure, Luis said, "We are ready, you all look better than I had expected. Think like guards. Matt be a beaten pris-oner, the other guards will ignore you, you may give us an advantage.

"Take this," Luis handed Matt a leather blackjack, thin and heavy, about ten inches long. "Tuck it into your thick belt. Used on the side of the head it will knock a person out with a snap of the wrist—too hard and it will kill. I have one also. Use yours only if we are in great danger."

Matt grasped the thin handle and slapped the weighted leather into his left palm, it hit with little sound and stung his hand.

While Matt practiced freeing his right hand and drawing the black-jack, Luis made his bed look occupied.

With one last sweep of his flashlight and after assigning the newly minted guards to their relative position around Matt they left and locked the cell.

Although the main hallway was the shortest route to the women's wing, it passed through the receiving office. So, Luis took his group through other hallways to enter the women's wing from an outside entry.

Inside the door, a holding area and double set of barred doors led to the hallway of cells. In an authoritative voice Luis ordered Matt and his two guards to wait. He took Camilo—because of his size—with him to the barred window of a small office.

"I am here to get this prisoner," said Luis as he handed over papers from a clipboard he carried. A sleepy guard got up from an office chair, leaving food and a thermos on his desk. The man looked at the papers, pushed a button and the first of two cell doors opened, Luis and Camilo entered the cage-like area, another buzz and the second door opened—Luis and Camilo walked through. The man left his office by another door and met them in the hallway. They walked to the far end of the hall where Tanya's cell, the largest, was on the right. The guard opened her cell.

Tanya was in her bed—awake.

Luis spoke in English, "Get dressed, take any personal items, we are moving you and your husband to new cells. Do not talk, move quickly."

Tanya dressed in front of the men, stuffed her pillow with the thin blankets and few toiletries she had accumulated, and walked out of the cell behind Luis, with the other two guards behind her.

The group was met at the office by two more people that the office guard must have alerted: the tall matron and the large guard who had taken the money from Matt.

The matron spoke, Tanya understood but pretended to be confused and frightened, "I must see your orders. I knew nothing about a transfer."

She took the papers from the office guard, read them carefully. Luis said nothing. She unhappily nodded to the large man, and they went into the lighted office so Luis could sign the necessary transfer documents. Again doors buzzed, one would only open when the other locked. The guard from the office escorted Tanya through the dual, barred doors. Luis signed the papers in the office, Camilo waited outside the office watching Luis.

With the papers signed, Luis turned to leave. From the office, the large guard caught a good look at Camilo highlighted now by office lights. He pointed, shouting in Spanish, "I know this man—he was in the cell with the Yankee. There is something wrong here."

Without hesitation Camilo smacked the side of the large guard's head with his baton. Luis grabbed the matron by the arms, saying, "Do not interfere or you will be hurt."

The matron shook him off and moved to the far side of the office, watching Camilo drag the unconscious guard into the office. The other night guard was quickly subdued by Lupe and Mario, who took obvious pleasure in clubbing the man into unconsciousness.

Both the male guards were dragged into the office, Luis worked the electric door buttons. Tanya and Matt came also.

Luis tossed several cords on the floor so Lupe and Mario could tie them up.

Matt, standing between the matron and the work being done on the two guards, freed his hands and found the handle of the blackjack when the matron snarled and lunged toward a button on the wall near the window to the holding area. It was yellow, with yellow and black slanted stripes painted in a square around it—likely the prison alarm. Matt swung the blackjack and hit her extended wrist, the woman cried in pain and reached with her other arm. Matt snapped the blackjack down on her forehead, she sank to her knees, down but not out.

The large guard began struggling against Lupe and Camilo's efforts to tie him up. Luis was on the other side of the room, watching the hallway. Mario, on his knees finishing tying up the first guard, had his back to the woman.

As Matt drew his arm back to strike again with the blackjack, Tanya's foot connected squarely with the matron's throat. Tanya dropped to her knees, straddling her, and pinned her to the floor, grabbing the thermos bottle off the table and, with both hands, brought it down onto the matron's head three times, the third accompanied by the sound of breaking glass within the bottle and a sigh of unconsciousness from the matron. Tanya gave the matron's head one more solid hit and stood up.

"There...," she said.

As Matt began to tie up the matron, Tanya grabbed his blackjack and turned to the men struggling with the big guard. Without hesitation, she hit the guard in the face and across the top of his head. As he slumped to his back, she kicked him between his legs. He was unconscious but the impact caused an involuntary jerk as he curled into a fetal position.

"And there," Tanya muttered again.

They ripped strips from the guards' shirts and stuffed them into the guards' mouths, securing them with shoelaces.

Luis checked to ensure each could breathe, saying, "They are Cubans and I do not wish them dead."

The commotion in the office awoke several prisoners, but none could see what was happening.

Luis checking the hallway, said to Matt, "We must go quickly! They will not awake for some time, then the ropes will hold them for awhile, but they will get to the alarm. The next office shift is not due for over two hours. I cannot break the alarm."

Matt brought up another problem. "We cannot all go out the door we came in. Someone has to buzz the doors."

Luis thought—then said, "We will go out through the main office, I have keys, and it is shorter to the boat."

The six walked back down the long hallway. Although many of the women saw them, none spoke—always afraid of the wrath of the night guards. They passed through two sets of locked doors and came out in the main office area where Matt and Tanya had first been detained for hours on its hard benches.

Matt noticed "Coronel Grosa" printed on the glass of an office door. "Our papers are in there, let's try for them."

Without waiting for permission or agreement, Matt rushed through the unlocked door. The desk was locked. He broke a letter opener on the desk's file drawer lock but, with one side of a large scissors, bent the lock's bar and opened the drawer. Their large envelope was on top of a messy pile of files and other envelopes. Feeling his watch through the papers, he jammed the envelope under his belt and covered it with his shirt.

Looking very worried, Luis said, "We have no time for this, we must get to the boat before dawn, we must be at sea before there is light to see us. We will now go to your boat. There is no need to lock your hands, just keep them together, in front of you—your wife should do the same carrying her bundle."

They exited through the same doors through which Matt and Tanya had initially entered this hell. The walk to the pier took longer than Matt remembered, the footing now slippery with morning mist. On the paving stones, the footsteps of the men in guard boots echoed loudly in the dark. They marched away from the spot lights over the office into the darkness of the long pier. There was no guard at the entry to the pier. They boarded the *Reefer* without difficulty. Matt saw the patrol boat tied up another twenty yards ahead, one anchor light, no guards in sight. The vessels were moored between weak overhead lights evenly spaced under the roof that covered the last half of the long pier.

Matt and Luis went up to the helm, Tanya and the others went into the salon. No lights were to be turned on until Tanya had the portholes and door covered. Matt reached for the ignition keys, which would turn on the engine instrument panel lights.

No keys.

Luis whispered, "Maybe my brother has them, he will be here soon."

Matt replied as he moved past Luis, "Let's not chance it, the ignition on a multimillion dollar yacht can be hotwired by an eight-year-old."

Luis understood the words but not their meaning, as Matt rushed by him, down the ladder and into the engine space. He returned with a small crescent wrench and a roll of electrical tape. He took the threaded ring off the ignition switch, removed the mechanism, located two large bayonet clips fitted into its base. Matt jerked them out, bound them with the electrical tape. Another twenty seconds to repeat the process with the second engine ignition lock. The helm's instrument lights came on. Luis gave a soundless cheer.

Matt pointed to a silhouetted figure, carrying a small bag, who stepped down the gangplank of the patrol boat.

Luis whispered, "My brother, don't worry."

Tanya came to the helm. "It is a mess down there, they took everything they could carry. What can we do about Alberto? Can't we try to rescue him?"

"We have had luck so far, I would be foolish to go after him, and I would need another guard." whispered Luis.

Mario stepped up behind Tanya and said in Spanish, translated by Tanya, "We have been in the salon talking about Alberto. I will go with you, we cannot turn our back on their friend."

Luis considered this, then went to the aft deck to meet his brother. They talked for a few seconds, then Luis motioned Matt to join them.

Luis introduced his brother—Jose Hernandez, who reported that he had his powerful radio jamming their military wavelengths and he had crippled the patrol boat. Luis then said, "We will try for your friend. I have papers, we will be back in fifteen minutes, hopefully not being chased by a dozen guards. My brother is armed, he will insure you do not leave without me. I am a dead man here.

"How long do you need to warm up the engines—they make much noise?"

Matt replied, "They will work cold if we go slow for a few minutes. I'll have us ready to shove off when you jump aboard. Good luck, and thank you."

Tanya organized the men to help with the lines. Matt gave her the envelope with their papers, rings and watch, then went to the master stateroom, opened the hidden storage area, and retrieved the black rifle and all the magazines and ammo boxes his pockets would hold. After reseating the tub to conceal the hiding space, he returned with the rifle and bulging pockets to the helm, past the startled looks of his cellmates and Luis's brother. "Now we have some firepower—we are not prisoners. There will be dead people before I go to a cell again."

On the bridge, Matt loaded the magazines. Slamming one in and charging the weapon, he put it on safe and leaned it near him against the helm console. Then he opened the helm chair back and took out the FN pistol, feeling for the little pin that told him it had a chambered round. He put the two magazines that were also in the foam padded compartment into his left front pocket. The silencer made it fit securely in the thick belt he still had around him. He pulled his t-shirt over the weapon.

He was thirsty, and just when he thought of going down to the salon, Tanya came up with a large, plastic mug of water. "This is one of only three drinking glasses left aboard."

Handing the mug to Matt, she whispered, "No ice, but it is wonderful to drink water that has no texture, smell or aftertaste, let alone little creatures I know I'd see under 100 magnifications."

As Matt gratefully drank the water, Tanya continued, "I'll never drink good water again without a little prayer of thanks. I'm going to take a shower as soon as we are in international waters—and we make hot water—which I'll selfishly use up. We have no soap—even the dish soap and laundry soap are gone—don't these people have anything?"

Matt said, helplessly, "Let me think about what we can do...maybe..."

Tanya interrupted, "I do have a little bar I paid $5.00 for from that bitch matron. I hope she and the guard remember me while their various lumps go down."

Luis's brother was on the helm, looking over the radio and other electronic gear, when he saw three people coming down the pier. "Here they come, we can start the engines. We must be past the fort before good light—there is a TGF observer there—he may be asleep but he also might like sunrises."

Matt pushed the port engine's rubber starter button. After a few seconds of worry, the engine's 1,200 horses came to life with a throaty roar. Then Matt awoke the starboard engine. Matt checked all the gauges—all off their stops with fuel showing over half full, more than 600 gallons, 300 mile range.

The three men came to the stern, where Alberto needed help boarding before collapsing to the cockpit deck. As Luis and Mario stepped on, the lines held around the old bollards were pulled in and the *Reefer* drifted away from the pier.

Matt engaged the propeller of the port engine, swung the wheel over, moving slowly toward the channel. After going a hundred feet, he brought on the starboard propeller, and eased away into the dark, conscious of his noise and wake.

The generator came on, and Matt knew Tanya had started the air conditioner, probably making ice and hot water, too—saying hello to civilization again.

Luis, his brother Jose and Matt watched the radar and the GPS. The brother was very familiar with the ship channel—Matt was glad for this as the markers were not easily seen in the darkness, further hindered by the blinding effects of various shore lights. As they came to plane, Matt could make out the rising hills, thanks to the scattered house lights, that ended at the heights where the castle and fortress had guarded the entrance to Santiago de Cuba for nearly four hundred years.

Matt looked up at the steep cliffs on his port side. Every pirate movie where the sailing ship slowly moved past the sinister barrels of twenty-pounders lining the walls of some dark bastion came to Matt's mind. He was now living the experience—he hoped he would survive to tell his tale.

They could identify the mouth of the harbor by the differentiation of the dark, rocky land and the lighter-colored ocean. The wall of fortifications rose to their port. The rising sun just touched the top of the two-hundred-foot wall of natural and manmade stone where it saw further east than their vessel. Dawn would be on them in just a few minutes.

Matt pushed the throttles forward. The meter showed their speed over water at 38 knots. The ocean swells were well separated and the chop was less than a foot. Matt remembered the black gunk in the fuel tanks and didn't want to stir it up with a bumpy ride. He steered 180 degrees magnetic—south being the shortest route to achieve twelve miles from Cuba. At nearly forty miles per hour, twelve miles would take…Matt worked on it—two-thirds of a mile per minute, roughly twenty minutes to go twelve miles.

He checked the helm clock—still working. The radar showed no ships in the channel. Luis's brother Jose worked with the radios, listening on various wavelengths wearing a headset Matt hadn't even known they had.

Tanya came to the helm carrying some items from the envelope Matt had handed her earlier. "Here is your watch, see my rings," she held up her left hand, "I tried the phone, something is wrong with it, maybe Jose can fix it—he really knows electronics. How much longer to international water?"

Matt looked at the helm clock while he reset his watch. "Eight—nine more minutes." He slipped his hand through the stainless steel bracelet and closed the clasp. "It feels good to have my watch back on my wrist."

"How's Alberto? He looked bad. The bastards, we should bomb the shit out of them!"

Tanya glanced toward Luis and Jose. Jose couldn't hear with his earphones on, but Luis looked a little stunned. She said, "Alberto's in bad shape—I've got him laying down, wet cloths on his leg and major bruises. They hung him from his bad leg, it's swollen and red, hot to the touch, even his toes are swollen and black from blood pooling in his foot. He was beaten all over. He is very thin and weak. We have no medicine, no food and ice will take some time."

Luis broke in. "Jose has a small bag with some of our personal gear, family pictures and some clothes, there may be some pills for pain. I will go look for what he might have."

Tanya continued, "We don't have any toilet paper! Otherwise, I've got things shipshape downstairs, we have AC working, water heating, ice making, but no booze, no food, and no TP…"

Matt thought for a moment then said, "Check the engine room, there's paper towels, instruction manuals, grease rags and you can use some degreaser spray as soap."

"Good idea, I know I should just worry about the next few minutes, but I couldn't stand the mess down there, and I want to get clean again. We need to call people—my folks, who will be crazy, Edward of the DEA and I bet Webb knows we're in trouble."

Tanya lifted the earphones and spoke to Jose in Spanish about the Westinghouse satellite phone. He said he would be down when they were out of Cuban waters. He was scanning many frequencies—difficult because the yacht's radio had all digital keys not the more flexible dials he was used to. He commented, "My jamming signal is still on and strong—someone will figure it out and turn it off. I'm using that as the time they know we are gone. Many people will have hatred for our leaving."

Tanya went forward to the helm lounge—happy to be on the boat, enjoying air that smelled clean, the freedom and joy of cutting through the sea.

Matt watched her in her tight blue dress, her skirt gathered up over her shapely legs as she scooted to the back of the lounge, the tight fitting top made Matt think about thoughts he had literally put on hold while in prison.

After another ten minutes of listening, Jose said in Spanish, "Ah, my signal, it is now off—someone knowing radios is on board the Zhuk and knows I should be on watch, also they will find they can't start engines. I took all engine batteries down and disconnected starter wires—nothing seen easy, they will repair all with a little thought and switching around some batteries or maybe with portable starter unit."

Tanya translated, Matt checked the time. "We are now in international waters as of one minute by my calculations and the GPS, but I want many more miles before we change course for...where? The DR would be my choice—get under the strong, protective wing of Webb. He can handle our cargo. I don't want to spend more time in any gray-bar hotel—the DR, PR, or any other shithole jail, on any island.

"Calling the Coast Guard could get our passengers a ride back to Cuba. We need to get to Webb. He's the expert in moving people around."

Jose, listening to the radio and watching the radar, Tanya interrupting between sentences, "Señora, there are ships coming out of Santiago de Cuba, and I think that dot that shows and then does not show is a helicopter coming toward us. I can hear the radio from the helicopter pilot.

He is military, but his identification is for a tourist service, *Aerogaviota.* Maybe that is all they could get into the air this morning."

Matt scanned the north horizon. He could see nothing but a dark shoreline.

Tanya spoke. "We need to call for help."

Looking at the radar, Matt suggested, "Let's wait until we see if they are armed. Their ships can't catch us. Or we could slow down, head east and maybe they won't be able to tell who we are.

"Ask Jose what he thinks."

Jose listened to the question with one ear and the radio traffic with the other, playing the frequency keys and knobs like an instrument, and in English answered, "If they send a gunship we have no chance, we are destroyed in seconds. Even help from your Guantanamo Bay would be too late. But we may be lucky, most of their Russian gunships don't work. They move them on trucks, just to show them at airfields.

"Look at the radar screen—these are passenger and cargo ships—they are not that far away. It might be good to have witnesses in international waters if the helicopter tries to attack us."

Matt noted the position of two large, southerly blips on the screen, he pointed the bow toward an interception course, and pushed the throttles up another two hundred RPMs. Their speed increased to almost forty knots—forty-five mph. He also realized he was burning fuel at one hundred and fifty gallons per hour. The blips he wanted to get close to were ships' masts twenty miles away, over his visual horizon from the helm, a half hour away.

The helicopter's intermittent reflection became a constant yellow blip on the black radar screen, and soon a red blinking light became visible through binoculars by scanning low over their wake. Tanya pushed some buttons on the side of C120 radar screen, bringing up MARPA—Mini Automatic Radar Plotting Aid. "I have the helicopter as a target on the radar plotting system, if it stays low enough, we may plot its speed, distance and direction. It's really moving, and directly toward us."

Matt glanced at the screen; the yellow dot took on a line indicating its bearing and showing speed and distance. Matt held the wheel steady as they hit some rougher water. "Damn, it's moving four times faster than we are. It will be on us before we are in sight of any ships."

Watching the chart window and glancing down their wake, the three on the bridge waited helplessly as the distance numbers went to zero. A collision alarm sounded at the same moment the large white helicopter, with its single, great rotor powered by twin turbine engines, screamed over the Hatteras. The power of its large rotor blades could be heard and felt on the bridge. Matt instinctively ducked. Jose identified it as a Mi-8, an old unarmed machine, piloted and owned by the military, but offered commercially by the government as an airline for Cuba's tourists. On the white body they could read AEROGAVIOTA in large print on the side. It made a tight turn and returned, matching the yacht's speed off the starboard bow. Its port door slid open and Matt could clearly see several armed men looking down at them. He could see AKs but no RPGs or heavy machine gun. The sun had just broken the eastern horizon and clearly illuminated its interior through the multiple windows of the big machine.

A loudspeaker blared in Spanish, "Turn back or we will attack"

Matt had Tanya take the wheel, telling her, "Keep course and speed. If they get close enough to fire their rifles they may be surprised when I fire back. They think we're unarmed."

Tanya took the wheel with one hand, with the other she brought down the radio mic and clicked the channel to 6—156.300 MHz—because Jose had said that was the frequency being used by the helicopter. Speaking in English and then in Spanish she announced that the *Reefer* was a US-registered vessel in international waters and the Cuban helicopter had no right to fire on them. She then put out an emergency call on channel 16 for anyone in the area. She felt that message would be heard by ships, the US Coast Guard and the Cuban monitoring stations.

The men in the helicopter threw out several objects as they moved ahead of the vessel, objects that exploded and created boiling domes of blue-green water twenty yards ahead of the speeding yacht. The *Reefer*, hitting the foaming water, bucked and yawed through it. Matt could clearly see the pilot and the men in the door from fifty yards away. It moved alongside, one hundred feet off the water and closing to thirty yards off their starboard side.

Two men lay side by side in the helicopter's port door, AKs leveled at the yacht.

"Get down," said Matt. "Hold her steady, we can't out maneuver them anyway. If they shoot, so will I." He held the rifle low behind the helm wall.

Matt saw the flash of the machine rifles, spouts of water stitched off their bow, a dozen shells struck the smooth white gel coat and exposed the pink of fiberglass on the long bow. The rattle of automatic gunfire reached them above the wind noise.

Kneeling by the helm, Matt brought up the M-16/C7. Working his arm into its sling he yelled, "Announce we are being fired upon, come off plane… slow down, I'll have a better shot."

He had arranged three magazines at his knee.

The *Reefer* slowed, its bounds and bumps quickly became a smooth, stable and quiet shooting platform for Matt. The helicopter matched their speed, seeming close enough to hit with a stone's throw.

The C7's fire lever was all the way back, pointing to AUTO; Matt had a relatively easy and close shot into the door of the Cuban 'copter. The rising sun illuminating his airborne target, Matt knelt in the relative darkness of the starboard side of the helm area. Full automatic fire released ten .223 Remington shells in quick succession. Then Matt touched off two more short bursts. The first burst went into the open door. Aiming at the shooters lying in the door, Matt saw them jerk and roll out of the doorway. Matt cursed, most of his second and third bursts worked high, hitting above the door. It was an impressive and unexpected return fire, however, but Matt felt he had wasted too many of his full-automatic shots. Before the pilot could react, Matt loaded another magazine, switched the fire selector up to R, cocked the rifle and fired well-aimed single shots into the door, then into the cockpit. The large, open window provided no protection, little better was the low-mounted, clear fiberglass that allowed the pilots to see the ground during a landing. Old, yellowed plastic cracked and flew as the military-grade shells peppered and shattered the helicopter's cockpit, the main target of Matt's second magazine.

Tanya, peeking over the helm, yelled, "You hit someone in the door and in the cockpit, I saw them jerk away and blood flew up."

Matt slammed in the third magazine and aimed, but the helicopter banked sharply, nearly plunging into the sea, its rotors bringing up a cloud of spray, the big machine shaking as it went to full power to keep itself in the air. A rainbow formed in the spray out of which the white monster slowly rose.

Matt, treating the large white Russian helicopter like a wounded partridge, yelled, "Go after it, I can finish it off, I think I got a few rounds in the pilot."

Tanya pushed the throttles forward, the *Reefer* leaped to plane. She headed away from the helicopter and back on their course toward the ships.

She yelled back at Matt, over the roar and wind of the moving boat, "You can keep them away now, and we are a harder target at speed if they come above us with more hand grenades."

"You're right," said Matt as he reloaded a magazine from a box of shells.

Jose was back on the radio, listening. Luis, worried about his brother, was back on the bridge and began filling another magazine.

Jose said in English, "They are hurt, returning to Cuba, requesting medical help. They wish the other ships to stand by in case they come down into the sea. I think we are free from pursuit."

Tanya slowed their speed. "We burned a lot of fuel and we were going south instead of east, so let's set a course for Puerto Plata and hope we don't have to tow ourselves with the Whaler."

Matt stowed the loaded rifle in a corner, took the wheel, and set the speed to 1300 rpm, 22 knots, their most efficient speed. Luis watched the retreating helicopter heading for Cuba. Tanya said she and Jose would work on the satellite phone.

There were two VHF calls from the Coast Guard. After the second one, Matt responded that the emergency was over, the Cubans were gone, they were fine and didn't need assistance. The Coast Guard station on Guantanamo asked several more questions. Matt confirmed several times they were fine, unless the Cubans sent jets.

Suddenly a West Texas, authoritative voice on a very powerful transmitter, boomed, "If those Cuban boys come out, they'll be lucky to swim back. You've got two Marine F/A-18 Hornets at twenty thousand feet over you right now. Tell the little lady who put out the first call we got y'all's back. The helicopter was too close to you when we got on station. What did you shoot at it? "

Matt answered, "A rifle, we may have nicked the pilot, over."

"Good shootin', pardner," said the Marine. "You'll be on Uncle Sam's radar from now on—where you goin'?"

"We're aiming for the Dominican Republic, coming from Jamaica."

"Good sailin', friend. We're here if you need us. *Semper Fi.*"

With the autopilot on, Jose at the helm and radios, Matt went down to the cockpit, Holding the fighting chair, he looked up—no planes could be seen, then a glint of sunlight on metal in the clear, blue morning sky. Matt still couldn't find its source.

He went into the salon to give the news to his shipmates.

VOYAGE
OF THE
REEFER

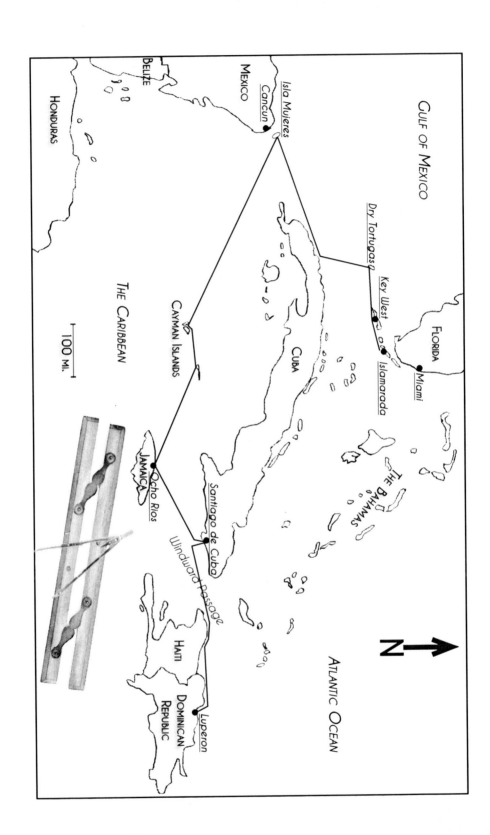

36

Windward Passage

Tanya sat at the navigation table, surrounded by Lupe, Luis and Camilo, as Matt entered the salon. He knew what they were discussing by the serious looks on their faces and the books, maps, parallel rule and dividers cluttering the desk's surface.

Matt glanced at the map and a book opened to diagrams of Caribbean currents and said, "Can we make the Dominican Republic—all the way to Puerto Plata?"

Tanya replied, "It will be a near thing. We used a lot of fuel going to Cuba and particularly in racing away. I believe we have enough to make Puerto Plata, but we will have no safety margin.

"With our passenger list of two Mexican and one Colombian —who are escaping prisoners without papers—and three Cuban refugees, all dressed in Cuban uniforms, we face great risk pulling into any port. Haiti is a quagmire, they are three hurricanes and an earthquake behind in their public infrastructure—run by officials that combine corruption with ineptness. We all agree their ports are out. The first good port in the DR is Monte Cristi, but we'd never get the Cubans past their custom officials and they wouldn't like unpapered Cuban prison escapees either.

Lupe mentioned turning back to a little island he knows off Haiti—a smugglers' nest. I think it's too risky and far from any help for us."

Matt looked at the current drawings, trying to understand the little arrows and numbers associated with them. "What about these currents?"

Lupe spoke up. "We are now on the east edge of the traffic separation scheme for all the shipping in the Passage—it runs through Cuba's twelve-mile territorial limit. We want to be out of it, and we are now going against a current heading southwest that gets stronger in the middle than at its sides. I suggest we should go east and skirt Haiti. The current is very little and in some places even flows north."

Tanya showed Matt the lines she had drawn on the map, noting waypoints and course bearings. "Here are my suggestions, we need to turn off the AC to save fuel, we will get thinner—we have no food, unless we slow down to fish. On the good side, all the material that was taken had lightened us, while—on the negative—our six passengers have given us the weight back."

Lupe spoke again, "As a veteran smuggler I worry about your navy stopping us as we go north."

Matt thought for a few seconds. "Maybe if we can fix our phone, we have some friends that can help us with the U.S. Navy. The DEA is responsible for most of the interest in northbound traffic, we have some contacts in that organization."

Lupe looked at Matt suspiciously. "How do you know the DEA?"

Tanya answered, "It is a complicated story, we really can't go into it now."

Matt changed the strained subject as Lupe kept looking at him. "How's Alberto?"

Luis spoke. "Jose brought some pain pills and granola bars, Alberto is dehydrated—we fix that, however, he needs nourishment, more than any of us. After some water and bars he is sleeping and seems comfortable. His leg is not good, but doesn't seem to be getting worse. However, I am no doctor."

Matt and Tanya went to the bridge, where Tanya worked on the autopilot and GPS. Jose went below to work on the phone—after first checking its satellite dome and its above deck coax cable connections.

Tanya came to Matt standing by the wheel, which was steered by the autopilot. She came into his arms, kissed him and pushed against him. "It seems like we have been apart for a year. You feel so good to me. I want us to sleep together." She reached under Matt's shirt. "Damn, it's a pistol, I thought you were just glad to see me!"

Matt kissed her ear and neck. "Do we have to sleep?"

Tanya patted the pistol lump. "You think you need to carry this?"

Matt, still kissing her ear, answered, "Did you see Lupe look at me when he heard DEA? I do not trust any of our passengers, except maybe Alberto."

Tanya whispered, while staying pressed against Matt, "I found some clothes in the back of the closet, on a ledge—some for both of us—shorts and sweatshirts, some socks and underwear, too. We can shower, get all clean and put on some fresh clothing, or not."

Tanya and Matt kissed and held each other, occasionally checking various screens and gauges.

They stayed at the helm, the *Reefer* moved easily over the light chop, behind a straight white wake and ahead of them the green Caribbean sparkled in the bright sunlight.

Jose yelled up to the helm, "I have fixed your phone—coax wiring had been pulled out of its connector, someone thought it was a regular telephone and started to take it. The phone is now showing a signal and will generate a carrier tone."

Matt yelled down, "Great, we'll be right down and make some calls."

He turned to Tanya and spoke confidentially. "We need to be on the phone without all those ears listening in. It will be too complicated to explain and we do not want them to know we talk with DEA people and Russian crime bosses."

Tanya suggested, "Let's put them up on the bridge while we phone. Alberto can stay in his room. We'll shut the door."

Matt agreed. "OK, I had told them to stay off the deck. There are a lot of white yachts in these waters, but I didn't want satellites to see a gang of uniformed men on ours. We'll send them one at a time. I'll get them started up."

Slinging the rifle over his shoulder, Matt went down to the salon and herded the men one at a time up the ladder to the helm.

The last to go was Lupe who questioned Matt, "Why cannot we hear your calls?

Matt looked into Lupe's hard, dark eyes. "We don't want you knowing our contacts, it is as simple as that. We are working to get you free. You just have to trust us."

Lupe paused, trying to read more from Matt's words and face, then he turned and went to the bridge.

Tanya joined Matt in the salon. "They will be fine up there, Jose is explaining all the electronic gear, showing them the radar screen—it can pick up both Cuba and Haiti right now. Lupe suggested we slow down and use only one engine—Camilo agreed with him. They are very experienced seamen. I explained we have good seas and perfect weather, we need to take advantage of it, and we have no food or help for Alberto. With the phone we can check weather with the service we use. I also mentioned eight knots will give us greater range, but take three times longer. I told them we will go at our present speed, that I have my Captain's Master papers and have been running these seas all my life. The macho Latinos just looked at my breasts and didn't say anything, so I added—if we feel us slow, we will read them the riot act, and there will be consequences for the person that touched the throttles."

Matt nodded at Tanya's impressive leadership, then went to the wall safe where she had put their papers. Retrieving his wallet with Edward's and Webb's numbers, he joined Tanya at the phone in the salon.

They tapped in Edward's number first: voice mail. Matt left a short, disrespectful message for Edward to call them, and questioned why government employees don't work regular hours, use call forwarding or answer their own friggin' phones.

Thankfully, Webb was in—Tanya talked to him, reminding him the DEA could be monitoring their call. Webb said he understood and had already talked to Edward twice when they couldn't reach the honeymooners for several days. He said Tanya's parents were very worried, finding out from Tomas when they had left Mexico.

Tanya explained their escape, describing each of the people they had on board, and explained that they were coming to Puerto Plata if they didn't run out of fuel.

Webb said, "I understand your situation. Let me do some planning and calling, I'll get back to you within an hour. We have much to talk about when we see you. I'm very happy you're out of Cuba. My darling Karen sends you her love, Carla is beginning exams at the university, but she is worried about you too."

Matt went outside and told the crowded bridge they were welcome to come down now. Only Lupe and Camilo came down. They sat together on the large couch in the salon watching Matt and Tanya as they moved in and out of the master stateroom, arranging clothes and talking about showering, leaving the phone unused, ready for incoming calls. Camilo got up, stretched and headed for the bridge.

The phone buzzed loudly. Tanya ran to answer it. It was Webb. He said hello, didn't identify himself, and told Tanya to listen and not talk. "Tanya, get a pen and paper, I have a substitution cipher for you."

Tanya was relieved to find a scrap of blank paper in the navigation desk, and a stub of a number 2 pencil. She said she was ready.

Webb spoke slowly and very distinctly. "D-M space J-T-O-B-Q-M-L space U-E-C-S-B-L space I-R space J-M-U-B-L-B-R-S.

"Got that?"

Tanya repeated the letters, they were clear and perfect.

Webb went on, "I hope to see you soon, you've both come a long way from that cabin in the north where my old friend died, I hope you remember him. If you have problems with my code call me back."

He broke the connection—total time less than two minutes.

Matt couldn't hear the conversation, just a few of the letters in Webb's low baritone. He watched Tanya print the letters on the page. When she whispered the letters back, Matt only heard a few. Lupe couldn't have picked up any.

Tanya took the tablet, "Let's go into the stateroom and work this out."

Matt commented, "Webb is one amazing dude," unmindful of Lupe still on the salon couch. Then Matt looked up, noticing Lupe and his expression as they left the room. Lupe was smiling.

In their stateroom, with the door closed, Matt watched Tanya print the whole alphabet across the top of the sheet. Next she printed IVAN below the ABCD of her first line, then put a B under the E, and kept the alphabet going in order, leaving out the letters in the word IVAN which already had their substitutes. In seconds she had twenty-six mixed letters under the twenty-six ordered alphabetic letters.

A B C D E F G H I J K L M N O P Q R S T U V W X Y Z
I V A N B C D E F G H J K L M O P Q R S T U W X Y Z

She explained, "This is a simple substitution code, Webb taught this to me when I worked for him, we had to know Webb's friend's name—I only knew him as Ivan. He died on your cabin couch. Now let's see what the message says."

DM became GO, JTOBQML became LUPERON—a harbor on the north coast of the Dominican Republic.

Tanya went through the cipher—in seconds she said, "Webb wants us to go to Luperon, use VHF 10—a little used commercial channel—and report 'AS LOVENEST.' I'm sure he will give us instructions from there."

Matt was amazed. "Webb sure knows his spy craft."

As Tanya tore up the code paper, she said, "This is kindergarten stuff. Webb at one time spends millions on computers and satellite phones all encrypted by the brightest people and the best technology available."

Noon turned to afternoon as the *Reefer* sprinted for the Dominican Republic. The fuel gauge slowly worked toward empty. They saw the clouds above the hills of Haiti, ran between a large island and the coast, the GPS set for the marker at the mouth of Luperon's harbor.

Tanya called her parents, they were frantic but very relieved Tanya was safe. Tanya cut them short, saying she was expecting a call she couldn't miss. She promised to call them soon and explain all that had happened. She reiterated she and Matt were fine and had had a great adventure.

Tanya made a quick call to their Caribbean weather expert, finding her instincts had been very correct—the weather would turn to squalls and a wind change by that evening. The winds would blow from the southwest, wind against current meant building seas. At their present speed they would reach Luperon in a little over six hours, beating the storm by several hours.

With Matt on the helm, Tanya gathered the group of men in the salon, explained in Spanish that they had a friend they could trust, a man that would get the Cubans to a "foot dry" situation in Puerto Rico, and the other nationals to their respective government officials—or wherever they wanted to go.

Lupe spoke up. "I have heard of this Señor Webb that your husband mentioned. He is a bigger smuggler than I am. Why should we trust him?"

Tanya paused, sorry that Webb's name had come up, before replying, "Lupe, would you like us to put you ashore on Haiti? We could give you the Boston Whaler and wish you to go with God. You will excuse me if I say you are an ungrateful person, not worthy of the help we are giving you. You would be very wise to forget any name you have heard. You will not be warned again. Our friend can be a very serious person and is helping you all because of his friendship for Matt and me."

Lupe said nothing, just shrugged his shoulders and smiled in agreement.

Tanya noted a reluctance in his dark eyes and suspected he was planning something.

She set up three two-hour helm watches—Jose and Luis to take turns on the first two, supported by Lupe and Camilo, on separate watches, effectively keeping them apart. Mario would watch Alberto. Anyone not on the bridge could relax and maybe get some sleep. She and Matt would take the helm in four hours, when they should be close to Luperon.

There was no argument, the men went where they were told, content with the speed of the vessel and the perfect weather.

While Matt took a quick shower, Tanya looked in on Alberto, who was awake, comfortable and happy with the prospect of getting to land, medical help and, most of all, freedom.

Tanya finally made it to the master stateroom, took a hot shower and joined Matt on the spacious bed: clean, glowing, warm and with just a faint aroma of commercial degreaser. She noticed Matt had the silenced pistol on the nightstand and the M-16 leaning on the bulkhead in the corner. She asked him why.

Matt mumbled his reply as he happily reacquainted himself with her ear, neck and breasts, moving toward other areas of special interest. "I told the men that if anyone came through that door he would be shot without warning or mercy."

37

Mutiny for the Bounty

Matt and Tanya lay naked in the hot sun, on a huge bed in the middle of the Roman Coliseum; thousands of Romans in multicolored togas were cheering and throwing laurel wreaths at them. They cheered rhythmically in French, "*Encore, encore, encore.*" The cheers changed into a distant buzzing sound. A large wreath landed on Matt's stomach. He awoke—the wreath was his old Levi shorts, the cheering crowd the satellite phone in the salon. Tanya had on her tan shorts and a Grateful Dead t-shirt.

She tied her hair into a ponytail with a rubber band as she opened the master stateroom door. Turning to Matt, she said, "You were having a wonderful dream my love, but now get dressed. That's probably Edward, and you've got a boat to run."

Matt looked at his sweaty body, the stateroom was hot, the mattress uncovered and damp, no air came from the ceiling vents, the motion of the vessel was steady and smooth. He checked the time, they had overslept. His helm watch started a half hour ago.

Matt got into his shorts, now loose thanks to the weight he had lost in the Cuban Club Med. He put on the Cuban belt over his shorts.

He tucked the locked and loaded, silenced pistol in the front of his waistband, checking that the safety was on, lest he do himself grave injury. He found a sleeveless sweatshirt in the pile of clothes Tanya had brought out from the back of the closet. He wanted the pistol concealed, and a t-shirt wouldn't do the job. In the head, he replaced the M-16 in its hiding space, grateful that the Cuban scavengers hadn't taken the plunger used to lift the small plastic tub. He splashed water on his face, ran his fingers through his damp hair and looked into the mirror—barely recognizing the thin stranger, unshaven, with tired eyes and looking like a member of The Village People.

Matt joined Tanya in the salon and found her speaking rapid and hostile Spanish. Finally, she took a breath. Matt gave a questioning look. She fired off another burst—ending in words Matt understood, *"Ahora, Edward, por favor."*

Tanya shifted back to English and a calmer voice. She said she appreciated his help and was glad to be alive and not on rent to anyone with one hundred pesos. Edward asked to speak to Matt.

Matt took the phone.

Edward said, "Matt, I'm glad you are free. I am in Guantanamo, or actually in a small building on the property border used for conferences between the Cuban army and the U.S. forces. At the same table is your Colonel Grosa, we were working out a deal for your benefit. It seems he was going to make me the same arrangement you had already made with him, money to a Texas friend in exchange for favorable treatment for some undetermined time. Tanya promised him she would tell the world, or at least several Miami papers how he had helped her escape with the aid of the guards on the women's wing. Now, the soon to be ex-colonel, wishes to seek his freedom in the good old U.S. of A. Tanya will fill you in. She intends to cook several ganders and one goose before she is done."

Matt thought about Edward's meaning, then smiled, asking, "Do you know where we are?"

Edward answered, "Not exactly, until about an hour ago we thought you were in prison. It seems the Colonel got the word before we did. His changing position started us looking for you. Tanya has asked we not look too hard for a few days. We trust you to let us know what you are up to at some time."

Matt replied, "We were looking for your help so we weren't stopped going through the Windward Passage—happily, we have avoided any inspections so far."

Edward broke in. "DEA inspections now are concentrating on the Mona Passage and the north side of Cuba. If you are headed east toward the Dominican Republic you are not as interesting as if you were going north toward the Bahamas. I can help you, I'll put out the word to leave the *Reefer* alone. Don't get me in trouble.

"I've got good news for you; you are heroes. Momo is in a U.S. jail, plea bargaining to fifteen years for various felonies. You were responsible for his capture and a major part of his conviction, you can pass go and collect one million dollars. We will work out the payment when we are both back in the states."

Matt smiled.

Apparently, Tanya already had this news and gave a thumbs-up. "I was thinking, we had help from a certain Cuban refugee—we can cut him in for some of that money, it would help him start a new life."

Edward and Tanya continued their discussions for a few more minutes, but she refused to commit to a time for their return. The conversation was finally over, and they hung the phone up.

At the bridge ladder, Tanya and Matt heard Lupe in a heated argument with the brothers Jose and Luis. Tanya whispered the translation to Matt—Lupe wanted to take over the vessel and change course toward La Isabela, a small port he knew on a river that Columbus first settled in 1493. Along with the history lesson, Lupe said they would be foolish to trust Webb—a Russian gangster—and La Isabela was closer and very remote with no police or government officials.

As Matt and Tanya came up to the bridge, the conversation stopped. Jose reported their position, the amount of fuel and the ETA to the mouth of Luperon Harbor. Lupe didn't say anything, just brushed past everyone on the crowded bridge and went down to the salon.

Luis spoke to Matt, "Lupe is not happy, he is worried about trusting your friend Señor Webb."

Matt replied, "Lupe has lived his whole life not trusting people. He was arrested because he was betrayed by a person in his own organization. I don't have an answer, except I have trusted Webb with my life several times, and I have saved his life several times—we have a bond. Also, he is like a father to Tanya. I will talk to Lupe, we have come too far to be divided now."

In the salon, with Tanya at the helm, Matt offered Lupe, seated on the larger salon couch, a plastic mug with ice water. Lupe took the water, seeming to enjoy having Matt serve him. He had Jose's travel bag on the floor between his legs. Camilo stood near by, leaning on the galley counter. Mario had remained on the bridge with the Cuban brothers.

Matt carefully listed several reasons for Lupe to trust Webb, including his ability to move people from country to country. He said Lupe was without money or power with the local officials, and Webb had both in abundance.

Lupe just smiled. "There is an easy way to get money, all you do is take it."

Then he reached into the bag and came out with Jose's TGF-issued pistol, saying, "We will go to the harbor at La Isabella, you will give us all the money I know you have in your safe. You will do these things or I will shoot you and your wife—which I would regret, but would do if you do not cooperate. I know who you are, it was all in the papers—but you never had a name. You helped capture Momo—I have learned in the prison yard he will pay one million pesos for each of you. When I heard you knew DEA people and then also Señor Webb, I knew you had to be the gringo couple Momo's people are looking for. You are very valuable, Momo's people will go to some trouble to take you, we will get money, maybe help getting out of the Republica Dominica. We will be heroes with cartels in Mexico and Colombia—we then buy a fine new boat and rebuild our business."

Matt looked at the black pistol held solidly in Lupe's hand, "It seems you have no loyalty except to money—what is a peso worth now? Thirteen to one U.S. dollar! We were just promised one million US dollars for capturing Momo—I will pay you your two million pesos for our lives, and you will not be repaying our rescuing you from the hell of Boniato with treachery."

Matt thought, *This a good argument to a Latin mind, also Lupe would not be so brave if he was staring at a gun barrel.* Matt had to get to his pistol.

Lupe thought for a few seconds then spoke to Camilo in Spanish. Camilo went into the master stateroom and returned, shaking his head. The black Makarov pistol in Lupe's hand continued its never wavering aim at Matt's midsection.

Lupe spoke to Matt, again in English, "You have hidden the rifle again, I would like to know where. No matter, we have gone too far to change our plans. If we took your money for our silence, someone would know, my family and I would die, the cartels are powerful by their use of vengeance and fear. I am sorry a little, but you will live in hope a little longer if you do as I tell you."

Lupe spoke in Spanish again—Matt caught the names *Tania* and *Mario* in the orders to Camilo. Camilo left the salon, returning with Tanya and Mario. Both were shocked by the pistol being held on Matt. Lupe explained his plans. Tanya stood beside Camilo in the doorway, looking at Matt, searching his eyes—seeing no fear.

Mario spoke in Spanish, obviously in disagreement with Lupe's plan and actions. He moved between Matt and Lupe, arguing with Lupe, partly in Spanish and partly in English for Matt's benefit. Matt picked up enough to realize that Mario was against the killing of the gringos who had won their freedom, telling Lupe he was a man without honor. With Mario in front of him, Matt saw the opportunity he had hoped for. He could draw his pistol, leveling it low behind Mario, with Tanya safely out of Lupe's line of fire. Matt might create the classic Mexican standoff, a balance of power. The Russian semiautomatic wasn't cocked, Lupe would have to pull hard to make the action work. Matt felt he could react faster than Lupe, and he was standing—easily a moving target—with some cover from Mario. All he needed was to avoid Camilo shouting a warning.

Tanya, seeming to understand Matt's options, moved between Camilo, just inside the doorway, and Matt. Matt tried, with a slight tip of his head, to convey to her to stay clear, but she either refused or didn't understand. She held her ground, probably hoping to slow Lupe down with two targets to choose from.

Matt mentally cursed, *Damn, no chance of a standoff—the little Mexican bastard will point at Tanya and he will know I can't bluff with her life.*

Actions began happening in slow motion. Matt pushed his hand under his sweatshirt, slipped the FN's safety off, closing his finger on the trigger. Camilo stood in the doorway, Tanya moved closer to Matt, blocking a side view of Matt's action.

Lupe spit back in venomous Spanish at Mario, motioning him away from his line-of-sight to Matt. As Mario moved to one side, Matt drew and fired the pistol at Lupe. Six feet away, Matt couldn't see where the shots were hitting, as he aimed for the center of the chest. The effect was immediate and deadly.

Pop... Lupe jerked, his eyes, previously confident and arrogant, showing complete surprise.

Pop... He jerked again, shock and pain replacing surprise. The Makarov still pointed at Matt.

Pop... Lupe jerked once more, as his eyes lost focus, life left them and the hand with the pistol dropped onto his lap. His head lolled forward onto his chest. His body began to slide sideways.

Camilo made a move toward Lupe, Matt brought the long, silenced barrel around and Camilo froze, raising his hands.

Tanya picked up the pistol that had fallen from Lupe's dead fingers. She moved to the other side of the salon, effectively keeping the large and powerful Camilo in the crossfire of two semiautomatics.

The three silenced shots were not heard topside, and the *Reefer* continued on speed and course toward Luperon. In rapid Spanish, Tanya barked orders at Camilo, who quickly lay down on the deck, hands behind his neck. Matt caught the word *muerte*—death—and knew she was seriously upset.

After Matt explained what Lupe had planned for them, Tanya spoke to Mario, now as white with shock as a handsome Latino can get. His response, translated by Tanya, was disbelief and an apology that his friends would repay being rescued with such treachery. He reminded the two people holding pistols that his words to Lupe showed the sincerity in his heart.

Matt nodded his agreement, then said, "We will throw Lupe overboard, tie up Camilo and see how badly I have shot up the couch. We need to show the consequence of mutiny to our passengers at the helm. I don't want Momo mentioned, just that Lupe was going to shoot us."

Tanya disagreed. "Camilo and Mario already know. I say tell the truth and pledge them to keep our secret in exchange for the help we have given. Honor is strong in these men. I would worry more that news of Momo's capture would leak from our government."

Matt agreed. Mario went topside to man the helm, and Matt brought the others to the salon to witness the scene, Tanya explained Lupe's death in Spanish. The men pledged to keep the secret of the death and the incident with the Mexican gangster.

All were moved by the drama around them. They weighted Lupe by tying the spare anchor to him with nylon rope and slipped the body overboard. Camilo, bound, seemed sure he would be the next to go overboard and broke down, crying and promising on the souls of his children he would be no trouble and a loyal crew member.

Matt let the decision play for some minutes as Camilo was placed in the fighting chair—staring, petrified, at the bubbling wake of the twin screws, then Matt and Tanya went to Camilo and slowly untied him. Tanya reminded him in Spanish, with a quick translation for Matt, "Upon your soul and that of your children?"

Camilo gratefully agreed, finally relaxing again.

Matt had good reason to leave Camilo unbound, knowing it would be hard to explain a bound man coming off the vessel in Luperon.

Matt inspected the couch, finding only one small hole, hardly more than a deep scratch, as all the power of the FN shells had gone into little Lupe.

Back at the helm, Matt and Tanya surveying the misty hills and cliffs of Luperon close on their starboard, the water getting shallower, the weather changing. A building storm building behind them rumbled ominously. Their fuel was nearly gone.

Matt considered how they had arrived here—after surviving Momo, a foul prison, helicopter attack, Lupe, fuel shortage, threat of a naval inspection. Matt gave a prayer of thanks, clicked off the autopilot and turned the wheel over to Tanya as they passed a large, well-organized resort with a beautiful beach that marked the entrance to the Bay of Luperon.

At the wheel, Tanya scanned the navigation information displays, brought down the radio microphone and prepared to begin her calls for Webb's next instructions.

38

Luperon

"This is Lovenest, Lovenest, Lovenest, calling Luperon Bay, over," Tanya spoke into the VHF microphone, broadcasting on channel 10. She waited a minute then repeated the call, increasing the power on the Raymarine.

A reply came back, in Webb's distinctive voice, "Lovenest, welcome to Luperon, enter the bay, bear right, watch for and proceed to the flashing light off your starboard bow. Over."

"Message received and understood, over and out." Tanya hung up the microphone. The slow speed reduced engine and wind noise, the radio's hiss on channel 10 now audible.

The *Reefer* entered the mouth of the bay. The hills on both sides were green and blurred with evening mist. Once around the headland, the bay opened to a large expanse of water, the main area running to the west, known to be a safe haven from storms. Many boats anchored at the southwest end that had a long public dock. Several small inlets broke off the channel, forming various-sized bays, each surrounded by thick mangrove foliage. The edges of the bay seemed to be unattractive swamp and mud banks with mangrove prop roots sticking up through the grimy and litter-strewn tidal flats.

Matt pointed. "There is the blinking light on the north shore, the chart shows shallow water, but a channel going toward the yacht club. Let's stay in the channel a while longer."

Just as Matt finished, Webb's voice came over the radio: "Lovenest, stay in the channel for another half mile, then follow the buoys to starboard."

Tanya ran west in mid-bay, with dozens of boats at anchor ahead as she found the channel markers to starboard. The bay was glass smooth, until it began to rain, first a few large drops pelted the water, then it came in sheets. The flashing light continued guiding them to a small dock, across a bay from the Luperon Yacht Club according to the chart. As the *Reefer* drew closer, Webb on the radio again gave brief instructions: "Tie up to the dock opposite the white trawler, you've got seven feet of water at low tide."

Tanya brought them in smoothly, pivoting and easing up to the wooden-plank dock occupied on the other side by a white Defever trawler, with the name *Miss Teak* in script on her bow.

Two men appeared on the dock, taking the *Reefer's* lines from Luis and Jose. The rain let up as they secured the fenders and lines. As Tanya was shutting down the engines, Matt worked at separating the hot-wire connectors. He could see Webb on the bridge of the *Miss Teak*, and got a smile and a wave.

The *Reefer's* foul-weather gear had gone the way of its food and bedding. They did find one umbrella for Tanya. The two men who had helped dock brought two more umbrellas. Jose and Luis helped Alberto off the boat, under an umbrella held by one of Webb's men, and they made their way down the dock to a van. Next, Camilo and Mario were escorted to the van. Finally, Webb stepped onto the dock and quickly came aboard the *Reefer*.

Webb hugged Tanya and gave her a kiss on each cheek. He shook Matt's hand, bruising it but not breaking any bones. "I'm very glad to see you. We will all go to the Yacht Club and eat—something you have been not doing according to my last talk with Edward. I guided you in from a friend's boat, they live aboard her, but I will still place a guard on your boat tonight. You are safe here, but it doesn't hurt to be careful."

Matt wondered, *Where will we be sleeping?*

Webb, "It seems your crew is one short. I made reservations for ten, including myself and Al. I thought it best that Karen not be with us until we are without our unpapered visitors."

Matt explained about the death of Lupe, showing Webb the pistol still tucked under his sweat shirt. "Al saved our lives twice with his wedding present."

Webb took the news of another killing matter-of-factly, asking only, "Did you put weight on the body? If not, you need to get rid of a very good pistol."

Matt answered, "We weighted poor Lupe. But we had three witnesses that would testify it was purely self defense."

After Tanya explained the sequence of actions of everyone in the salon during the shooting, Webb extended his hand.

"Better give me the pistol. Two of your witnesses are friends of Lupe. They can change their stories if they make a deal with some prosecutor or have fear of their gang leaders. It is best to have no body and no pistol—in these matters."

Reluctantly handing over the pistol, Matt thought, *Yes, Godfather, we'll take the cannoli, leave the pistol...*

Webb unscrewed the silencer, put it in a pocket and, after checking there was no round in the chamber, tucked the pistol in his waistband, covering it with his shirt.

Al appeared in the salon doorway. "We are taking the van up to the Club. The wounded man says he is very hungry, and we will make his leg comfortable. The Jeep is waiting for you." Looking around the *Reefer*, Webb commented, "This was always my favorite boat. I designed the interior myself, it is too bad they stripped all the things they could carry—actually, the US authorities do almost the same thing, all the food and packages go—drugs can be hidden in a cereal box, flower or sugar containers or pillows, even toilet seats can be hollowed out and filled with drugs—you still have yours. Sometimes the Coast Guard will take a power saw to the beds and couches, then dump all the dry goods on the deck.

"Anyway, let's go have some great lobster and homemade breads and soups."

After a crowded drive—with five people, including Webb's driver and Al, Webb's body guard, in a four-person Jeep—they made it up the wet, dirt hill that flattened into the Luperon Yacht Club parking lot.

Inside the open great room, round and seventy feet in diameter that looked down on the bay, seating for the group had been arranged— the table already filled with various hors d'oeuvres and a large green bottle of *El Presidente* beer at each place. Alberto had an extra chair and cushion for his battered leg. Three of Webb's men were seated at another table near the entranceway. There was only one other couple dining at a table at the far side of the large room. The night was dark and the rain now came in a steady downpour, dripping off the over-hanging thatched palm roofing.

Tanya and Matt took their seats, the three Cubans were seated across from them, Mario and Camilo were at one end, Webb and Al moved to the other end of a large table. Webb ignored the menu and ordered for the group, everyone agreeing with his choices—soup, Caesar salad, then lobster with side dishes served family style. The second round of beers came in bamboo tubes to keep them cold while the first bottles were finished.

The food was perfect, hunger being the best spice. Matt and Tanya talked about the prison and their escape—avoiding discussing Momo and Lupe.

When all had eaten, Webb rose and walked to the far end of the table. There was no noise except the steady rain on the fronds of the roof. He looked around, confirming that the other couple had left. In low but easily understood Spanish he explained, without using names, that the Mexican and Colombian would be taken to Santo Domingo where their national consulates would arrange papers.

Webb put his powerful hands on Camilo's large shoulders and, look-ing directly at Mario, spoke earnestly in Spanish while Tanya whispered the translation to Matt. "Do you remember a man named Cortada?"

Camilo nodded yes, Mario just looked scared.

"I tried to teach him to fly from a helicopter, but he would not learn quickly. You must understand Matt and Tanya are very special to me. Camilo, you have a family to go to and Mario, you can live a long life—but only if you honor your obligation for being rescued from prison. Repeat nothing about the actions on the boat. I would have not been as generous with your lives as Matt. Do we understand each other? You will now leave, and hopefully, I will never hear of you again."

Webb's men at the far table rose and came to stand behind Mario and Camilo, then led them out to a waiting vehicle.

The Cubans looked worried as Webb returned to his seat at the end of the table.

Webb poured a half glass of the cold, excellent beer, took a long swallow, waited a few seconds to establish a dramatic moment, then addressed them. "We will get you three to San Juan, you will soon walk off the dock onto *Calle Marina* in the old city. Alberto, you may be limping, but we will have you under a doctor's care this evening. In three or four days you may be walking on a road of blue glass, near the walls of the large fort—a very historic street, paved, interestingly enough, with cobblestones that were once Spanish glass furnace slag, used for ballast by the Spanish galleons—but legally you will be stepping on them 'foot dry' and on U.S. soil. You will be walking, maybe limping, as free men."

Webb raised his half-filled glass. "Salud, to freedom and new lives."

Everyone at the table echoed the toast.

Webb went on, "Tanya and Matt, I have a special place for you to sleep tonight. I own part of a large hotel complex just up the coast. It went bankrupt, got it for almost nothing. We are refurbishing it, trying to make it a little Monte Carlo—high-stakes gambling, five-star rooms, three-diamond food, several huge suites looking over the sea. You will be there several days."

Webb addressed the Cubans in Spanish, "There are rooms for you also. If someone asks who you are, say I hired you as sheet metal workers, your materials haven't arrived yet, so you are just resting, with my blessing. Alberto, you had a fall off a ladder—poor boy."

Al got up and stood by the three men until they understood they were being dismissed. Jose and Luis thanked Matt, kissed Tanya. Alberto hopped over to Tanya, kissed her and, taking Matt's hand, said, "I owe you my life many times, and I will always be in your debt. You will be in my thoughts and prayers every day."

Tanya, not knowing when she would see Alberto again, scribbled an address and two phone numbers on a napkin. Giving it to Alberto, she said, "It is very important you contact us. Your help in the capture of Momo will be worth money to you. Promise to contact us when you have reached our shores. We live only a few hours from Miami."

Alberto nodded, hugged everyone again, even Webb, and with Jose's help limped out of the room. Both Jose and Luis helped him up and down some difficult steps to the parking lot, where Al waited with the car.

Tanya, Matt and Webb ordered coffee and cognac. They were served as the table was cleared. They sat in the middle of the room, watching the pelting rain, enjoying a cool breeze that occasionally wafted through the open dining room. In the large harbor, several dozen anchor lights glowed, sparkling and reflecting off the rain-swept water.

For Webb's benefit, Tanya reviewed everything that had happened since their encounter with Momo up to their arrival in Luperon. Webb listened attentively, asking no questions.

Matt listened, but could not suppress a yawn after their grueling ordeal.

When Tanya finished, Webb drank the last of his cognac and said, "I have a presidential suite waiting for you. We will work on new clothes tomorrow. We need to talk about the *Reefer* and your plans for the rest of your honeymoon—let's wait until you are both rested.

"The hotel's restoration is less than half done, you have one of three completed rooms. Our kitchen is also just getting organized, but the chefs can make a gourmet dinner on a campfire."

Al returned with the Jeep. The three diners paid their respects, and Webb the bill to the Canadian couple that ran the Yacht Club, then all three hurried through the rain to the vehicle.

At the hotel, construction evidence was everywhere—walls with scaffolding and corners piled with boxes of material. Webb escorted the honeymooners to the elevator and the third floor. He opened a double door with a gold key, exposing a large, onyx and gold, Italian-tile foyer, which flowed into a room furnished with high quality, tropical furniture. The large room looked out through floor-to-ceiling sliding glass doors to a patio that ran the length of the apartment, overlooking the beautiful bay. There was a wet bar, a small dining nook and a conversation center facing the ocean. The carpet was thick and champagne colored, the walls papered and flocked in golden fleur-de-lis with matching draperies. Lamps and accessories were in hammered copper and black leather. The master bedroom had a king-size bed, its own sliding glass door and access to the patio. The bathrooms were both large and beautifully appointed in white tile and gold fixtures.

Tanya smiled, held Matt's hand and commented, "This will do."

39

Beached

Tanya and Matt had spent a wonderful night: unlike the *Reefer*, the room offered spacious hot showers, clean sheets and pillows, a magnificent bedroom featuring a large stationary bed. They reveled in the space and in each other, their freedom and the joy of having choices.

At 9:00 in the morning, a light tapping at the door announced a young Dominican girl pushing a breakfast cart. She also brought a note from Webb.

In fluffy white robes, they rolled the cart set with coffee, juice and croissants out to the patio. They selected from sliced fresh fruits, fruit jams and appreciated the finger bowl with a perfect hibiscus flower floating in it. The note from Webb asked them to join him at 10:30 for a brunch on the dining patio that overlooked the pools and gardens.

About the time they started to worry about getting dressed, the knocking came again. Another cart rolled in with t-shirts, jogging shorts for each of them, top-of-the-line flip-flops and two flowered cotton shirts. They dressed, approving Webb's judgment of their sizes, and headed for the main floor.

Webb and the Cuban brothers sat at a table at the edge of the large tiled patio, in the shade of the building. Across the open area was a buffet with silver servers and hot cooking surface—behind which stood chefs ready to cook eggs, pancakes and a variety of other foods upon request.

Matt, deciding he was still hungry, directed the ingredients for a two-egg omelet. Tanya also ordered an omelet—choosing diced ham over Matt's bacon, green peppers over cheese. When the eggs were given to them on warm plates, with sliced toast and a garnish of strawberries dusted with powdered sugar, they joined the table with Webb, Jose and Luis.

Webb rose to help seat Tanya, explaining, "Alberto is in bed, with an IV. He is already showing improvement according to the doctor. He will need to be able to walk in two more days. These young men will join the throngs of tourists coming off the three cruise ships that will make their port in San Juan at that time. They will push carts of garden products landed from service boats that ferry across the bay. It is the old wheelbarrow maneuver. There is a joke about a worker taking a wheelbarrow of sand from his manufacturing plant every week. The guards searched the sand very carefully and always had to let him through. They didn't realize the man was stealing wheelbarrows. In coveralls, moving wheeled wagons of fresh produce, the only items getting inspected and checked will be the tomatoes, peppers and cabbage."

Matt saw the brothers beam with the prospect of getting to Puerto Rico. They talked about how they would get to the States and about relatives and friends they would see. Then they excused themselves and made up a plate to take back to Alberto.

Webb signaled a waiter for coffee all around. When he had taken a sip, he began, "You need to bring the *Reefer* to the main dock below the Yacht Club, immigration and customs people will be there at noon. You may want to put beach towels over the bullet marks. Then I suggest you take the *Reefer* to the marina and fuel dock—it's the only fuel at the dock on the north coast and the best mechanics on the island—except maybe in Santa Domingo. They can clean the tanks before refueling.

"But before you spend $6,000 for diesel fuel, and the time and money to patch bullet marks and outfit the galley and staterooms, I want you both to consider another arrangement—I can buy the *Reefer.* I've already phoned the man that bought the marina from Mr. Vega. I offered him a good price—it would take him years to realize the profit he could make by just signing a paper, with no risks, insurance costs or expensive maintenance. I get a fine yacht, special to me for its design and history.

"So you come to our villa, you have your own wing, Carla's little convertible to use, you honeymoon with us as long as you wish, maybe go around the island, dive, sail, lay on beaches. My wife and I would be honored to have you. I can use the Hatteras to bring guests from Puerto Plata—18 miles by sea, an hour's cruise along a beautiful coast— versus over two hours driving on narrow curving roads.

"You can use it while you are here. What do you say? You fly back when you want to."

Tanya looked at Matt—his eyes only reflected his love, with no opinion except that they would be together.

Matt's words confirmed his loving expression. "I'm very flexible. We've spent as much time as we originally planned on a boat, our honeymoon should be everyday for the rest of our lives. I really wouldn't mind going north—finishing the summer house, walking in the woods, maybe catching some walleye or lake trout, speaking some Yooper again—hey—breathing cool air, hearing the wind in the white pines, splitting wood, watching the flickering fireplace."

She continued to search Matt's face, thought a few seconds, then said, "I can give up the *Reefer,* but I want to see the Cubans reach freedom, we can help them. It will be like my parents and your grandparents, making a choice, taking risks, giving up one country for another—learning a new language, new foods, maybe adjusting to a different climate, new friends, new laws, bringing very little except courage and hope."

Tanya turned to Webb. "I love your villa and your wife, we will be happy to be with you."

40

New Life in Old San Juan

Matt, Tanya and Alberto's uncle Max sat on a tree-shaded bench bordering a large parking lot, near the southernmost set of gates that marked the end of the massive dock complex, bordered on the west by the massive walls of the old fort. Four huge, white cruise ships, like suckling piglets, nosed into the old city docks of San Juan, Puerto Rico.

Matt was happy, he enjoyed watching the bustling dock activity, after three restful days in the Dominican Republic.

He and Tanya had left Webb's Luperon hotel on their first day ashore to spend an afternoon of meetings and making payments to a parade of immigration officials, sanitation inspectors and several other Dominicans whose official functions they really didn't understand. They then moved the yacht to a very well organized service marina where they were expected. Bidding farewell to the *Reefer* was more emotional than they expected. The fiberglass and chrome boat would be inanimate to most people, but she held many memories for the couple. A heart throbbed in her diesels, the sea gave her a pulse, she had been a magic carpet to beautiful worlds and many adventures. Webb taking the boat helped ease their feelings of abandonment. Following Webb's instructions, the M16 stayed in its hiding place. They carried very little from the Hatteras except their memories, their papers and money from the safe as Matt helped Tanya hop from the deck to the marina dock.

Late that afternoon, Al drove them the fifteen miles from Luperon to Webb's villa. He promised that the rifle and the pistol would get smuggled back to Matt in a month or so.

For two days, the honeymooners enjoyed the Webbs' hospitality at their palatial villa and estate west of Puerto Plata. They literally spent their money and time for nearly a whole day on a shopping spree to rebuild a tropical wardrobe and purchase other necessities: toiletries, a new digital camera, cell phones and bags to put everything in. They enjoyed the unhurried pace at the villa: sleeping, sunning and enjoying lunches around the pool, talking for hours with Webb and his lovely wife Karen. Their time together often extended into stargazing on the large patio during the pleasant tropical evenings.

On the third day, after a drive through Puerto Plata's crowded, narrow streets with their driver skillfully avoiding collision with a frenzied populous on motorbikes, they were delivered to the airport. An early-morning commuter plane brought them to San Juan, where Alberto's uncle Max, who had flown in the day before from Miami, met them. He worked for a large brokerage firm in Miami and, through business, knew San Juan very well.

The drive from the airport introduced Matt and Tanya to Puerto Rican traffic. Max, driving defensively, humorously commented as they pulled into traffic, "The rules are different here. A green light means you may be hit from the right. A red light means three or four vehicles may still go through the intersection. Passing on the right includes the sidewalk. Honking means the driver only has one hand on the wheel."

They made one stop on their drive to the city. The impressive sign and driveway of the Ritz-Carlton led them to a magnificent group of buildings. Tanya and Matt went in and registered at the desk, checking their bags with the concierge. The beautiful pools, awesome landscaping, perfect beach and distance from the cruise-ship crowds made a lovely place to continue their honeymoon for several days. Webb had suggested the hotel as one of the finest in the city. Matt numbly handed over his black credit card and tried not to think of the cost of the three nights in terms of his former monthly take-home salary as a teacher. He decided he would take a lot of their shampoos and soaps back to the hunting cabin for the guys in November.

Leaving the hotel, Max made good time driving them through the sprawling communities that held half the population of Puerto Rico, who lived in and around the modern city of San Juan and into the area called *El Viejo San Juan*, the old city. They arrived shortly before 9:30; they were early and had the large lower parking lot almost to themselves. Webb had told them the three Cubans would be brought to them through the old historic and unguarded dock gates around 10:00 that morning.

Observing the empty parking lot, Matt concluded that San Juan was not a morning city—the cruise ships were just beginning to disembark their thousands of eager sightseers. Tourists streamed ant-like from the white ships, making San Juan the busiest port in the Caribbean. Most moved toward the narrow cobblestone streets and small shops of the old city. Others walked along the harbor's edge and climbed the steps to the Fort called *El Morro*—Matt had learned that *Morro* literally meant headland or promontory, explaining why Havana, Santiago de Cuba and San Juan each had an *El Morro*. All also had a unique name honoring a king or saint: *Felipe* in San Juan, *San Pedro* in Santiago de Cuba and *Tres Reyes* – the Magi—in Havana.

After several minutes of watching the ever more active dock area, Max and Tanya reviewed their upcoming tasks. Max assumed the responsibility of taking the three Cubans through the complexities of the immigration center, dealing with the forms and data needed by U.S. Homeland Security and then escorting them to Miami—they would be granted legal permanent resident status and offered steps toward U.S. citizenship. Tanya would give each Cuban an envelope containing an American Express debit card made out in their name, plus a letter from the bank with contact information for a personal banker, and instructions to set up a PIN and an official welcome as a new bank customer with an account balance of $100,000 US.

Matt had rationalized, with no little consideration, that they could recoup the money from the DEA reward they were promised, and the substantial sum would be a major jumpstart to new lives for the Cubans. Their personal banker in Gibraltar had transferred the money and provided the plastic within twenty-four hours.

Minutes passed. The three waited in the shade of palm trees as 10:00 came and went. Twice they excitedly rose, preparing to give hugs of joy as several groups passed by, only to receive curious looks by young men who had no idea what a precious gift they already possessed and generally never thought about: freedom.

The morning was warm. Uncle Max shed his sport coat and tie, having dressed more formally in anticipation of meeting various government functionaries. The envelopes with the debit cards got wrinkled as Tanya checked them several times, mentally rehearsing her speech to each man—thanking him for his bravery, for making the escape possible or, in Alberto's case, rescuing Matt from the engine room of the *Reefer* and helping to defeat a Mexican gangster. Matt noticed Tanya's nervousness and tried to reassure her that Webb's men knew their business, and at least, they had a beautiful place to wait.

The sun rose higher, under the trees, the puddles of shade melted and the temperature climbed into the low 80s as 11:00 came and ticked by. The breeze from the bay quit. The waiting three became uncomfortable, their excited anticipation turning to worry, with spoken and unspoken cascades of dire scenarios that put the three excellent young men back in the grasp of a monstrous, communist system.

Max got up, folded his coat and tie, placing them next to Tanya, and said he had to move around, maybe walk down by the docks. He'd keep them in sight.

Matt eased closer to Tanya, who was holding and staring at the envelopes. He put his hand over hers. "Don't worry, they will get here.

We're giving them a life-changing amount, I bet they'll know how to use it wisely."

As Matt sat next to Tanya, Max returned, looking hot, tired and worried. He found some shade under a tree near them. No one spoke.

A squeak of brakes from an old, green-and-rust stepvan came from behind them, its main door slid open, followed by an excited shout of "*Tio!*". Alberto ran to his uncle with a limping gait. They hugged, cried, whooped with joy and voiced praises to Mary and to God. Finally, Alberto went to Tanya and Matt, who were hugging Luis and Jose.

Al came from the driver's seat of the van and walked up to Matt, while machine-gun-speed Cuban Spanish shot between Tanya, Max and the three newly free young men. Their words included introductions, their relief emotions and a cacophony of joyous shouts for the goal they had reached.

In contrast, Al spoke quietly and slowly to Matt. "We got hung up along the docks, had to go to another area to off load our cargo. Then we had to load it in this van and deliver it to another dock area. The whole scheme relies on the men being real dock workers, they can't just touch land and quit or it wrecks the system for the next person."

More cries of joy from the Cuban group drew Matt's attention. Luis and Jose actually were spinning and dancing, holding the white envelopes above their heads while Alberto just stood quietly mute and stared at the little card. Tanya continued to explain the amount and how a debit card works. Another wave of excited disbelief came across the men as they realized the money was in US dollars and represented many lifetimes of accumulated wealth in a little piece of pressed plastic. Max was also shocked at the amount of money, but Tanya made him understand the reward for freedom was beyond price, and she and Matt fortunately had enough money to afford these gifts.

People along the walkway watched and listened to the loud celebration. Al suggested they keep a lower profile and get on with their business. He had to return the van and get on the boat that would take him back across the bay. Max had offices to visit. Tanya and Matt had a honeymoon to continue without a Cuban chaperone. They all promised to call each other and maybe meet at Tanya's parents' home at Christmastime, phone numbers and addresses were exchanged and, after final tears, hugs and handshakes, the group broke up. Tanya and Matt watched the others pile into vehicles and head into busy San Juan.

Matt kissed the tears from Tanya's beautiful eyes. "You know, that was a little like giving birth, or at least watching a new life begin. I wonder at all the potential that goes with those men. I'm emotionally whipped."

"Me, too," she agreed. "What now?"

"Let's have some cold beers and a little lunch, play tourist for a while, then see if we can survive a cab ride to the Ritz-Carlton. And I think we should consider heading north for the black fly and tick season. There are a lot of projects we can afford now."

Tanya kissed him, "I miss the whisper of your pine trees and a cozy fireplace, do you think your road has the snow off it? You know, a honeymoon in a remote cabin isn't all bad."

Hand-in-hand the loving couple walked across the old blue-green glass cobble stones, past fountains, plaques and shade trees into the historic old city.

The End

Acknowledgements

My wife Ann did all the initial editing and plot discussions. She handled a very difficult job with her usual skill and sensitivity.

Walt Shiel, consummate literary, publishing and production guru, did the final edit and typesetting. His very talented wife Kerrie conjured the cover art to capture the spirit of the novel. Lisa Shiel took time from her many writing projects to update my website.

The seagoing knowledge of many people was tapped to bring validity to the voyage of the *Reefer*. I've been to all the ports described, except the ones in Cuba, but not in a 54-foot Hatteras. My son, Ben, captain of many yacht trips on the Great Lakes, kept me in touch with reality and helped work out many very important plot points. Aric Chaltry of Nestegg Marine in Marinette, Wisconsin, let me on and in their 54-foot Eggharbor and gave answers to all my questions. Friends John and Mary Lachat, experienced yachtsmen, advised me on nautical terms and were wonderful hosts aboard their beautiful 40-foot Tiara moored in Fort Myers, Florida. Capt. Don Reichert helped with Islamorada and yellowtail fishing information.

So much is owed to Luis Ruiz and his family, the Cuban connection for the novel. His life story would make a fine and inspirational first-person book. We spent many very pleasant hours together. His wife Silena's flan was the highlight of one of our sessions.

Their accounts of two highly educated, industrious and skilled parents raising two young daughters in a communist country are heart wrenching. Limitations of food, medicines, education, healthcare, and pay—caused by constant and cruel government control—beggar our perception.

Also, a "thank you" to Father Frank Lenz, PhD, a treasure of a man, who read and advised on many chapters. He can solve the world's nuclear waste problems.

Doug Dawson posed for the picture of Hunter with the M16 and behind prison bars. We needed a Hunter without the heavy coat and hat of the previous two novles and a new rifle that fit the story.

The prison scenes were aided by an interview with a US citizen who spent two years in Cuban prisons—18 months in the infamous Boniato Prison.

And finally, a tip of the dark blue—made in the USA—USCG GANTSEC cap (Greater Antilles Section) given to me by my best buddy Master Chief Archie Davies for the times we roamed the docks of old San Juan, and for his forty year history with the U.S. Coast Guard.

Author's Note
The Reality of Cuban Prisons

I could not write about *all* the inhumane tortures that the Castro government inflicts upon its prisoners. I had nightmares just researching the *gavetas* (drawers) and the *tapiadas* (steel isolation cells). I could not bear to put Matt or Tanya in them.

My story is a superficial look at the real Cuban prison system. On my website, I'll write more about the atrocities that are happening just 90 miles from the lights of Key West.

Interested in this topic?

Spend some time researching the life and ongoing works of the remarkable Armando F. Valladares, and for the treatment of women in Castro's prisons, read work by Maritz Lugo Fernandez!

About the Author

Born and raised in Michigan, John (J. C.) Hager earned a B.A. and M.A. in Biology and Science Education from Western Michigan University, taught high school science and coached football and wrestling. He retired from IBM after 27 years on quota. He and his wife Ann live in Michigan's Upper Peninsula on the shore of Little Bay de Noc. They have two grown sons. John dilutes his writing time with hunting, fishing, boating, traveling, and providing laughs and lost golf balls at the Gladstone Golf Club.

The Matt Hunter Adventures
by J.C. Hager

Hunter's Choice

With the sound of snapping pine tops and tortured metal skidding across a frozen lake, a peaceful deer hunt becomes a rescue mission. Hunter's choices quickly become life-and-death decisions as a barrage of life-changing events thrust him into a fast-paced, page-turning adventure.

> "A powerful and intelligent thriller!"—Steve Hamilton, author of the Alex McKnight novels

Hunter's Secret

Diving into the cold depths of Lake Superior, Matt and Tanya follow the algae-coated links of an old anchor chain to a mysterious shipwreck. The discovery locks them in a vicious struggle with powerful, and deadly, businessmen determined to keep the past buried and catapults them into a wicked world of kidnapping, bribes, corporate subterfuge, and murder.

> "The locales depicted are bang-on, the human characters are well-crafted and many return as the reader's old friends."—Joseph Greenleaf, Publisher, Swordpoint Intercontinental Ltd

---

Looking for the perfect gift for an outdoorsman, a fan of adventure thrillers, or somebody in need of a great "summer read"?

The Matt Hunter Adventures can be purchased:
- At your local bookstore
- At online book retailers
- Direct from the author at **www.JCHager.com**

Available in popular eBook formats, too!

CPSIA information can be obtained
at www.ICGtesting.com
Printed in the USA
FFOW02n0422141216
30152FF